The Hotel Between

SEAN EASLEY

Simon & Schuster Books for Young Readers

NEW YORK LONDON TORONTO SYDNEY NEW DELHI

SIMON & SCHUSTER BOOKS FOR YOUNG READERS
An imprint of Simon & Schuster Children's Publishing Division
1230 Avenue of the Americas, New York, New York 10020

SIMON & SCHUSTER BOOKS FOR YOUNG READERS is a trademark of Simon & Schuster, Inc.
For information about special discounts for bulk purchases,
please contact Simon & Schuster Special Sales at 1-866-506-1949 or business@simonandschuster.com.
The Simon & Schuster Speakers Bureau can bring authors to your live event.
For more information or to book an event, contact the Simon & Schuster Speakers Bureau
at 1-866-248-3049 or visit our website at www.simonspeakers.com.
Jacket design by Chloë Foglia
Interior design by Hilary Zarycky
The text for this book was set in Goudy Old Style.
Manufactured in the United States of America
0818 FFG
First Edition
2 4 6 8 10 9 7 5 3 1
Library of Congress Cataloging-in-Publication Data
Names: Easley, Sean, author.
Title: The Hotel Between / Sean Easley.
Description: First edition. | New York : Simon & Schuster Books for Young Readers, [2018] | Summary: Twelve-year-old Cameron discovers a magical hotel through which, with the help of new friend Nico, he hopes to find his long-lost father and help for his twin sister Cass's spina bifida.
Identifiers: LCCN 2017043726 | ISBN 9781534416970 (hardcover : alk. paper) | ISBN 9781534416994 (eBook)
Subjects: | CYAC: Hotels, motels, etc.—Fiction. | Brothers and sisters—Fiction. | Twins—Fiction. | Missing persons—Fiction. | Spina bifida—Fiction. | People with disabilities—Fiction. | Magic—Fiction.
Classification: LCC PZ7.1.E247 Hot 2018 | DDC [Fic]—dc23
LC record available at https://lccn.loc.gov/2017043726

For Lizzie and Becca, and all the places they'll go;
and for Shelly, and all the places she takes me.

1

Here, There, and Everywhere

I'm going to die in this stupid locker.

I stare at the strips of light in the door, kicking myself for getting stuck, again. And on the last day before winter break. When everyone comes back from the holidays they're going to be surprised to find a shriveled-up mummy with a bag of Skittles in his pocket encased in this locker-coffin.

This seemed like a perfectly good hiding spot when we started this fateful game of sardines, but I've waited over an hour for the other teachers' kids to find me, and I'm the only fish in the can. It's over. I'm through.

I throw my head back against the interior of the locker, tracing the page displaying my pencil sketch of a tree with a cramped, crooked finger. I can almost hear the leaves rustling, as they have been lately in my dreams. It's the same tree that's on the wooden coin hanging from my neck. Dad's coin. It might not be able to save me from the clutches of evil combination locks, but I feel better wearing the one thing Dad left me before he vanished. As long as I have it, I have hope I'm not going to vanish too.

Footsteps. Some angelic soul is coming down the empty Social Studies hall to free me from this death trap of my own making.

"Hello?" My dry voice cracks.

The footsteps pause. I can't see much through the vents, but I imagine this heavenly hero gliding down the hall with shimmering wings and a staff of love.

"Cameron?" a familiar voice says. It's Oma—my grandmother. Thank all her weird dreamcatcher charms it's not some stranger.

"Please get me out of here."

She crouches so I can see her through the vents. No wings, no staves . . . just Oma, who's been both mom and dad to me and my twin sister our whole lives. "How long have you been in there?" she asks in her long Texas drawl.

An eternity.

"I don't know," I say, not wanting to be dramatic. "Can you get me out?"

"Cammy . . . ," she says—the most awfully cutesy nickname in all creation—, "I think there's a latch inside."

Of course there is.

I feel around and find the metal release. The door opens like magic. I stumble out on tingly legs and lean into her. It's almost a hug, but I play it off. I'll be thirteen next year . . . too old to be hugging my Oma in the Social Studies hall.

"I'm sorry," I tell her, about nothing in particular.

"Are you okay?" She's dressed in her typical flower-print blouse and khakis.

I nod. I really . . . *really* don't want to talk about how, once again, the other kids abandoned me and our game.

"I'm going to have to stay at school a while longer," she tells me. "Just a bit more work today."

That's a lie. Oma's a sub—she hasn't taught full-time since Dad disappeared, so there's no reason for her to stay at school longer than everyone else. And the look she gives me sets off every nuclear alarm in my head.

She was supposed to talk with my sister's doctor today. Something must be wrong—again.

"Why don't you head home and make your sister dinner?" she says, giving me a droopy-eyed smile. "I'll be late."

On the walk home, I stop at 7-Eleven for an orange Creamsicle pop. Something about choosing a brain freeze in December makes me feel like I'm in control. My sister, Cass, makes fun of me for it. "No one eats Popsicles in the winter," she says every time. But she's wrong.

Just like she's wrong about Dad. He didn't abandon us. It's like Oma always says: *Someone stole him away.*

I finger the painted circle of wood hanging from my neck. My coin matches my sister's in every aspect except one—mine is gold, and shimmers a little when it catches the light, while Cass's is a dull, gray wood. Her coin belonged to Mom. Oma says hers is gray because Mom died. The only logical assumption is that, since mine is still shiny, Dad's still alive out there.

Cass may not believe it, but I do. I'll prove it to her one day, too. I'll find Dad, bring him home, and everything'll be the way it's supposed to be. I just . . . don't know how yet.

I debate sitting at the picnic table outside the gas station to eat my Popsicle, but one of Cass's morbid, educational TV shows said sitting too long can cause blood clots. On my list of Worst Ways to Die, "deep vein thrombosis" is one of the least exciting.

Instead I continue to walk through the parking lot behind the 7-Eleven, scanning the shopping center between it and my neighborhood as I go.

Something's different about the shopping center today. It's the only new building development in our area. The place was supposed to be a mini-strip mall, but not a single business has moved into the twenty or so glass storefronts during the whole two years since they finished. Now it's a ghost town, complete with plastic bag tumbleweeds.

But today, a new sign on one of the doors screams for my attention. Big, shiny letters with delicate, curly flourishes sparkle even under the cloudy sky.

THE HOTEL BETWEEN
HALFWAY BETWEEN HERE, THERE, AND EVERYWHERE.

A giant, etched tree rises behind the letters, split down the middle with one half on each of the glass double doors. The sign is almost blinding, but at the same time so entrancing I can't help but stare. Most businesses around here have cheap, off-kilter letter stickers or those plastic, sun-faded OPEN signs, but these letters glitter like New Year's Eve confetti.

The tree behind it looks so familiar, too. I know that tree. Same as the drawing posted inside my locker, and carved into our coin necklaces. I've run my fingers over that symbol so many times. And ever since I turned twelve, it's been invading my dreams, too. Like its presence should mean something to me.

I hurry to the door and peek through the glass, but can't see anything inside. Must not be open yet. I cup a hand and press my face against the pane, and . . .

Wham!

The door slams into my nose. Glass and metal rattle, along with my ice-pop-frozen brain. I stumble back, dropping my Popsicle in the process, and crash to my butt on the sidewalk. It feels like my nose was shoved way back into my skull. I'm definitely going to have brain damage (number 43 on my Worst Ways to Die list).

A man peeks around the door as I pinch the bridge of my nose to keep it from bleeding. I'm doing everything in my power not to cry, but holding back the tears is like building a Lego ship with no instructions.

The tall man laughs and says something in another language, offering a hand to help me up. He's bald, wearing a long robe with bright yellow and green shapes that look like those tangram puzzles in math class. My probably-crooked-now nose barely comes to his chest.

Two more people step through the doors behind him: a bearded man in a linen suit, and a woman with a headscarf tied around her face. The woman sounds like she's apologizing for Tangram Man almost knocking me out, but I can't understand her. Linen Suit Man steps out into the parking lot and gazes upward to the Texas sky.

I turn back to the door and catch a glimpse of . . . something unbelievable. Thick, velvety maroon carpet stretches deep into an open foyer and up a twisty staircase. Warm light shines from old Thomas Edison–style bulbs in intricate brass fixtures. A sparkly chandelier with long, dangly chains of crystals casts rainbows everywhere, flooding the enormous space with warm, smoky light. I can't even see the ceiling, it's so high. And I think I smell blueberries.

Maybe the door knocked me out and I'm dreaming. But do dreams usually hurt like this?

Before I can process it all, a fourth person pushes me with a "Step back, sir," and the spectacle inside disappears as he closes the door behind him.

It's a boy who looks to be around my age. His skin is light bronze, and he's dressed like money. Black suit with wide lapels and a professional name tag that reads NICO. White gloves. Two long coattails drag at the backs of his knees, and his dark hair swooshes to one side, slick with gel. The only thing he's wearing that doesn't shine is a pair of black Converse sneakers.

Nico leans against the door, watching me as he addresses the others in a language I don't recognize. When he finishes, they all laugh.

"Don't worry," Nico says, this time in perfect English, "I told them you don't work for the Hotel. Besides, we're not looking for a tour guide today. Thanks, though." He winks.

"What?" I'm totally lost.

He says something else to the others and motions them back through the door. That warm, pie-in-the-oven glow reaches me again. I catch another whiff of blueberries, mixed with a wood-burning stove and the sharp aroma of curry.

I gaze back up at the crystal chandelier over the room, but something's off about it. The chandelier has to be attached to a ceiling I can't quite see, three floors up at least—maybe four. But the shopping center is a one-story building.

I step in to take a closer look, but the boy in the coattails pushes me back.

"Nuh-uh, kiddo." A smile creeps across his face. "That ain't for you."

"But—"

"No vacancy at the Hotel tonight."

"That's a hotel?"

"The Hotel Between," Nico says, pointing to the sign. "The vacation of your dreams, located halfway between here, there, and everywhere." His gaze flits to my necklace, and he grins. "Come back when you can afford a room."

"Am I dreaming?" I ask.

Nico chuckles. "Nope. Dreams aren't really my thing."

He steps through the door, snaps his fingers, and a coin appears between his thumb and forefinger. He rolls the coin over his knuckles . . .

. . . flicks it into air . . .

. . . and it's gone.

He raises his other hand and pats my chest. "There are magics in the world, if you know where to find them."

And he closes the door behind him.

I back away and stare at the door. Nico's words bounce like a Super Ball in my head.

There are magics in the world . . .

Oma's always told us stories about magic and spirits creeping into our world, ever since we were little. Magic's neither good nor evil, she always says . . . it just *is*. It's the person who uses the magic that determines whether it helps or hurts.

She also says it was magic that took Dad from us.

But I don't believe in magic. Magic doesn't help the ones you love get better or give you more friends. It hasn't brought Dad back, either. And Oma's stories about magic and Dad and all that never make sense. She has hundreds of postcards Dad sent to her from all over the world—Japan, Botswana, Queensland, everywhere in Europe—but when we ask her what Dad was doing there, she won't say. She acts like she's forgotten all the important bits, like how he could travel to all those places in so little time, or who would have taken him, and why.

A drop of something wet falls from my nose, and I wipe it with my hand. Blood. And not just a little. Full-on Niagara Falls. I was so distracted by the door, I didn't even notice how badly I was bleeding. I try wiping it, but all that does is leave a big smear of red across my hand and probably all over my face. I must look like a preschooler who's been finger painting.

I feel in my pocket for a used tissue from this afternoon, but my fingers close around something hard and round instead.

Nico's coin. The one he used to perform his magic trick. The smiley face scratched into the worn-smooth front grins at me. He must have slipped it into my pocket somehow.

I turn the coin over, and freeze. It's the tree again. Nico's coin is an exact replica of the ones Cass and I wear around our necks. The coins Dad left with us when he dropped us off with Oma twelve years ago.

I glance back at the door, emblazoned with that same gold tree. Is this where Dad got them? Did he stay here, at The Hotel Between? A twinge of excitement bubbles deep down inside me. I have to figure out a way in.

Another drip of red falls from my nose, so I finally dig out the tissue and pinch it closed. Oma says nosebleeds are a normal part of growing up, but I'm pretty sure this represents a subdural hematoma or a brain aneurism (numbers 458 and 459 in my WWTD list). She should take me to the hospital to confirm, but I know she'll tell me to suck it up instead.

The hospital. Cass. She's probably waiting for me.

Sorting out this hotel stuff will have to wait. I need to get home and make sure Cass is okay.

. . .

My nosebleed stops before I get home, which is a good thing, because Cass is in a mood. She basically assaults me with her wheelchair as I enter.

"Where have you been?"

I juke out of the way and take off my shoes. "At school."

"Oma said she sent you home, like, hours ago."

"Don't be mad. I got . . . detained."

Cass huffs. I get why she's annoyed. It's not about dinner or needing help. She's capable of doing most things on her own these days. It's because bad things happen when she's alone. Ever since the home health care nurse stopped coming last year, we've all been more worried about her.

"I'm sorry," I say, and hurry to the kitchen to make dinner.

"What happened to your face?" she asks, rolling behind me.

I throw a hand up to cover my nose.

"Did you get in a fight again?"

"No."

"Liar."

I *am* a terrible liar, but this time I'm not lying. Unless fighting with a door counts.

She folds her arms, giving me her best disappointed-Oma impression.

"I only got in *one* fight this year." I never had the heart to tell her it was because Jaeden called her a . . . well, just thinking about it makes me want to hit him all over again.

I ignore her look and grab a skillet from under the stove.

"Put that away," she says. "I already ate."

"Ate what?"

"Pop-Tarts."

I groan. "You should have waited."

She groans back. "If I waited for you, I'd starve."

Oma's been "working late" a lot lately, so Cass has been taking the accessible bus home. I should probably ride with her, but I can't stand the bus. It smells like the fumes of a dirty gas station, and Oma says it's good for Cass to do things on her own. Besides, I'd rather walk so I can be aware of any changes in our neighborhood. Like the hotel.

My hand jumps to my pocket to make sure Nico's coin is still there. I want to talk to him, to find out more about this Hotel Between, and why he has a coin just like Dad's.

I glance at the almost identical coin hanging from Cass's neck. Has she been having dreams too? I want to ask—to tell her about the door and Nico—but it feels like a bad idea. Talking about Dad always makes her angry, and when Cass gets angry, we might as well flush the whole evening down the toilet.

I pull the Pop-Tarts out of the pantry and pop two in the toaster, glad I don't have to make anything special. It's not pretty when I cook on my own. She was smart to eat the Pop-Tarts.

"Something's up with Oma," I say.

Cass slouches in her chair. "I know. She was talking to Aunt Jeri on the phone last night."

"What about?"

She shrugs.

"I thought she might've heard something else from your doctor," I guess, hoping for a clue.

Cass twists her lips to the side, which means Oma *did* hear something, but they're not going to tell me just yet. Typical.

She goes back to watching a *National Geographic* show about hunters in the Congo. It's her favorite channel. She calls it "preparation" for when she gets to travel the world. I don't know why she tortures herself like that; we've never left Texas. And I'm pretty sure Cass will never go to any of those places—not with her condition. One of these days she'll realize what I've already learned: It's safer and better for everyone if we all stay home.

I head to my room and flip on the ceiling light. My fan whirls, blowing up the corners of all the safety posters and foldouts I've collected from our endless trips to the hospital. Someone's got to be ready to take care of Cass in an emergency. *Her* room is plastered with maps of the exotic places from Oma's stories. Photos of South African cities, a painting of Peru, a cuckoo clock Aunt Jeri sent from Germany, even a didgeridoo Cass's friend gave her after a vacation to Australia. She may think Dad abandoned us, but her eyes still brighten every time Oma leans in for another fantastical tale of Dad touring the temples of Burma, or sleeping under the stars in the Sahara.

I flop onto my bed and a tiny cloud of dust poofs from under the mattress. Oma doesn't believe in dusting. She told me why once—something about needing as much dust as she can get in her life to bind her to one spot—but really, I think she just doesn't like cleaning.

I lie back and untie my necklace, comparing Dad's coin to the one Nico slipped into my pocket. Dad's is light, thick, and so scratched up I've never been able to read the words imprinted on it. The embossing on Nico's is clear and bold. The words "Hotel Between" swirl under the tall, regal-looking tree on the front, and the design on the flip side—a grand castle-like building—bears the words "Halfway between here, there, and everywhere." A smiley face has been carved over the building, winking at me.

There are magics in the world . . .

After all this time I can't possibly have found something to help me, can I?

I pull my Dad-box—a shoebox full of clues I've collected over the years—out from under my bed. It's mostly pictures and notes and used ticket stubs I found in Oma's closet. I flip through some photos of Dad and Mom together. One shows them atop the Empire State Building. Another has them on a rocky, snow-covered mountain, the wind blowing Mom's long, dark hair.

Oma says that on the night Dad left us with her, he was scared. He told her that Mom was gone, and that they'd be coming for him too and she needed to keep us safe. And then we never saw him or Mom again. I've always wondered what they could have done to cause people to come after them. Who—or what—was he running from? Are they the reason he never came back? And if Mom's "gone," what happened to her?

I stop at a photo of Mom and Dad at a fancy party. Dad wears a suit and a prickly mustache, and Mom's dressed in a silky, cherry blossom dress. In the background, I spy the pair of gilded doors engraved with that same tree symbol.

Nico's coin is proof—I can feel it. Proof Dad's still alive. Proof that someone's keeping him from us.

Proof that Dad's out there, waiting for me to find him.

2

The Dallas Door

Oma comes home a couple of hours later, pretending nothing's the matter. But when she says she needs to talk to Cass before bed, I know exactly what's wrong.

Another surgery.

"To bed," Oma tells me, waving me away like she's swatting a housefly.

I grumble and head to my room. Oma never talks about Cass's condition in front of me anymore, except to say that the coin around Cass's neck can only protect her from evil spirits, and not from her health problems. Apparently I make things out to be worse than they are, or something. Even so, Oma still only talks about it with Cass when she has to.

Cass was born with spina bifida. It's a weird condition that does lots of things and some people who have it never show signs, but Cass isn't one of those. The real issue is the complications. Hers could be a lot worse given the type she has, but it's bad enough that she'll never be able to walk and still needs tons more surgeries to keep her healthy.

Friends at school tell me it's weird to worry about my sister the way I do, but they don't know what it's like. She's always in danger. If we aren't careful, aren't ready, everything could change. I don't want to think about that, but I have to. Every moment matters.

It doesn't take long before I drift off to sleep, dreaming of that enormous tree again.

The monstrous trunk rises before me, as big around as our house. Roots twist and curl beneath my feet. Leaves rustle under a blinding sun.

Open doors hang from the branches like fruit. There's something odd about these doors, and it's not that doors don't normally grow from trees. That part seems strangely normal. It's that when I look through them, I don't see the tree, or the leaves, or even the sky. Each door reflects a different scene from around the world. I see snow-capped mountains. Shimmering oceans. City streets. Windows into other places.

A door at the base of the trunk cracks open, spilling amber light across the gnarled roots. A hand reaches through the sliver of light, curling a finger to invite me inside.

The sky darkens, the breeze whispering . . .

Come

A noise in the house wakes me.

I grip Dad's coin around my neck and roll over to stare at the picture of Mom and Dad on my bedside table. There has to be a way to find Dad. Everything's been so hard lately. If only he were here to help. Oma's always tired, and she keeps leaving unpaid bills on the table. And then there's Cass. If I could get Dad back, he could help us. He could be there to make sure nothing bad happens. To guide me on how best to help her. He could . . .

Knock, knock.

I sit up. That's strange. Sounded like it came from outside my window.

Knock-knock-knock.

I slide out of bed and slowly draw the curtain.

A face pops up on the other side of the glass, and I stifle a yelp. "Nico?"

"Hey buddy," the slick-haired boy says in a slightly muffled voice. "Let me in. *Hace frío.*"

I unlatch the lock, and Nico climbs through like he's done this two thousand times before. He's wearing a black T-shirt and jeans instead of the coattails and satin lapels of his uniform. Four horizontal loops of fabric have been stitched into the shirt where a pocket would normally be—same as his suit.

"I thought Texas was supposed to be warm," he says, rubbing his arms. "It's stinking *cold* out there."

I shut the window and lock the latches to keep out the various WWTDs that lurk in the night. Then again, I just let in a stranger, so I don't know why I'm worried about what's outside. "What are you doing here?"

He grins. "Just being friendly."

Sounds suspicious. "You don't even know me. How'd you find my house?"

Nico digs in his pocket and pulls out a coin, which he flips in the air and snags just as quickly. "Magic." He wiggles his fingers around the shiny disc. It looks exactly like the one he snuck into my pocket, smiley face and all.

"How—" I start, and then I pull out my Dad-box and shuffle through the pictures. I left the coin right here. It's gone.

"It's the same coin, buddy. My coin."

"H-How'd you get it back?"

He smirks. "You know what they say about magicians."

Oh, he's good.

Nico flops onto my bed next to the photos. "I'm pretty skilled at finding people. You were an easy mark."

"Finding people?" My eyes dart to the picture on my bedside table.

"It's part of working at the Hotel," he says, lying back on my pillow. "We find all sorts of people, places, things. It's what makes a good concierge." He says the word "concierge" with awe, like it means something special.

"Are *you* the concierge?"

Nico laughs. "Not yet. But one day . . . one day I'll be master of my own House."

I have no idea what he's talking about. Master of a house? What does that even mean?

He rolls the coin over his fingers, staring at me like he wants something but he's not sure how to ask. "You never told me your name."

"Cameron." I gather up the pictures and stuff them back in the Dad-box. "Everyone calls me Cam though."

He sits up to shake my hand. "Nico. Pleasure to meet you. So"—he squints his eyes—"I've got a question for you."

"Okay?" I've got questions for him, too.

"Why were you hanging around the Dallas Door this after-noon?"

"Dallas Door?"

"Yeah." He waits, as if I'm supposed to know what he's talking about.

"Uhh . . . it's on my way home from school. First time I've seen any businesses in our new strip mall so I stopped."

"Uh-huh." His eyes remain narrowed. "And when was the last time you were in the Hotel?"

"That place on the other side of the door? Never."

"Never?"

I shake my head. "Now for *my* questions," I say. "What is that place?"

"Magic." He leans back on my pillow and flips his coin. "You sure you've never been to the Hotel? Not even in your dreams?"

Okay, this is getting annoying. "I don't believe in magic and of course I haven't. I don't even know what it—" but I stop myself. All those dreams I've had lately of the tree and the places beyond the doors . . . they are just dreams, aren't they?

"I knew it. You *have* been to the Hotel. How else would you get a coin?" He points to my necklace.

I unclasp it and rub my thumb over the smooth surface of Dad's coin. "It's my dad's. He gave it to me when I was little."

Nico laughs. "Your dad must've stolen it, then."

"My dad didn't *steal* anything," I snap.

Nico holds his hands up in surrender. "Whoa, whoa. I didn't mean—"

"My dad's gone," I say in a cold whisper. "Someone stole *him.*"

"Oh." Nico lowers his gaze.

Uh-oh. I shouldn't have said that. I've never told anyone at school about what happened to Dad. I always figured that if he was on the run from someone, and he left us with Oma to keep us safe, then it's best we stay under the radar.

"Sorry, I mean, that's not what I—"

"No, it makes sense, actually," Nico says.

I flinch. "How does it make sense?"

He grits his teeth. "I didn't mean to say that. Forget it."

"No, tell me." I lean in. "What do you mean?"

Nico scoots away. "I-I can't."

"Why not?" I ask, letting my irritation show. This kid better not be pulling my leg.

"Because the secrets of the Hotel are not mine to give," he says, seriously. "You don't know how privileged you are to have gotten just a peek. Most don't even see the doors. And *no one* gets to keep their coin when they leave."

I shoot him a skeptical look. "You've got one."

"Of course I do. I'm staff. I can come and go, but I've always got to end up back there. Or at least, the *coin* has to."

My fingers rub the disc harder, as if squeezing it can press the truth out of him. This night is getting weirder by the minute.

"Well, I mean, you *do* have a coin. . . . I guess that entitles you to something." He draws his lips into a thin line. "You won't tell anybody, will you?"

"Tell anybody what? I want to know what you meant about my dad."

His face lights up in a birthday-boy grin. "It's better if I *show* you."

Normally there's no way I'd follow some strange, slick-haired kid out into the night in my pajamas. Lots of entries on the Worst Ways to Die list start with following strangers into the night. But tonight's different. The tree, the coins . . . everything's telling me I need to go with him, even though my stomach's shriveling like a raisin. This may be my only chance.

I keep one hand in my pocket to hold on to the photo of my parents as we weave through the streets toward what Nico calls the "Dallas Door." I'm trying not to think about the possibility that Nico's one of the greedy spirits from Oma's stories. But he couldn't be. He's a kid, like me. The spirits in Oma's tales *take* kids.

Besides, those stories aren't real. And I'm pretty sure a spirit wouldn't ramble like this guy does. Nico talks, a lot. Like, a lot a lot. So much that I barely have to say anything, which is fine by me. He tells me about the busy streets of Paris at night, and the aurora borealis above Reykjavik, Iceland, and how much bigger the sky is there. He asks where all the horses are, and what's the point of Dallas without horses, and says the "Old Man" should have opened a door to Orlando instead.

I can't keep track of what he's saying. Still, as weird as he is, listening to him makes me feel at ease. He's a little like how I always imagined Dad—a world traveler telling stories of his adventures, reminiscing about the best dishes he ate in the forests of Lebanon and the mountains of Peru.

But Nico can't have been to all those places. He's too young. Something's off about him; I just can't figure out what. It's like he's trying to sell me on something, but I have no idea what I'm buying.

We round the corner of the shopping center and the shimmering script of The Hotel Between comes into view.

"It's so small." I picture the chandelier on the other side, the warm light, the second and third and fourth stories. "A whole hotel couldn't possibly fit here."

"Exactly."

"Where is it, then?"

"Right here. And everywhere." Nico pulls out a brass skeleton key and inserts it into the door.

But he doesn't poke the key into a keyhole, like he should. Instead, he shoves the key right into the middle of the door. Shimmering foam expands from the glass around the key, glittering with copper-tinted smoke. I can't believe my eyes.

My mouth falls open as he turns the key in the rippling glow and opens the door. Warm light poofs out like a cloud of hot air from an oven. The familiar smell of blueberries and woodsy smoke and spices wrap around me like a blanket.

Nico taps the threshold. "The Hotel Between. A very old establishment with doors that open all over the world."

"You're joking with me. This has to be a trick," I say.

"Not everything in life is so black and white, Cam," Nico replies. "Sometimes you need to take a risk."

I step up to feel the heat rolling through the door, but Nico presses a hand to my chest to hold me back.

"To pass through always costs something," he says.

"But . . . " I touch my dad's coin. "I thought this meant I could go inside."

Nico shakes his head. "That doesn't mean you *should*. The Hotel isn't a place you enter lightly, you know. It's dangerous."

My arms prickle at the word. "It's a hotel."

"The Hotel Between is more than just a place to stay. It's got an agenda—a mission—and you do *not* want to get caught up in that."

I lean in and breathe the warm, blueberry air, taking in the bubbling fountain in front of the grand staircase. The chandelier above is bigger than I remember, brighter, with its long, flowing chains of sparkling crystals. I'm really seeing all of this.

"It's . . . wonderful," I say.

Nico clasps his fingers behind his back. "This is the North American Lobby. Lobbies are typically the first thing our guests see."

A girl with dozens of tiny braids in her hair shuffles papers behind a counter on the far wall. People in colorful shorts and sunglasses meander through the velvety curtains on one side and climb the curling staircase to the upper level.

"When you cross the threshold of The Hotel Between, you pass from one place on the globe to another." Nico waves his hand over the glass door front. "This side is Dallas." Then he runs his hand over the dark wood inside. "And this is the Hotel."

As nice as it seems, it almost reminds me of the Gingerbread House in *Hansel and Gretel.* Everything in me screams to get away, even as the warm light beckons me inside. I should listen to the uneasiness in my stomach. I don't do risk.

Nico pushes us back out and closes the door. The colors of the hotel are sucked away into the night, leaving the strip mall looking even bleaker and dirtier.

"That's pretty much it." He leans against the wall and gives his coin a flip. "You've seen magic. How do you feel?"

I don't mean to say it out loud, but I've wanted to ask the question ever since Nico's comment earlier. "Could you find him?"

Nico snatches his coin out of the air. "Who? Your dad?"

I hesitate. I can't believe I'm going to trust an absolute stranger with my secrets. That I'm going to trust magic, of all things. But Nico said this is what he does: finds people. And he's the only lead I've ever had.

"He's been missing since my sister and I were babies," I tell him. "Oma worries about him, and we—"

Nico pulls a picture from his jacket pocket. "This him?" It's the photo of Dad and Mom all dressed up at a fancy party. The one I brought with me.

I feel for the picture in my pocket, but it's not there.

"How did you . . . ?" I glare at him. He swiped it from me, like a common thief.

"Just practicing." He smiles. "But why would you want to find him? If he left you—"

"He didn't leave," I say, snatching the photo back. "I told you, he was taken. Someone was after him, and I think whoever took him . . . killed my mom, too."

Nico shakes his head. "Trail's too cold. The magic has to have *something* to go on. If no one's heard from him your whole life . . . " He glances once again to the coin at my neck. "Then again, if I had his coin—"

"No." I can't give Dad's coin away. It's the only connection I have to him.

He shrugs. "Then there's nothing I can do."

I grip the necklace tighter. This is such a bad idea. Or maybe it's all just one long, bad dream.

"I'll make you a deal," Nico says. "You keep my coin." He flips the disc to me. "Call it collateral. Meanwhile I'll take your Dad's, and the picture, and bring it back once I've figured out whether I can help. What do you say?"

This isn't what I expected. Nico's coin is the same as mine, so maybe it offers the same protections—if they offer any kind of protection in the first place. If he was some sort of greedy spirit, he wouldn't offer the same thing in return, would he?

"I don't know. . . ."

Nico winks, and places a hand on the Dallas Door. "I'll be back before you know it."

A sick feeling grows from within the pit of my stomach. This coin is the most important thing I own.

"Don't worry," Nico says. "It's a touch."

"A touch?"

"Hotel lingo. It means 'don't be a baby, it's no big deal.'" He reaches out a hand. "You'll get your coin back, safe and sound. I promise."

I can't believe I'm considering this. I saw on TV once that there are brain parasites that can mess with your mind and cause you to do things you wouldn't normally do. WWTD number 637. I feel fine, but maybe my brain's already deteriorating.

"Okay." I untie the necklace and hand it to him. I feel naked out here in the dark without it. "Bring it back, all right?"

"Hopefully, I'll bring *him* back, yeah?" He turns his key in the door. "See you soon, Mr. Cam."

"Wait."

Nico stops, key sparkling in the magic keyhole.

I swallow the cottony dryness in my throat. "Do you really think you can find him?"

He opens the door and smiles. "I'm Nico. For the right price, I can do anything."

3

Tricks in the Cards

The tree looms over me. Honey-colored light spills from the open door in the trunk. I don't want to go in there. It feels like something bad is waiting for me on the other side. But at the same time, I do want to. I have to know.

One of the rustling leaves breaks loose and drifts downward, letting me pluck it from the air. Only it's not a leaf. It's a playing card. The four of hearts. On the back of the card are the words "Find Your Destination." The phrase makes me happy, like I've been invited to an exclusive party.

But the happiness quickly fades. The door in the tree trunk is coming toward me now, fast. I turn to run away, but it catches me. I'm drowning in a swirling vortex of chandeliers and marble and kids in fancy suits.

I've made a huge mistake. Some stranger shows up at my window and I place all hope of finding my dad in him . . . how is that supposed to end well? I thought the hotel was some sign, a clue that this ridiculous hope wasn't for nothing. I should have known life doesn't work that way for us.

Two days pass, and nothing. No word from Nico. I've gone by the Dallas Door four times, bundled against the winter chill, but every time I look through the glass all I find is an empty concrete building. No evidence of anything existing beyond those doors.

I can't believe I trusted him. And I've lost Dad's coin, to boot. This is what I do . . . I make dumb decisions. I lock myself in lockers and give away what's important and trust the wrong friends. It's why I never want to *do* anything in the first place.

On the third morning of break, I wake to Oma hovering over me.

"Get up."

"Is it time for breakfast?" I ask—the only logical reason she'd have for waking me before noon.

"You need to get up!" Her relentless smile is like a blowtorch. I'm in danger of being lit on fire with her enthusiasm. "Can't sleep your whole vacation away."

Now that I've lost my last connection to Dad, that's *exactly* what I want to do.

Then I notice the flour on her nose. Nose-flour can only mean one thing: biscuits and gravy. Oma must *really* want to cheer me up—she never makes biscuits and gravy anymore because it's not on her current diet plan.

I get dressed and head to the kitchen to help. Cass rambles on about some waterfall in South America while I start to crumble sausage. My gaze wanders to the gray, mottled coin dangling between her collarbones. At least Cass still has Mom's coin.

I dump the sausage into the frying pan. "Oma, how did Mom die?"

"Hmmm?" She looks up and wipes more flour on her cheek.

This topic is usually off limits, unless Oma's telling us her stories, but now I'm committed. "You've never told us how Mom died."

Cass cocks her head to listen. We've asked these questions before, but Oma never gives us much. She only wants to talk about far-fetched adventures and places around the world . . . how Dad was wild and free-spirited, and his life was too big to be kept in one place, and how Mom was rooted into the soil of the earth. They always sound like fairy tales. But whenever the fateful events that led to his disappearance come up, she goes silent.

"I'm afraid I don't know," she says. "Your father didn't tell me. And if he had, those secrets wouldn't be mine to share." She grabs a strip of bacon cooling under a paper towel and passes it to me. "Chewy enough, or should I make more?"

Cass scoffs and rolls into the attached living room to watch a bunch of barely clothed men riding in a Jeep, armed with spears. Oma lets her go. We both know what happens when Cass starts dwelling on our parents.

I wish Cass didn't hate Dad. There are times I want to hate him for not being here, too, but then I picture him rotting away in some dank, wet cell, and I can't. Flesh rot: WWTD number 340. Rare, but extremely gross.

Oma returns to kneading the dough. "You know, your father

used to make all sorts of food I'd never seen before. He'd fry up these little meat pastry things . . . oh, what were they called . . . sammy-so-somethings."

I'm not going to let her dodge my questions again, though. She has to tell us eventually. "If you don't know what happened, how do you know for sure she died?"

Cass turns her head slightly, pretending not to listen.

"Reinhart told me so," Oma says, calling Dad by his first name. "When he dropped you off, he said that Melissa . . . " She trails off, as if she forgot what she was saying. "How is that bacon?"

"But he didn't say how?" I ask.

Oma sighs and flops the dough over on the flour-dusted counter in a huff. "He was in such a hurry. Said they'd be coming for him soon, and that those coins would keep you safe. Always wear the coins. Always, always. They'll protect you kids." She points to the fridge. "Could you get the milk out, please?"

My shoulders slouch. Nothing new. No mention of hotels, or who might have taken him. And of course, still nothing about Mom.

I head for the refrigerator. "But if he left his coin with us, doesn't that mean he's *not* protected?"

"That's different," she says. "Reinhart wanted *you* to be protected. Those greedy spirits would possess the world if they could, but as long as you've got your coins, they'll think you're already owned, and they'll leave you alone."

I pull my collar up to hide my coin-less neck, and finger Nico's coin in my pocket. Is this why Nico carries one too? So the spirits will think he's "owned" already?

"If you could find Dad," I say after a moment, "would you?"

Oma shakes her head. "I can't."

"But—"

She sighs again and wipes her forehead. "Your father is a good man. If he could be here, he would." Oma presses her knuckles into the dough with more force than necessary. "I would pay any price to have my Reinhart back."

By the time afternoon rolls around and my biscuits are half-digested, I'm back in my room, turning Nico's coin over and over and wishing it would magically transform into Dad's.

A knock comes at my door, and I shove the coin back in my pocket before Oma enters. "Cammy, you have a guest," Oma says. "Nice boy. Very snappy dresser."

Nico! I hop off the bed with a "Thanks!" and rush to the living room. Sure enough, there he is, sitting on the couch in the tail-coat of his hotel uniform, a cup of Oma's tea pinched between his thumb and forefinger.

"Hey there, Mr. Cam." He nods toward Cass, sitting across from him. "I was just getting to know your sister."

"I—" I pause, unsure what to say. Part of me wasn't even convinced Nico was real, and here he is, talking to my sister, who is one hundred percent the *last* person I want to know about the Hotel. "What took you so long?"

Cass laughs nervously. "Don't be rude, Cam."

Nico gives her a wink, a sparkle in his eye.

My pulse pounds in my ears. Could he really have found some information about Dad? But Cass can't know anything about that. She'll pitch a fit, and probably think I'm nuts—trusting strangers who claim they can do magic.

Am I nuts?

"How'd you guys meet?" Cass asks him. "You're not in our class at school."

"Homeschooled," Nico says. "My family travels all over the world."

Cass's eyes flutter as if he just told her he's Santa Claus. Ugh. She can be so embarrassing. She doesn't even notice how Nico dodged her question.

He sets his teacup down and pulls out a deck of cards from his jacket. "Wanna see something amazing?"

"Sure!" She almost rolls over my foot to get closer.

"Wait," I say, "what about—?"

"One trick, Mr. Cam. Then we'll talk." He fans the deck for Cass to pick a card.

She pulls one from the deck and shows it to me. Four of hearts, with little Japanese cats holding each of the hearts.

My breath catches. That's the—the card from my dream. Outside, the wind picks up and rushes through the trees.

No. No. I'm imagining things. I only *think* I saw that card in my dreams. I'm remembering it wrong. There's no way . . .

"Now," Nico tells Cass as he shuffles the deck, "fold the card in half and slide it into my coat pocket."

Cass creases the card and gives it a kiss before sliding it in.

"And that's the trick!" Nico claps his hands, and the deck disappears. "*Et voilá!*"

She eyes him skeptically. "That's no trick. You just waved your hands around."

Nico turns to me. "Well, Mr. Cam?"

I wait for him to finish, but he just stares, like he's waiting for *me* to do something. "What?"

"Give her the card."

"I don't have it."

He nods with a sly grin. "Check your pocks."

"My what?"

"Your pocket."

I reach into my pants pocket and pull out a folded card—the four of hearts, complete with cats. The dream of snatching the card out of the air flashes through my mind. I jerk back and drop it like a hot pan.

Cass squeals and rocks her chair back and forth. "You were in on it?"

"Umm . . . " I don't know what to say, what to think. My mind is a tornado of cutesy cat cards.

She clucks her tongue and turns back to Nico. "Do you know any more?"

"Lots. But I think your brother wants to talk." He motions to the door. "Outside?"

. . .

"Okay," I say once we're on the back porch, trying not to think about the bizarre connection between my dream and what just happened inside. "How'd you do that?"

"The card?" He laughs. "A magician never reveals—"

"No, how'd you know? How . . . ?"

The look on his face tells me he has no idea what I'm talking about.

I decide to change tactics. "Okay, whatever then. What'd you find?"

"Who says I found anything? Maybe I just wanted to check in on my favorite Texan." His tone sounds cooler than the December air. He pokes at the dying plants in Oma's flowerbeds with the mini shovel she had leaning against the back door. "It's called 'building relationships.' You should try it."

I flash him a glare. He's toying with me. Hiding behind that dumb grin.

"Okay, fine." Nico twists the shovel in the ground, turning up the top layer of soil. "Maybe I needed something else before I commit to searching for him."

My heart collapses. Total cardiovascular failure. Death by disappointment.

He digs a little deeper into the sprinkler-damp earth.

I study him. "Dirt?" I ask. "You need dirt to find my dad?"

"For a start." He digs out one last scoop and places the shovel back against the siding. "I wanted to learn more about who I'd be helping, too. See, if I'm going to be master of my own House, I have to be able to tell who's good and who's not."

He rakes his fingers through the soil, scooping a handful into his white-gloved palm.

"What's the story with your sister, anyway?" he asks, pouring the dirt into a tiny jar that he's taken from his pocket and sealing the cap. Cold wind rakes through the fallen leaves.

"Spina bifida," I tell him. "She was born with it. Hers is one of the worst kinds."

"So"—he considers me—"she's the reason you want to find your dad so bad?"

"Yeah, I guess. We do our best to take care of her, but it's hard sometimes. If Dad was here he might be able to do something . . . more."

He pockets the jar. "But Cass doesn't seem all that helpless to me."

"She's not anymore," I say. "But sometimes her body doesn't do all the things it should. Today's a good day."

"You should give her more credit. I bet she's more capable than you think." He dusts off his glove and starts toward the gate. "I've gotta get back. Big tasks today."

"That's it? You're leaving?"

He stops with a hand on the fence and tosses something to me. Dad's coin. He gave it back. Now I feel bad for not trusting him. Cass always says I get worked up about nothing.

"Be ready," he says. "And figure out how you're going to pay me." He wiggles his dirty, gloved fingers. "Gotta get something for services rendered."

"I-I don't have any money."

"You'll figure something out." He pulls his hand back and opens the gate. "If you need me, just knock on the Dallas Door. A knocked door is always opened."

He starts to leave, but something stops him.

"You hear that?"

I listen to the wind. "No, I—"

Then it comes again. A sound, like someone gagging.

Adrenaline prickles up my arms. "Cass!"

I race inside to find her on the floor, a dribble of vomit running down her shirt. Her head bobs forward and back, like she's trying to shout, but nothing comes out.

Oh no . . . What if it's a shunt malfunction? What if . . .

I drop down next to her and help her to sit up. The doctor said if this happens we're supposed to face her downward so she doesn't breathe in the sick. But she's coughing and pointing to her throat like she already did. Not good.

"What should I do?" Nico says, entering behind me.

Be calm. I'm supposed to be calm. This is what I stay ready for. "The phone!"

I yell for Oma as Nico hands me the phone to dial nine-one-one.

The operator answers. "What is the location of the emergency?"

Nico supports Cass's head so I can go through the normal back and forth with the operator—address, problem, details of Cass's complications. He holds her hand, watching her intently.

Halfway through the operator's spiel, Oma snatches the phone away from my ear, freeing me to go to Cass. "It's gonna be okay," I tell her, brushing her hair back. But the worry strikes again. What if it's not? What if it's worse this time? What if . . .

"Complications" are number 3 on the WWTD list, partly because they're so nasty, partly because it's the most likely way my twin is going to be taken away from me.

And everything gets taken away eventually.

Hours later we're settled in at the hospital, like always. When your sister's had thirty-three surgeries and counting, you get to know hospitals really well. It's like a labyrinth of cursed memories—whenever I come, I always worry I won't be able to get back out. And that seems like a very bad way to die.

Nico stays with us a while, pacing and nervously shuffling his deck. It takes a few tries, but I eventually convince him it's okay for him to go. He doesn't know this procedure the way we do. Waiting in the hospital is boring, and he's got things to do, I'm sure.

Still, it's nice of him to stick around as long as he did.

Later, the doctor comes to tell us Cass is going to be okay, for now. Those are the words we always wait for. It's hard for me to know whether to believe him, though. There's still this new surgery Oma won't tell me about, and they'll have to run a bunch of tests, but for now they don't think it was one of the more serious complications.

The doctor says it's good we heard her, but I know the truth. Nico's the one who heard, not me. I could have missed it. One day I *will* miss it, and Oma will too.

And I can't be a twin without my second half.

The nurse takes Oma down the hall to go through whatever it is they need to talk about, leaving me to sit in the uncomfortable chair in Cass's room pretending to look at my phone.

If Dad was here, he could come with us to the hospital and stay with me while Oma does the paperwork. He could be there. Here. With me. Figuring it out with us. Our family wouldn't feel so incomplete.

I'd pay any price for that.

A knock at Cass's door grabs my attention.

"Hey, kiddo." It's Nico, changed back into his black T-shirt. At first I grimace at him calling me "kiddo," but it's nice to have a friend. Even if we just met, he's been more of a friend to me than anyone else, outside my family.

"Hey," I say, acting like I'm not super glad to see him again so soon. In the dim light, I recognize the horizontal loops of fabric sewn where his shirt pocket should be. This time one of the loops holds a wooden peg, about four inches long, with a flat head on one end and a point sticking out through the loop at the other. "What are you doing here?"

"Had to meet someone." He steps up and places his hands on Cass's bed. "How's she doing?"

"She'll probably go home in the morning. She just needs rest." And new lungs. And a new spine. And a new digestive system. And . . . wait, "You had to meet someone in the middle of the night?"

"The Hotel does stuff all over the world. Times don't always sync up." Nico holds a flat straw hat close to his chest as he watches her sleep. "Your sister's nice. Like you."

All over the world. "Because you work at a magical Hotel."

I don't know when this is all going to sink in.

"Yep." Nico pulls his coin out of his pocket and rolls it over his knuckles, eyes still on Cass. "This kind of thing happens a lot?"

"It happens enough."

"Another reason you want to find your dad. You hope he'll have the answers you've been looking for."

He gets it. No one ever gets it.

Nico pops the hat on his head. "I want you to meet someone. Someone who I think can help."

"Help what?" The thought hits me like blast of hot air. "Help find my dad?"

He nods. "But you have to do what I say. Every little word."

My heart explodes in mini fireworks. "Who are we meeting?"

Nico gives me a sideways smile. "Come on. He's waiting."

I bite my lip and glance back at Cass. "I can't just leave her."

"It's a touch," Nico insists. "You'll be back before you know it."

If I find Dad, maybe I won't need to worry as much. With all of us together, I could finally feel more assured that she'll be all right.

Nico steps up next to me, reaches into his pocket, and pulls out a card. The four of hearts, from his trick earlier. He sets it on the table next to Cass and gives her a gentle smile. "We'll take care of her, Cam."

A flood of warmth spreads through my chest. "Okay. Let's go."

I scribble a quick note on a notepad and place it on the table beside Nico's card.

"I'll find Dad for you," I whisper. "Whether you want me to or not."

4

The Man in the Pin-Striped Suit

Outside the hospital, the cold night air sinks its teeth into me. I wrap my arms around my body, trying to ignore the hiss of the wind and the flutter of the grackles' wings as they gather in the trees.

A murder of grackles: WWTD number 52.

"Okay," Nico says as we round the back of the hospital, "here's the thing: Don't go asking a bunch of questions. Trust me, there are some things you don't want to know."

That doesn't sound promising. I fold my arms and clutch my sweatshirt tight to guard against the vampiric wind. "Who is this guy we're meeting, anyway?"

Nico stops at a plain metal door hidden in the shadows. "Someone who knows the Hotel's secrets."

"You keep making it sound like the Hotel's a bad thing."

He pauses, and the look on his face tells me that might not be too far off.

Nico pulls the peg from its loop on his shirt.

"Hinge-pin," he says, holding up the peg. Then he raises a

separate, gun-shaped device with brass barrels on both the top and bottom of the grip. A little iron spike protrudes from the top of the lower barrel, curled in a shiny spring. "And this is a plug."

I reach out to touch the smooth brass.

"Pins and plugs are two tools every staffer should be familiar with," Nico continues, kneeling next to the door. "Hinge-pins— 'pins' for short—are bound with binding magic to a specific place. When a pin is put in the hinge of a door, it turns that door into a shortcut to the location connected to the pin. Plugs aren't magic though . . . they're just a little mechanical tool we use to insert and remove the pins."

He lines up the plug around the center hinge. The spring-loaded spike fits perfectly underneath. He pulls back the hammer, and . . . *flick!* The spike punches the original metal pin out, and it clatters to the concrete.

"Just a touch." Nico spins the wooden peg—*his* pin—in his fingers. "Now, we install the new pin"—he slides the peg into the hole, flips the plug so the spike faces downward, and hammers the pin into place—"and we have a new door." He waves his hands like a game show host. "Ta-da!"

The door crackles like it's charged with electricity.

"Aren't those kind of pins usually metal?" I ask.

He clucks his tongue and pulls a shiny, silver skeleton key from his pocket. "Hello? This is magic, buddy. Gotta do things a little different."

Nico sticks the key into the door, just like before. Silvery foam blooms up from the new keyhole as he turns and pulls. The door opens to a deep, cold darkness that's not at all like the warm, welcoming lobby from before.

I clench my teeth. I do *not* want to go in there. "This doesn't look like the Hotel."

"It's not," he says. "Stripe isn't in the Hotel."

"I thought you said he knows more about the Hotel than anyone?"

"That doesn't mean he *stays* there."

"But—"

"I told you, it's complicated. The Hotel isn't the only place with magic." He disappears into the dark hall.

I lean over the threshold to see inside. A tiny jolt buzzes in my head, and my ears pop. "It's so dark," I say. No response. "Where'd you go?"

"Hey." Nico's voice, inches from my face, makes me jump. "Come on. I'll turn on the lights."

He shuts the door behind us and flips a switch.

Doors line both sides of the straight, checkerboard-tiled hallway. Scarlet wallpaper with twisting silver designs curls off the walls in sheets, revealing dirty brown beneath. The doors are all the same—simple wood with tarnished brass hinges and crystal handles. There's at least fifty, extending to a single door at each end of the hallway—one with a swirling, silver M, the other with a crooked, wooden H.

"Follow me, and no matter what, *don't* wander off." He laughs.

"Always wanted to say that." This is not at all what I expected.

Nico marches, shoulders squared and tense, toward the M door.

"What does the M stand for?" I ask.

"Museum," he says. "Stripe's Museum is one of the great old Houses, like the Hotel. It uses the same magics and all—like the doors—but it's got a different purpose. Stripe's kind of like a . . . curator there. A collector of history. This Corridor is a hidden back door that connects his Museum to the Hotel."

Hidden? Why would it be hidden?

I stop and press my hand against one of the in-between doors. A shock of static zips through my fingers to my elbow, warm and tingly, like steam from a cup of hot tea. Dad could be on the other side. He could be right there, waiting for me.

I grab the crystal handle, and turn.

The door opens to a riot of flashing lights. Blaring rock music assaults my ears. Neon greens and pinks and yellows and reds scream for attention. "It's like a giant arcade."

Nico pulls me back and slams the door. "What are you doing?"

"I—where was that?" I ask as the noise and lights vanish.

"Vegas." He checks his pocket watch before marching on down the hall.

My shoes squeak on the tile as I jog to keep up. "*Las* Vegas? Nevada?"

"Yeah." He points at the doors as we pass. "And that one leads to Baghdad, and Nairobi, and . . . look, we don't have time for this. Stripe's waiting." He leads me to the end of the hall and rests his knuckles on the M door. "He's a great man, you know. Meeting him . . . it's a big honor. Don't mess it up."

Great, like I needed any more pressure.

Nico knocks, and a boy in a gray suit opens the door.

"Orban," Nico says, giving him a slight bow.

Orban bows back. He looks a little older than me, but not by much. A big patch of furry hair rests under his right eye like a giant birthmark. "Stripe's coming," he says, adjusting his red satin pocket square.

I stand on tiptoes to look past Orban through the door. The hall beyond is carpeted royal blue, and lined with glass cases displaying ancient weapons, pottery, and scrolls of parchment. Paintings and tapestries hang from the walls. The air inside smells sweet, like moldy paper.

At the end of the hall, a man passes through an arch flanked by suits of armor. He's dressed similar to Orban, in a gray pinstriped suit with a red satin tie and feathery brown hair. The man hobbles with a wooden cane carved to look like a twisted rope, gathered up in a knot where his hand grips it. He leans on the cane with every step.

"Nico!" the man says, holding his free arm wide in greeting as he passes Orban on his way into the Corridor. "So good to see you!"

"You too, Mr. Stripe." Nico shakes his hand. "Thank you for meeting us."

"Wouldn't miss it." Mr. Stripe leans in to fake a whisper in Nico's ear. "I hear we have a development."

Nico turns to me. "Stripe, this is Cameron. . . ."

"Kuhn," I finish my name for Nico, before gripping Stripe's warm hand. "It's good to meet you."

"So polite!" Stripe laughs. "You could learn something from him, Nico."

Nico laughs nervously. "Yes sir, I'm sure I could."

Stripe motions Orban to shut the door. "So," he says, placing a hand on my shoulder and leading me back down the Corridor, "Nico tells me you're looking for someone."

"Yes sir." It's hard not to believe this guy can help me find my dad as he squeezes my shoulder encouragingly. There's something so certain and powerful about him.

"Nico showed me your father's coin." Stripe stops and turns me to face him. "I think I am in a very unique position to help you. You see, I knew your father."

Nico gives me a big grin, and it takes all I've got to hold back the burn in my eyes. Don't get emotional, Cam. Not now.

"Reinhart was a good friend," Stripe continues. "We worked together. He collected valuable artifacts for my museum. We had plenty of . . . unusual adventures." He pulls a photo from his breast pocket and hands it to me. "How I've missed him these long years."

I lose myself in the picture. It's Dad, all right. He's young—just a few years older than I am now—dressed like Nico was when I first met him. And beside him stands Mr. Stripe, one arm around Dad's shoulder, tipping his hat with the other.

I trace Dad's grinning face with my finger. I can't believe it. It's all true. "Dad really traveled the world?"

"More than that," Stripe says. "Your father hopped doors like few others. Never could keep track of him properly. I'd wondered what happened to you and your sister after Melissa . . . " He trails off.

"It's okay," I say, handing the photo back. "I know she's gone."

He smiles warmly. "Then surely you know I would do anything for Reinhart Kuhn's son. Of course I'll help you."

A thought niggles at the back of my mind. How do I know this guy wasn't the one Dad was hiding us from? The one who was chasing him? But that doesn't seem right. Dad looked so happy in that picture with Stripe. And Stripe's a museum curator, who Dad worked for and went with on adventures. He doesn't seem like he'd hurt anyone. What harm could he do, put me to sleep with a boring history lecture? And I need help. I'm never going to be able to get Dad back without them.

Stripe claps his warm hand on my shoulder again. "Are you okay, my boy?" The way he says the words "my boy" makes me melt. I always imagined Dad calling me that. *Good job, my boy. I'm proud of you, my boy.*

"Yeah," I say. "It's just a lot to take in. I mean, thank you, sir."

"Don't thank me yet," Stripe says in a serious tone. "You don't know what I'm about to ask you to do."

I look to Nico, who gives me a shrug.

"This isn't easy business." Stripe leans close to whisper

confidentially in my ear. "Only the Hotel can reveal what happened to Reinhart. Which means someone bound to him must go there to find out."

"I-I don't understand."

Stripe points to my necklace. "The answer's right there, around your neck." He straightens up, leaning on his cane once more. "Let me guess: You've recently had dreams. Dreams of doors that lead to places you've never been. Of banquets and—"

"And trees?"

Stripe smiles. "You have!"

"What do they mean?"

"It's the coin." Stripe says. "That coin was bound to your father. Objects bound to a person contain a piece of them. The Museum is full of such artifacts. Like owning a piece of people who existed long ago. Their memories and dreams. That coin is a key—the key to Reinhart's memories from his days working at The Hotel Between."

"Dad . . . worked there too?"

"Yes. And the Hotel was his downfall." Stripe takes a slow breath. "The Hotel guards its secrets well. It's why I asked him to go inside and bring its secrets back to the Museum. But Reinhart was deceived by the promises of the Hotel. He couldn't see how it would destroy him. In the end I tried to save him, but I . . . failed."

I gulp. "What happened to him?"

"Only the coin can answer that." Stripe draws me close. "The coin always wants to return to its owner. But not just anyone can access his memories. Only those bound to him by blood—his family—can learn Reinhart's secrets."

I grip Dad's coin tight. So Oma was right, there *is* something special about it.

Stripe leads me to the door at the far end of the Corridor, with the crooked letter H. "'The Vacation of Your Dreams,' they call it. Ha! If only those who stayed in the Hotel knew how they were manipulated—"

"Sir," Nico says, "are we really taking him . . . inside?"

Stripe grits his teeth. "I'm afraid so."

"What's so bad about that?" I ask.

"I would think you of all people would know the answer to this," Stripe says. "Many enter those doors, but not all return. And many who are invited end up . . . changed."

I shudder. "Why? What does the Hotel do to them?"

Nico joins me at the door. "The mission of the Hotel is its most closely guarded secret," he says. "Even those who know can't share."

Stripe looks down at me, eyes sparkling. "Mr. Cameron, I want to know what happened to your father too. He was my friend, and I failed him." He touches the coin at my neck. "You came to me for help, but it's your help we need. Will you brave the Hotel to find your father?"

I hesitate. "If it's so dangerous . . . "

"It's only dangerous if you get taken in by the Hotel's sheen.

What happened to Reinhart happened because he got distracted. Focus on finding your father, and you'll be fine." Stripe places a hand on Nico's shoulder. "Besides, you will have friends—allies— like Nico here. He'll introduce you to those you can trust." He looks long and hard at the boy who brought me to him. "You will take care of Cameron, won't you?"

Nico bows. "Yes sir."

"Good." Stripe gives me a pleading smile. "Son, are you up for this challenge?"

"I—of course." I smile back, struggling to contain the emotion bursting from my chest like some alien in the movies. Death by exploding-chest-alien . . . not really one I want on the list, I don't think.

Stripe places a hand over his heart. "I am so glad to hear it. We may save Reinhart after all."

Nico and I step through the door to the Hotel, leaving Mr. Stripe behind to return to his Museum. The smell of dust and paint remover washes over me as soon as Nico closes the door.

The cramped, short hall on the other side is littered with junk. Dirty shelves covered with rusty tools and paint cans. Rolling tray tables with broken wheels. Cobwebs hang from every dim, gray corner, giving the alcove a creepy, horror-movie feel.

"It looks like a janitor's closet," I say.

"Well duh." Nico weaves his way through the junk. "Can't exactly walk through the front and say, 'Hey, looking for my missing dad. Seen him?' We've got to sneak you in."

"I just thought the Hotel would be . . . friendlier than this."

"It is. *Mira*, there are two sides to the Hotel. The lobby you saw before was part of the facade. Front-of-house stuff. Staff keeps the facade shiny and clean and warm for the guests." He waves a hand. "These are the back halls. The dingier parts. It ain't glamorous, but at least down here the Alcove Door stays secret."

I glance back at the door to the Corridor, filing it away as the Alcove Door.

"You will keep it secret, right?" Nico says, grabbing my shoulders. "No matter what, you won't tell anyone about the Corridor?"

"Who would I tell?"

"Things tend to go wrong in the Hotel." He looks over my shoulder, as if making sure the door's still there. "You should consider this hostile territory now."

I don't like the sound of that. "Really, though, what'll happen to us if we're caught?"

"We get the beef."

I picture a herd of stampeding cows trampling us underfoot. I know that's not what he means, but it would sure be an awful entry to the list.

Nico leads the way around the corner and under a wooden arch. A snapping sound pops in my ears as we pass from grungy linoleum into a hall of ancient, pockmarked stone and tamped earth. Caged vintage bulbs tinge the crumbling walls with warm yellow light. The smell of dust and damp makes me cough. If there ever was a place where greedy spirits stole kids, this would be it.

"Who is he, anyway?" I ask as we pass under another archway. "Stripe, I mean."

"I told you, Stripe's the Curator. He collects magic from all over the world, and displays it in his Museum."

"But why? And what does that have to do with the Hotel?"

Nico shrugs. "Why not? If you'd known all your life that magic existed, wouldn't you collect it too?"

"I guess." I try to piece it together. "But museums don't typically just take things they want, do they?"

"It's not just taking things." he says, continuing down the dark hall. "The Hotel has some grand ideas about what's good and what's not. It seems all right and all, but a lot goes on behind the scenes. Stuff that'd make your nose hairs curl. That's why you need to leave all that what's-the-Hotel-up-to to me and Sev, who you'll meet in a bit. That's *our* job. Yours is to find out what that coin says about your dad. Do that, and we might make it out of here with our bindings intact."

As we round another dusty corner, I can't help but think something's off about the layout of this place. Like one of those brain-melting optical illusions where stairs lead to nowhere and halls turn in on themselves. The passage splits like tines of a fork under three wooden arches, with a wall between each. But as we enter the far right hall, it curves left and *through* the others. Windows that should look into the adjacent passages instead overlook rolling hills, as if the other halls didn't exist.

"The halls cross but never touch," I wonder out loud. "How can they both be in the same space?"

"The Hotel's just a mishmash of places magically stitched together. These halls *look* like they're in the same place, but like I said earlier, you're actually moving from one spot on the globe to another with each arch or door."

We spiral down a staircase that should take us below ground level, but when we pass through the next arch the windows show us being higher than before. Sunny hills give way to snowy mountains. We cross another threshold, and the snow turns to rocky desert.

"So, the Hotel isn't just one building?"

"Nope," Nico says. "The Hotel is everywhere. A lobby in Dubai, guest rooms in Naples . . . most of our closets are somewhere in Portugal, I think. Even these back halls are hidden under sections of the Great Wall of China."

"That's why they look so old."

"Yep." He leans to look through the window. "*And* it's why you've gotta stick with me. The back halls are a labyrinth. Last thing we need is you running into a maid."

I trace the stones with my fingers as we walk. The Great Wall of China. Cass would love this. When I get back and tell her . . .

No, I can't. She'd be packed to leave before I finished the first sentence. It already takes all I've got to keep her from running off to join the circus.

Nico leads me up a thin metal staircase to a burgundy door marked COURTYARD.

I stop him before he opens it. "Why are you doing this? If bringing me here is so dangerous, why risk it?"

"Because Stripe asked me to. If he thinks it's worth it to track your dad down, then I do too." He grins. "Besides, it's fun, yeah?"

"Putting myself in danger isn't exactly my idea of fun."

"Then you haven't lived, my friend." He opens the door, and the warm, blueberry-spiced air wraps around me. "Welcome to The Hotel Between. We hope you find your destination."

5

Dancing in Russia

Nico and I step into a warm, sunlit courtyard. I breathe in the smell of wet grapes and fresh-cut grass. Birds chirp in the cedar trees under a clear sky. A wall of carved marble encircles us, glittering like snow cone ice and hung with curtains of climbing vines. Huge potted floral arrangements and rosebushes wave in the breeze.

And doors . . . so many doors, set into the curved wall every few feet. Their painted wood frames reflect the sun in dazzling colors, each completely unique. One arch features white mosaic curls dotted with sapphires over a door etched with starbursts. A carving of an elephant is set so deep into another one that the door itself must be two feet thick. The next, two pillars encircled by dragons, support a crossbeam that bows at the corners, like the entrance to Oma's favorite Chinese restaurant.

The doors look identical to the ones hanging from the tree in my dream. They continue around the courtyard, similar only in how different they look from one another—each a mash-up of cultural icons. What I take to be Hotel staff in maroon slacks and suspenders roll brass luggage racks and trays of food along the walk-ways. The yard is greener and sunnier than our yard back at home ever looked. It's the most beautiful place I've ever seen.

Though . . . wasn't it just nighttime? And cold?

Nico continues left down the covered patio like this change isn't even a big deal.

I step onto the grass and gaze up at the cloudless sky. "It's day-time."

"Yep." He rounds a column and cuts across the yard toward a fountain—a grand, multitiered pool with an enormous marble tree at its center. Water pours from the gold-flecked branches like the boughs of a willow.

"But . . . it's daytime," I say again, running to catch up.

"So?"

"It was just night."

"In *Texas.*" Nico rolls his eyes. "Night in Texas is day on the other side of the world. Try to keep up."

This can't be possible. I mean, part of me believes, or I wouldn't have come, but this—the intricate doors and glittering murals, the warm sunshine and shimmering orange koi in the fountain . . .

"Okay then, where are we?" I ask as a girl in a colorful, jangly outfit and gobs of jewelry sidles past.

Nico stops at a large, angled board with a sheet of splotchy tan paper stretched across it. The words FIND YOUR DESTINATION flow across the top in bronze script. "The Sundial Courtyard is like a shortcut." He points to the Roman numerals carved above each of the doors. "See those? They're time zones. Twenty-four of them."

The sundial . . . the Roman numerals . . . the Courtyard's a giant clock, with the marble tree fountain casting shimmering, watery shade toward my own time zone, where it's the middle of the night.

I spin slowly, taking in each and every door set into the circular wall.

"These frames down here are staff-use-only." He leans against the parchment board and nods to the railing around the top of the Courtyard wall. "Guests use similar doors up there on the Mezzanine."

"There are people up there." Whole groups lean over the balustrade, watching the staff hurry back and forth across the paths below. A young boy spits over the railing, and it lands close to a girl in maroon slacks leading a luggage cart.

I'm suddenly very aware of how exposed we are out here. "Everyone can see us."

"Guests on the Mezz can, but they don't have access down here." Nico fishes in his pocket. "To them, the Sundial Courtyard is just another mystery of the Hotel. The only ones we need to make sure we keep you hidden from are the maids."

"Maids?" I laugh.

His eyes widen. "Trust me. You do NOT want to get on the maids' bad side."

He pulls out his coin and inserts it into a slot on the board.

The paper bursts to life. Sparkling strokes and glittering honey-colored lines zip across it, drawing a series of concentric circles and decorating them with sketches of trees and rivers and doors.

The swirling lines of amber light finish by scribbling the words YOU ARE HERE at the center of the innermost circle.

"It's a map," I proclaim.

"More like . . . a representation." Nico points to the paper. "If you could see all of the pieces of the Hotel at once, it wouldn't make much sense, so the map-boards make sense of it for us. The boards only show what we need, and track our coins so we can find one another."

I touch my finger to the paper, and an electric hum vibrates through me. The ink begins to swirl, tracing a winding line through the map. New paths emerge across the paper. Words like "United States" and "Texas" scribble themselves over a couple of the doors.

Nico snatches my finger away, and the ink fades. "No touching. We don't want anyone to know you're here."

"Right. Sorry."

He taps the marker at the center, and the ink springs to life again, drawing names like "Rio Hall" and "Pyramid Foyer" onto the board.

"The Courtyard is basically the core of the Hotel," he says, indicating the circle we're in. He drags his finger to the circle that surrounds that one, and the ink in that section grows bolder, flaring to life like sparklers. "The Courtyard is set into the middle of the Mezzanine." He points to the rail above us. "Together, the Mezz ring and Courtyard form the heart of the Hotel. The doors in the cliffs surrounding the Mezz lead to the ring with the Elevator Bank, and beyond."

More circles exist beyond those two we're in. The outermost ring reads "Lobby Level." Smaller circles fit between the others, but I can't tell if they're actual places or just extra lines.

"Now"—he gives the map-board his full attention—"where would Sev be?"

The lines continue to twist across the map, scribbling words like "Couples' Dinner Party" and "International Bingo" and "Dim Sum Banquet." My stomach grumbles at the thought of food . . . all I had for dinner was snacks from the hospital vending machines.

I hope Cass is all right.

"There." Nico plants his finger on a door marked "Russian Mixer," and under it a circle that reads "Vsevolod Pronichev." "Follow me."

He veers onto one of the spoke paths that stretch away from the fountain tree, to a door flanked by columns twisted in a rainbow of colors and topped with onion-shaped domes.

"This way to the Russian Branch," he says. "*Dobro pozhalovat!*"

My ears crackle annoyingly again as we pass into the next hall. I want to ask Nico what that's about, but it's all I can do to keep up.

"I like Russia," Nico says, nodding to a boy around my age pushing a mop bucket as he passes. "The buildings are so cool."

"Oma has a postcard Dad sent to her once from Red Square."

"Oh yeah. So many colors on those domes."

We take the third door down—marked with a sign that reads

POCCNR with the N and R backwards—and pass through a panel hidden behind a flowered tapestry to enter the rear of a grand ballroom. The sounds of upbeat string music mix with the powerful aroma of perfume as men and women in tight suits and sparkling gowns hold conversations I can't understand. Long-stemmed glasses filled to the brim with drink fizz at their lips as they laugh and smile and dance.

Russia. We're in Russia. I've never even been out of Texas before.

A heavy weight sinks to the pit of my stomach. I don't know if I can handle all of these new experiences at once. "This is a bad idea," I say as Nico edges past couples spinning and dancing under the colored lights. "We should leave."

Nico gives each guest a professional bow as he crosses the polished floor. "Too late now, kiddo."

He points to a boy who looks like he's in high school standing beside a table covered in food. His skin is dark with a cool tone to it, and a bold crimson sash with ochre fringe hangs across his shoulder. He's talking to a girl much shorter than him, also in staff tails, with a black satin hijab wrapped under her chin.

"Wait here." Nico grabs a tiny sandwich off the brass platter carried by a passing staff member. "Do. Not. Move."

He scarfs down his sandwich and hurries to grab the boy's attention.

Everything's happening so fast. I try not to think about what we're doing, but alarm bells sound off in my head. Oma's stories, Stripe's warnings, Nico's promise that passing through the Hotel doors always costs something, the thought that I'm actually in a *magic* hotel. What if this is all a trap? I could be handing myself over to the very people Dad hid us from, and not even know it. And Cass—I just left her. What kind of brother does that?

The girl in the headscarf storms off across the ballroom, and Nico and the other boy push me out a different side door into a dark hallway.

The boy closes the door behind us, and the noise of the party dies instantly. "So," he says, his Russian accent grumbly and deep, "this is the one Stripe sent?"

I swallow hard. He's a big guy—tall and stout enough to make two of me. I feel like I'm standing completely in his shadow.

A tiny smile curls up one corner of his stubbled lip. "Vsevolod Pronichev." He offers a hand. "I am called Sev."

I hesitate, but after a trusting nod from Nico I shake Sev's hand. His grip is strong; his hands, rough and calloused.

"Come," Sev says. "We go somewhere private."

He leads us down the hall and through another before hitting the call button next to a pair of shiny elevator doors with the image of the tree engraved across their surface.

I run my fingers along the engraving. My tree is everywhere in this place. The elevator looks just like it did in the picture of Mom and Dad. They were here. For the first time, I am somewhere they have been. I bite my lip to hold back the strange mix of emotions welling up inside me. This is the closest I've ever come to doing something with them.

The elevator dings, and the doors slide open, splitting the metallic tree down the middle. I imagine a hand coming through the doors, beckoning me inside.

Nico glances down the hall. "Should we be worried about Rahki?" I assume he's talking about the girl who stormed away from them.

Sev's bass-y accent echoes as we board the lift. "She will hold back. Trust her."

The walls inside the elevator are made of glass, but it's what lies on the other side of the glass that takes my breath away. Each wall is a window to another place. In one, I see a city of sky-scrapers aglow with traffic and streetlights. In another, craggy, moss-covered hillsides are wrapped in fog. And in the window across from it, white, cracked earth that looks as if it hasn't seen rain in years stretches out under an ocean-blue sky.

Sev presses the button for floor twenty-one. "This elevator is typically for guests," he says, "but I think is good for you to see."

The elevator ascends, but it feels like we're moving sideways as well as up. At one point, I'm pretty sure the elevator even changes directions. But the landscapes beyond the glass never change. Looking at them, it's like we're not moving at all.

I rest my hand on the wall between me and the flat, white desert. The heat of its sun warms my palm. When I touch the wall with the green, foggy hills, a chill prickles up my arm. Will I ever get used to this? I can't wrap my head around it just yet. I'm basically in two places at once.

"Is it real?" I ask, gazing out over the bustling city below.

Nico grabs the rail and looks through the glass with me. "Yep. The whole world, just a step away."

My lifelong search has finally started. Dad's out there, I can feel it. Before long I'll have him back, and everything will be the way it's supposed to be.

6

The Doorman in Room 2109

The elevator opens into a hallway with plush, patterned carpet. Dim bulbs with corkscrew filaments flicker in sconces. The heavy doors are numbered—2103, 2104, 2105—with framed paintings of bears in between.

Sev stops at room 2109 and inserts a key with a soft, silvery twinkle. "*V gostyah horosho, a doma lutshe.*"

Nico translates, "Visiting is good, but home is better."

They have no idea how true that is.

Sev's room is small, cozy, with dull slate walls and a smell like woodworking class. Shelves loaded with books and jars and little carved figurines line the room. A cloud of dust hangs in the air, lit by the gray light cast from the window. Sawdust lies in mounds on the floor, covering the leather chair, even curled in shavings next to the bed.

"Goodness, Sev." Nico wipes a finger through the sawdust on the table. "Don't you ever clean this joint?"

"Would not do any good. At least it keeps me warm." He clears the tools from his desk. "Did you bring land for me?"

Nico digs the jar of dirt from Oma's garden out of his pocket. "I bound another door, too."

Sev raises an eyebrow.

"I was practicing," Nico says. "Besides, it was the only way to get him in to meet Stripe."

"I do not believe that *you* of all people need practice binding things." Sev holds up the jar and gives it a shake, then sets it alongside the hundreds of other tiny, dirt-filled jars. "And Stripe approved of bringing him here?"

"Practically ordered it." Nico flops down in the leather chair. Dust billows from the cushions. "Gotta hear this story."

I hesitate; I've never been one for lots of talking, but now I feel like I'm spewing my life out to everyone. Nico already knows all of this information, though, so what would be the point in keeping it a secret from his ally?

So I tell Sev everything, along with the bits Stripe shared. Sev listens to every word. Never looking away. Never interrupting. It's as if he and I are the only two people in the world.

When I'm done, he pinches his brow. "It will be difficult to keep you secret if you stay."

"Wait, I can't *stay* here," I say, sitting on the edge of the twin bed. "I just came to figure out what's in the coin and go back home."

Nico shakes his head. "Doesn't work like that."

I don't like the sound of this. "If I'm not back soon, Oma and Cass will worry. They'll probably have the police out looking for me."

"It will take awhile to access your father's memories," Sev says. "And the only way to unlock them is by spending time in the Hotel."

"Then I'll leave my coin here!"

"The magic won't work without you," Nico says. "We can hide you."

Sev frowns. "Every moment he remains puts our task in jeopardy."

"He's part of the task!" Nico snaps.

"What task?" I ask, and they both look at me as if they momentarily forgot I existed.

"Don't worry about it." Nico watches Sev's face carefully. "All you have to do is find your dad. We'll keep you safe. Promise."

Sev sighs. *"Bez truda, ne vitashish i ribku iz pruda.* Everything worthwhile requires a push. You must stay."

"And what happens when we find him?" I ask.

"You leave. It's a touch." Nico's eyes darken. "Digging around into the Hotel's secrets will complicate that, though. That's why we only want you to find your dad. We're stuck here. You're not."

Sev nods approvingly.

"I-I can't," I say. The sun is high outside Sev's window, but I have no idea what time it is in Dallas. Cass and Oma will be coming home from the hospital. Cass'll need someone to help her over the hump of getting back to our normal routine, someone to lock her chair into place in Oma's van. Oma gets so tired; she's getting too old to do it herself.

But that's why I'm here, isn't it? To find someone who'll take care of us all.

Sev's eyes soften. "It is your choice, but it is a choice. We will not blame you either way."

All these choices play tug-of-war with my emotions. I'm pretty sure my destiny is to one day stay home and never leave again. But this is about my dad. More than that . . . it's about Cass, too. She and Oma both insist she doesn't need me worrying about her, but I want her and Oma to be taken care of. I want *me* to be taken care of. To feel like a kid.

Still, I can't leave her alone that long.

"I can't," I say again. And I hate myself for it. It makes me sound so scared. "My family needs me."

Sev locks my gaze. "Your family is not lost. Your father is."

My fingers clench the bed sheets. There's so much I don't understand about this place. Oma said she'd pay any price, but I don't think I can. Finding Dad was a dream. I can't travel the world. I'm just Cam. Scared, unremarkable Cam.

Boom-boom-boom!

We all jump at the pounding on the door.

"Maid service!" a voice yells. "Open up!" *Boom-boom-boom!*

"It is the Maid Commander." Sev points to the window. "Hide him. Out there."

Nico throws the window open and a gust of icy air whips around me. Sev helps me over the ledge into the powdery snow outside his first-floor window. Twisted iron bars dripping with icicles fence the building in. The street beyond is wet and steamy. Gray sludge rolls in mounds in front of a large, historic-looking building that's all pointy towers and wrought iron and lots and lots of barred windows. The air is so cold, my nose and ears and fingers contract.

"Bust it open," the woman's voice says on the other side of Sev's door as Nico closes the window, locking me outside.

I duck behind the bushes and press my back against the chilled brick. Muffled voices escape through the glass as a woman barks commands. This is ridiculous. I'm hiding out in the snow because they're worried about a maid? What's she going to do, dust them to death?

I draw my arms close to my body, taking in the view of the cathedral across the street. It's real. This definitely isn't Dallas. I'm not even sure where it is. Cass would be amazed. She'd be giddy if she was able to travel anywhere, given how difficult it is for her to fly, but this would top the charts. She'd be fascinated by the way everything in the Hotel sparkles like a new penny; we're not used to new things. Oma has to scrape together money to take care of us. Almost everything we own is used. Cass would stay. I know she would. Maybe not to find Dad, but she'd stay all the same, to visit all the places she never could before. She'd be brave enough to face the unknown. So why can't I?

I peek over the ledge to see inside, but someone's drawn a thin, sheer curtain. Through the gossamer I can make out Sev, and Nico, and a third person—the so-called Maid Commander, I guess—flanked by two more imposing, suited shadows.

The Maid Commander's silhouette isn't shaped like a maid at all. She's wearing slacks and a jacket that looks more like something a soldier would wear than a cleaning lady. The shape of a sheathed sword hangs on her hip, and she's shouting Nico and Sev down like a general reaming out soldiers.

WWTD number 899: death by maid-rage.

The wind whips through my ears. There are lots of ways to die in the cold. Number 221: Frostbite sucks the heat from your hands and feet, leaving them black and stiff until they fall off. Number 224: Breathe air that's too cold, and it turns the water in your lungs to ice. Number 237: Hypothermia drops your body temperature so low your brain shuts down. None of them seem like good ways to go.

"Come on," Nico whispers, offering a hand to help me over the windowsill and back inside once the Maid Commander leaves. "We've got to get you back to Dallas before anything *else* goes wrong."

My body is stiff and achy. I relish the warmth from Sev's heating vent. My teeth chatter as Sev and Nico rub my arms to warm me up.

"Y-y-y-you g-got r-r-rid of her?"

"For now." Sev throws a heavy wool blanket around my shoulders and gives Nico a cautious look.

"Wh-wh-what ab-b-bout the p-plan?"

"We do not have a plan for keeping you hidden when Maid Service knows you are here." Sev sighs. *"Vek zhivi, vek uchis."*

"Live and learn," Nico translates, though I can tell those aren't the words he wanted to hear. "I told you, we can't trust Rahki."

"T-t-that g-girl f-f-from the b-ballroom?"

Sev hangs his head. "Rahki intends for good."

"I'm s-s-so c-cold." It's all I can think about. Cold. Cold. Need to warm up.

Nico leans his ear against the door. "I think they're gone. We have to leave. Now."

"T-t-thanks." I hand the blanket back to Sev.

He takes it and grips my hand. "Remember us fondly. I wish we could do more." His smiling eyes tell me he means it. *"Shastlivovo puti."*

Nico and I hurry through the passages. The running warms my joints, but not enough to keep up with Nico.

"Put a rush on, kiddo," he says, and I flex my fingers, knowing I've hit my limit. I swear if he calls me "kiddo" one more time I'm going to pop him in the mouth. We're practically the same age!

"Where are we going?" I ask. "Isn't the elevator back there?"

"Magic doors, remember?"

Nico pushes on a section of the wall, and it gives way to a hidden passage. We take the stairs two at a time, and head down to a dimly lit hall with wood paneling and musty green carpet, before another swiveling panel puts us back in the dark, musty stone back halls.

Leaving this place is a mistake, but I can't stay. I have too many responsibilities.

A few more turns and we're back at the alcove where we came in.

"Told you," Nico says. "Just a touch. We'll be out of here before you know it."

He rounds the stairs into the cluttered hall that leads to the Alcove Door.

A noise behind us draws my attention. Footsteps. I turn to see a man and woman dressed in black suits marching down the hall, followed by the girl from the ballroom, and the tall, imposing figure of what I assume to be the Maid Commander.

The Maid Commander drills me with her stare. Her graying hair is pulled back into a tight bun, and a burn scar trails down her severe face. Compared to the suited staff in front of her she seems willowy and thin, but the sharp way she walks makes me think she could easily do a WWTD number 136 and snap me like a pencil.

"Uh, Nico?" I dodge into the alcove to find him squeezing through the pushcarts. "They're here."

Nico stops and listens to confirm, the silver skeleton key already in hand. "Not good." He shoves the key in his pocket.

"What are you doing?" I say. "Open the door."

"It's okay. You still have that coin I gave you at your house?"

"No, you took it back."

He rolls his eyes. "Check your pocks."

I reach into my pocket and pull out the small, gold-painted disc. He must've slipped it to me. Again.

Nico grabs my hand and shoves it back into my jeans. "Put it away! Just follow my lead."

Rahki and the others round the corner, holding their heads high in a dignified stance. The woman on the left cracks a knuckle. The man flattens his shirt. Rahki pulls a long wooden baton from her belt and hefts it with both hands.

I shrink behind Nico, wishing the Maid Commander's eyes would stop stabbing me.

"Ms. Rahkaiah told me I'd be rewarded if I waited." The Maid Commander's vowels roll off her tongue, as if she's not sure which to land on. I think the accent's French, but I'm not sure. "Mr. Nico, all intruders must be brought directly to me or the Old Man. You know this."

Nico bows. "Forgive me."

She pushes Rahki aside and steps up to face me. I smell her perfume—something almost nutty. "And who is our intruder?"

I swallow. "Cameron."

Her eyes narrow. "Cameron what?"

My mouth hangs open. I can't tell her my last name is Kuhn, can I? They'd surely recognize it, if Dad used to work here.

"Uh, Jones," I say, remembering Oma's maiden name. "Cameron Jones."

"Are you sure about that?" the MC says.

I nod, and Nico nods with me.

One of the staff rifles through a clipboard. "He's not on the guest list."

"No, I should think not." Her gaze digs deeper. "How did you get here, Mr. Cameron? Through which door?"

"The . . . uh . . . Dallas Door?" Not the Alcove Door behind us, that's for sure.

"He snuck in," Nico adds. "I was going to report him, but he had a coin, so—"

The Maid Commander turns her bludgeoning stare on him. "A coin?"

I pull the necklace out from under my shirt.

She grabs at it and yanks me toward her, humming to herself as she turns Dad's coin over. "Not your own, I presume?"

I'm not sure what to say. Stripe warned me—many who come to the Hotel never leave. They disappear, just like Dad. If I answer incorrectly, will I disappear too?

"Answer me, boy!"

"No ma'am." I gulp. I can't tell them it was Dad's. If they're the bad guys, like Stripe says, they might lock me in a cell and I'd never get out of here. "I just . . . f-found it."

"Hmph. Why bring him down here?" she asks Nico.

Nico glares at Rahki before turning back to the woman. "I wanted to hide him somewhere the guests wouldn't see him. I was going to find you and ask what to do, but I mean . . . since he's got a coin, I thought it'd be okay." His lie sounds so convincing, I almost want to believe it myself.

She nods to the door behind the shelf. "I do not recognize that door. Is it bound?"

He shakes his head. "I don't know."

"Open it."

Nico obeys. I can tell he's accustomed to taking orders from her. I wonder if he's used to lying to her, too. It doesn't matter though. She's about to see where that door leads, and this whole thing will end up becoming an even bigger disaster.

But when Nico opens the door, it reveals nothing but a closet full of cleaning supplies.

The Maid Commander scowls. "You know what I mean. Open it with your staff key."

Nico fishes in his pocket and inserts his skeleton key into the door. Once again, the key embeds itself in the metal with a sparkle. He turns it and pulls, revealing . . .

The janitor's closet. Still just a closet.

Then I notice the key. It's not silver, like the one he used before. This one's brass. It's the one he used on the Dallas Door.

He switched them.

My hand is drawn to my own pocket. My fingers wrap first around Nico's coin, and then around a long piece of metal.

He slipped the silver key to me. Smooth.

The Maid Commander scoffs. "Come. We will take the boy to the Old Man. Mr. Cameron must settle his account."

7

An Old Man in the Sea

It's over. The Hotel caught me, and now I'm going to be carted away to some deserted island off the coast of Bali where I'll have to survive on coconuts and my strength of will. And I don't really have strength of will. Which means one of the many WWTDs tagged "starvation" is going to make me its victim.

The Maid Commander folds her hands behind her, waiting for us to get into the elevator.

This box is different from the one we took to Sev's room. Instead of the gilded doors engraved with the all-too-familiar tree, this elevator lies behind a pair of drab iron doors decorated with florets and swirls. On the inside, the previous elevator's traveling windows have been replaced with a rickety cage suspended in darkness. Not exactly something I'd trust to carry me to another floor.

Rahki steps on first. I follow Nico and gaze through the wire cage that prevents me from leaning out over the edge.

"The Shaft," Nico whispers.

A perfect blue circle of sky countless stories above provides the Shaft's only light, illuminating the empty column of rock wall only halfway down. It feels almost like looking up from inside a volcano.

"The cages were added to these lifts later," he says, nodding to the wire mesh that extends above the railing. "Rumor is someone fell into the pit and died."

Rahki clears her throat.

"Oh shut up." Nico sticks his tongue out at her.

"Enough," the Maid Commander snaps, still standing in the hall outside the elevator. She looks even more general-like up close. Multicolored epaulets decorate the shoulders of her maroon jacket. Her slacks are creased in perfect, straight lines. She leans in past the metal inner gate, glances at the console, and barks "sublevel" to Rahki. "Take them to Agapios, and report back to me. I want to know what the Old Man decides."

"Yes ma'am." Rahki slides the metal gate closed.

"And Mr. Nico," the MC says through the bars, "I will see you at your designated time tomorrow. If you are still with us, that is."

The doors beyond the gate shut, locking us in with Rahki.

The platform starts down with a rickety shake. I grip the railing and focus out over the giant, open-air column, tracing the walls of the Shaft down, down, down. The pit below is so deep, I can't see the bottom. Across the gap—which seems so far away—more elevators hang like roller coaster cars on cabled metal tracks. Some are closed-in gold boxes like the one we took before, but others are cages, like this one. The tracks lead up, down, side to side, even diagonally, carrying the elevators every which way to the doors cut in the Shaft wall.

Nico said elevators were everywhere in the Hotel, but those doors must all lead to this Shaft.

"That was a bad move, Rahki," Nico says as we descend. "Why couldn't you just leave it alone?"

Rahki's voice is full of venom. "You don't bring unauthorized people into the Hotel, Nico. You know that."

"Cam *is* authorized." He points again to my necklace. "Coined and everything."

"We'll see about that."

The cage shakes, and I grip the rail tighter. A metal lattice is all that stands between me and that pit of doom. Oh, how I wish we had the window-walls instead.

"Sev trusted you to stay quiet," Nico continues. "I keep telling him he should steer clear of you, and you always prove me right."

"All I did was point the MC in the right direction." Rahki shoves a stray tuft of hair into her headscarf. "I didn't get *Sev* in trouble when you obviously had the kid outside his window, because I knew it was *your* fault. You're the one he shouldn't trust. I don't know what you're up to, but rules are rules."

"Tattle-tale."

"No-good weasel," she shoots back.

He growls as the platform rattles and switches to another path leading us deeper into darkness.

"I don't know what Nico's told you," Rahki says, looking at me, "but you need to be careful around him. He's always up to something."

Nico flutters his lips. "The only thing I'm 'up to' is making your life as difficult as possible."

"There's one thing we agree on."

The elevator dings, and Rahki pulls back the cage gate as the doors open on the other side. My ears pop as we cross into a cluttered metal hall lit only by dim red bulbs.

Rahki stations herself outside the doors as Nico drags me down the hall. "It's only a matter of time until I figure you out," she calls after us.

Nico straightens his back in a mock salute, and with a sarcastic, "Good evening, ma'am!" to Rahki, he turns and pulls me through the porthole into the next compartment.

Everything in these cramped halls is a similar dull, painted metal. Our feet clang on sheets of it. Pipes and cabling run across the ceiling, and a damp, iron smell stings my nostrils. Weight presses in on my body from all sides. The cables, the metal rivets, the caged lights . . . it almost reminds me of an old submarine.

"Thank goodness that's over," Nico says as we make our way down the straight hall. "Rahki's with the Maid Service, a.k.a. the enemy. Best keep her at a distance."

"She doesn't look like any kind of maid I've ever seen." I glance back to see her standing in front of the iron doors that hide the cage elevator. "And is this a submarine?"

"Yeah. Sub-level." Nico ducks under a low-hanging cable and through an open metal door with a spinning lock mechanism—the first of many in this long hall. "Maid Service aren't your typical maids. The maids of The Hotel Between don't clean rooms; that's Housekeeping's job. The Maid Service cleans up messes of a more . . . dangerous sort. And they report to that nasty troll of a woman who calls herself the Maid Commander. Trust me: You do not want to be on the receiving end of *her* duster."

I block his path before he reaches the next metal door. "Stop."

"What?"

I don't even know where to begin. "We weren't supposed to get caught, but we did. What happens now?"

"We get the beef from the Old Man."

"Will you please speak English?"

Nico sighs. "The Old Man is Agapios. He's kinda like . . . head concierge, or the owner, maybe. But like I said before, to enter the Hotel always costs something. I'm not sure what it'll be for you. The Hotel will decide."

I glare at him. "This is your fault. If you and Mr. Stripe hadn't—"

Nico claps his hand over my mouth and shoves me into the metal wall.

"Do *not* say that name here," he whispers. He glances back down the corridor, but Rahki's too far away to be seen. "Names are important. It was good thinking to give the MC a fake last name, but you still have to be careful. If the Hotel figures out why we're here, we're through."

"Why?" My voice muffles through his fingers. My heart's racing. What am I doing? This kid shows up with some card tricks and I trust him with my life just like that? I don't even know him. He could snuff me out right here in this hallway.

I've got to be more careful.

"You have no idea what they could do to us. What *he* might do. You've come this far; you have to trust me. We've got to play this cool." He releases me, straightens his shirt, and runs a hand through his hair. "Follow my lead, and it'll all be just a touch."

Nico's reaction to Stripe's name bothers me. Why would the staff at a hotel care about a museum curator—no matter how special he is? There's definitely more to this story than Nico's telling me.

I follow him up clanging metal stairs to a heavy iron door that reads:

AGAPIOS PANOTIERRI

CONCIERGE/MANAGER

He pokes a finger to my chest. "Whatever happens, let me handle it."

I give a silent nod, and he spins the wheel lock.

The door squeals open, and warm candlelight floats through. I cross the threshold, expecting to feel the rough cast of metal as I run my hand along the inside of the sub door, only this side isn't metal at all. It's wood—aged, worn, with deep, long splits and a moldy smell. An old ceiling fan whirrs over a stripped oak desk covered in papers. Sunlight streams through slats over the windows. Shelves line the clay dome all the way to the top, packed tight with books and trinkets.

And at the desk in the center of the room sits a man who looks like Death on his way to the prom—flat, angular forehead with a receding hairline and slick black hair. His pale face is long—way longer than it should be—and his cheekbones look like someone surgically inserted dice into his face.

A gold cross-keys pin hangs from his shiny lapel.

The man waves us forward. "Please, sit." His accent is crisp and deep and decidedly not English, though I can't tell where it might be from.

Nico takes a seat in one of the saggy chairs in front of the desk. A wood-burning stove flickers off to one side.

Agapios—a.k.a. Viktor von Dracula—watches me with blank, emotionless eyes as I sit. His face, the wrinkles around his mouth, it all looks like he might be around Oma's age. But when I look into those cloudy eyes, I can't help but feel like I'm gazing into centuries past.

"Mr. Nico." Agapios leans back in his creaky chair and locks his long, crooked fingers. "Won't you introduce me to your friend?"

Nico looks up from under his brow. "His name's Cameron. He came through the Dallas Door."

Agapios hums. "And *why* did this young man come through the Dallas Door?"

"I dunno. Ask him."

What? Nico's supposed to help me, not throw me onto the fire.

The man leans forward. His tone makes the room shrink. "I'm asking *you*. Because I believe you encouraged him. Yes?"

Nico's face reddens. "He came through on his own."

Agapios stares as if he's analyzing Nico's soul. I know this tactic. Oma's really good at it. He's waiting for Nico to make a mistake, hang himself with his own anger. It's a mean, underhanded way of playing out an argument, but it works.

"I met him when I showed the new door to the Saudi ambassadors," Nico says, tightening the noose. "All I did was show him the door."

"*You* showed him the door?"

"No, I—" Nico bites his lip. The noose is cinched. He's going to hang.

"So, you gave away the secret of the Hotel without considering the consequences."

"I—"

"Its secrets are not yours to give. There are many who would go to great lengths to obtain access . . . "

"But the Hotel—"

" . . . and many who would be enticed to enter without means to pay. Like your friend, Mr. . . . "

"Cameron," I remind him.

Agapios pauses, boring his gaze into *my* soul.

Secrets, just like Stripe said. I bet it's those secrets that forced Dad to run. That kept him from us all this time. And those who would "go to great lengths" . . . he must be talking about Stripe.

Agapios turns back to Nico and pulls a page from a folder on his desk. "You have made a grave error, Mr. Nico. The Hotel recognizes a new debt to your account on behalf of Mr. Cameron, and demands payment."

"But he has a coin!" Nico shouts.

Agapios leans back and looks at me again. "Is this true?"

I swallow, and pull the painted, wooden disc out from under my shirt.

"I see." He tents his fingers. "Is this coin bound to you?"

Silence overtakes the office as Agapios waits for an answer. I look to Nico for help, but he avoids my gaze.

"I-I don't know," I say finally, deciding it's best to play dumb until I figure out what I'm going to do next. "What does that mean, 'bound to me?'"

Agapios raises an eyebrow. "Our particular establishment runs on a magic we call 'the binding.' That coin is one such binding. Each individual who enters our doors is bound to a coin when they first arrive." He pauses. "However, it seems you managed to acquire one apart from us."

"See?" Nico says. "He had payment. I didn't know what to do."

"Hmm . . ." The Old Man squints at Nico, and pushes the page from the folder across the desk. "And yet, the Hotel has added the cost of his passage to *your* account."

Nico scoffs. "Add it to my tab."

"Additionally"—Agapios places his palms on the desk and rises—"your key has been forfeited."

That gets Nico's attention. "What?"

"The Hotel cannot abide a bellman who allows intruders, especially now. We must be diligent."

He settles back in his chair, and my heart slows. I didn't realize until now how much he sets me on edge. Intruders, military maids, a submarine . . . it's almost as if the Hotel's at war. And somewhere in all of that, is Dad. If he got mixed up in whatever terrible business the Hotel is keeping secret, the situation could be worse than I thought.

"You are to be demoted," Agapios says.

Nico's face looks like it's about to pop. "That's not fair!"

"The Hotel has decided." The Old Man holds out his long, bony fingers. "Please relinquish your key."

Nico stares, open-mouthed, then turns his glare on me. I've seen that look a thousand times on Cass's face. But this isn't my fault. I asked for his help, sure, but *he* was the one who took me to Stripe and said I had to come inside.

"Fine." Nico produces the brass key and places it in Agapios's bony grip.

I slide a hand into my pocket and feel the silver key—the one Nico used in Stripe's Corridor—still where he last put it. Interesting.

Agapios opens a large cedar cupboard behind his desk. The doors jangle as they swing wide, revealing thousands of keys on small hooks. Big keys. Small keys. Iron and silver and shiny and corroded keys, and keys that look like they're made of stone.

I glance at Nico while Agapios's back is turned, and he gives me a wink.

He *knew*. Nico knew his key was going to be taken. All his bluster and anger—it's an act. He's pretending to be upset, playing it up for Agapios. But why don't they know about his other key? Is it separate from the hotel?

And what should I do in return?

Agapios returns to his desk. "Please step outside, Mr. Nico. I have some things to discuss with Mr. Cameron." He scowls at me under a shadowed brow. "Alone."

I shift in my seat as the door closes on Nico and my hopes of escape from Mr. Tall, Dark, and Deathly. Agapios's hair shines in the low light of the ceiling fan over his desk. The cross-keys pin on his lapel glitters like costume jewelry.

The Old Man slices through the silence. "I would normally welcome you to our Hotel, but it appears you have already acquainted yourself. I am Agapios Panotierre, Grand Concierge of The Hotel Between."

He leans forward and extends a hand for me to shake.

I lean back, wondering whether shaking it will allow him to suck out my life force.

"I am certain you have many questions," he says, pulling his hand back.

I do have questions. Questions like, *What are you going to do to me?* and *What do you know about my dad?* But those won't get me out of this mess. This guy's probably collected punishments from all over the world. If I don't play this right, he could turn me into a gorilla chew toy (WWTD number 764).

No, I have to keep my cool. "Why did you demote Nico?"

Agapios arches an eyebrow high on his gigantic, shiny forehead. "It was the decision of the Hotel. Mr. Nico knows his contract. He tempted you through the door, and there are consequences."

"Tempted." The word makes me feel uneasy, like I was tricked. "I came through the door on my own."

"Yes," he says, almost like a hiss. His gaze wanders to my neck-lace. "I must ask: The Hotel has misplaced very few of its coins over the years. To whom did yours belong?"

I hesitate. Should I tell him the truth? Not if the Hotel's the reason Dad disappeared. And I don't know the answer to that yet. "I don't know. I've always had it."

"Hmm . . . " He leans back and turns to face the open key cupboard.

"What kind of Hotel is this, anyway? What do you do here? You said secrets—"

Agapios raises a hand to shush me. "The Hotel Between is a . . . unique establishment. Our doors allow quick and easy passage to all manner of destinations for those with means to pay. Ours is a singular experience." He turns back to me, an awkward smile creasing his pallid lips. "The vacation of your dreams, located halfway between here, there, and everywhere."

The vacation of your dreams . . . "I think I've dreamed about this place," I say.

"Yes. You must have, with that coin around your neck. Ever since you turned twelve?"

"How did you—?"

Agapios stands and rounds the desk toward me, pivoting on long, skeletal fingers. "Those who stay within our walls may dive the deepest lagoons and climb the highest mountains in a single day. Here, one can enjoy arepas for breakfast in Venezuela, the most authentic Philly cheesesteak for lunch, and dine luxuriously on the Rhine for dinner." He leans close. "And Chef Silva's ooey-gooey butter bars are . . . to die for."

The flickering light from the fire in the wood-burning stove casts shadows over his sunken eyes. He turns back to the cupboard, fingering a long, pearlescent skeleton key.

"But the Hotel is more than just doors," he says. "Our walls are rooted with secrets, yearning to reveal themselves to those bound to it. But you, Mr. Cameron"—he turns to me—"are not bound. The cost of your passage has been added to Nico's account, and therefore you are free to go."

Free to go. Free to return home, leaving all my hopes of finding Dad behind. I picture Cass in her hospital bed back in Dallas. Everything's been so hard for her . . . she deserves to have something good happen for once. Oma too. She's sacrificed so much for us, and all she wants is her son back.

"Or," Agapios says, holding the pearl key tenderly, "the Hotel could allow you to stay."

Surely I didn't hear that right. "You'd let me . . . stay?"

"Not as a guest." He replaces the key, clasps his hands behind his back, and begins to pace in front of the fire. "Since you are the accountable age for service, the Hotel could offer you a position. Provisional, of course. A ten-day trial period, if you will. You would be assigned a room and a coin of your own to aid in performing your various . . . duties, while the Hotel decides whether—"

"Yes!" The word explodes from my mouth like an unexpected burp.

Agapios stares as I try to rein in my emotions.

"I mean . . . " I grip Dad's coin in my fist, wishing I could stuff the words back in. This could be a trap. Why else would this guy offer a nobody like me this position? Then again, almost all the staff I've seen here are kids. Maybe this is how they get all their employees. Kids like me, vanished by the Hotel.

But if what Stripe said is true, this is now my only chance to figure out where Dad went. Nico and Sev work here. Dad worked here. Maybe I can too. And if it's only ten days, Cass and Oma should be able to manage. I'll ask Nico how I can get in touch with them the first chance I have, so they won't worry and they'll know I'll be home soon.

"I mean, yes sir." I lower my head. "I think I'd like to stay."

The Old Man smiles. "Excellent." He raises a hand and inclines his ear to the ceiling, as if listening to something I can't hear. "The Hotel is intrigued. It seems to like you."

Okay, that's creepy.

Agapios pulls a sheet of paper from his drawer and scribbles on it with a strange wooden fountain pen. I lean in, trying to read his beautiful, flowing letters, but I can't. His handwriting reminds me of pictures I've seen of the U.S. Constitution.

He scratches a sharp line at the bottom and passes the paper to me. "This is your contract. It states that you are welcome to work here until the ten-day trial period is over, or until the Hotel determines this arrangement is no longer beneficial. And you must protect the Hotel's secrets, at all costs."

I scan the curling, looping letters, struggling to read what it says. Is this how it happened with Dad? Did he sit in this very office and sign a contract? Did Nico?

"What if I want to leave?" I ask. "Does this bind me to the Hotel, or whatever? Can I visit my family?"

"Of course you can leave. This contract is very limited. The Hotel offers such terms to those it wishes to . . . evaluate. If you decide to leave at any time, you are free to go. But if at the end of your trial run the Hotel deems you suitable for service, it will determine your role with us for the foreseeable future. If you accept those terms, please sign on the line."

He passes me the pen.

I quickly scrawl my name at the bottom. I have to know what happened, and going forward is my only option. Though it feels weird writing the name "Jones" instead of my real name. I'm glad this guy didn't ask for it. I'm not a very good liar. I wonder if the contract even counts if I don't sign my real name.

Though, as I finish, a crackle zips through my ears.

"Wonderful." Agapios offers me a small, painted wood coin from his drawer.

I take it and shake his hand. It's like shaking hands with the Grim Reaper. When I try to let go, Agapios tightens his grip and pulls me forward. I can smell his breath—hot and damp and a little odoriferous—as he whispers, "The Hotel lifts high the low, and bridges the gap. If I find you pose a risk to its mission, you will no longer be welcome here."

He releases me and flashes a wary half-smile. My now-aching hand tells me there's more to that threat.

"Mr. Nico will see to your accommodations, and will orient you in the morning." Agapios motions for the door. "We hope you find your destination."

I watch his stony eyes. I have absolutely no idea what the concierge is thinking.

And I thought I was scared before.

8

No Longer a Guest

The tree stands majestic and bold before me. For some reason, that seems silly. It shouldn't be bold. It should be afraid.

The door at the base of the tree opens, but this time there's no hand beckoning me inside. Instead, I hear the massive branches crackling overhead.

The hanging doors fall, one by one, crashing into the earth below.

One falls right through me—and the tree is gone. I'm standing on a pier now, looking out over an enormous lake reflecting the city lights on the other side. Mountains rise up all around this valley, and in the distance a statue with arms outstretched watches over the people from its mountaintop.

Another door engulfs me, and I'm riding a camel across a sandy desert, under a midnight blue sky. A third, and the camel transforms into a weird bicycle with a carriage seat in the back. It's raining, then the rain stops, then it begins again as door after door swallows me up.

At last I trip forward into an open elevator platform. The metal clangs, sparking with amber light. Boom-boom-boom. Boom-boom-boom.

• • •

Boom-boom-boom. "Wake up!" *Boom-boom-boom.*

I roll over in my bed, doing my best to chase away the lingering nightmare.

"Mr. Cam," a voice shouts through the door, "if you don't get up, you won't have time to eat."

I squeeze the pillow against my chin. Nico. The Hotel. It wasn't a nightmare. It's my reality.

I roll onto my back to stare at the popcorn ceiling over my bed in Poland, where Nico brought me after I signed my contract. Poland. The air in my seventeenth-floor room is cold, because I'm in Poland. The sky outside is dark, because I'm in Poland.

Boom-boom-boom.

"Go away," I yell.

A pause, and then, "I'm coming in." A key turns in the lock, and Nico bursts through like he's being chased by rabid monkeys.

I pull the covers over my chest. I went to sleep last night with just Dad's coin around my neck, and my underwear. "Hey! You can't come barging in my room. Why do you even *have* a key to my room?"

"We call them screws," he says. "And it's not like you're a guest. You're staff now, and you've gotta get to work."

He marches toward the bed, fully dressed. He's in uniform, and I'm in my boxers. Which might not be a big deal for some people, but I'm not one of them. Once, at a second-grade sleepover, I naively walked out of the bathroom in my tighties, ready for bed. I didn't know any better. . . . I did stuff like that at home all the time. But all the guys in my second-grade class laughed at me. They pointed . . . *actually* pointed. It was mortifying. Even Cass called me "Briefs" for weeks after she heard about it.

"What time is it?" I ask, pulling the blanket tight to hide my scrawny chest.

"End of second shift."

"Second what?"

"Get up!" Nico tugs on the blanket.

I pull back with a grunt. "It's not even light out."

"It's night in Poland, but it's morning in South America. And we're working South American hours."

Nico's clothes aren't like the ones he wore when I met him. Today's getup is maroon slacks with a burgundy sash around his waist, and an upside-down dog bowl hat—a bowler, like from those silent comedy movies. No coattails, no satin lining.

"Where's your other uniform?" I ask.

He groans. "I'm not a bellman anymore, remember? The Hotel says I'm indebted to you, so the Maid Commander made me your valet."

"What's that supposed to mean?"

He rolls his eyes and grabs the covers again. "It means I have to dress you."

"*Dress* me?"

"Look, don't make this difficult. I got in trouble, and now I have to serve you like we do the big shots on floor twelve. I don't like it either, but the MC will break my binding if I disobey again.

That'll mean no job for me and no friend in the Hotel for you."

He gives one last pull and rips the bed sheets out of my hands.

The cold air makes my backside shiver. "I'll dress myself, thank you."

Nico sighs, turning around. "Fine. Go ahead. Try it."

At first I'm not sure if it's a trick. If last night showed me anything, it's that Nico could tell someone they're a bunny rabbit and they'd believe him. But when I'm satisfied he's not going to help me like a little baby, I hop out of bed and snatch my jeans from the chair.

He motions to a stack of clothes next to the door. "I brought you a uniform."

The perfectly folded clothes are just like his. A sparkling yellow stripe runs down each leg of the maroon slacks. The white button-up is crisp. Stretchy suspenders, gold fasteners, even the same felt bowler.

"Need help?"

"No."

Though as I start to pull the slacks on, I realize I might have jumped into the deep end. There are too many buttons on the fly, inside and out, and a strange clippy thing I've never seen before at the waist. And I have absolutely no idea how to work the suspenders.

"What's with these pants?" I ask.

"You have to do it in stages."

I try a couple of different arrangements, but nothing feels quite right.

"Sure you don't need help?"

"Nope." Stupidest pair of pants, ever. Seriously, why would anyone need five different ways to secure the fly? I clip and button, button and snap, snap and clip, until finally I give up. "All right. How do you do this?"

Nico instructs me on how to button my pants. I feel like a two-year-old. And it's not over yet. The shirt has extra clip-thingies too, and a tie. The hat uses weird pins to hold it to my head. Even the socks are held up by these tight suspender-garter-thingies around my calves.

"Feels like I'm getting dressed for the circus," I say as he tugs the front of my shirt. "I thought valets just parked your car."

"Ugh. You Americans have ruined so many perfectly good words. A valet is a personal servant. It's old-world custom in some countries. Many of the older Embassy guests are used to having things taken care of for them, so all staff must learn the procedures."

I've never worn something so stiff and restrictive. It feels like I'm made of wood.

I look at myself in the mirror, remembering the picture of Mom and Dad all dressed up with the reflective elevator doors behind them. Dad wore the Hotel uniforms once. He could have stood right here, in clothes just like this. I bet they were never scared like I am. I wonder if they knew the answers to all the questions I have. What they'd think if they saw me standing here, filling Dad's shoes.

I poke my finger in one of the four horizontal loops of fabric where my breast pocket should be. They're like the ones Nico pulled the pin out of at the hospital.

"Don't stretch out your pin-sleeves. They might rip." Nico hands me a pair of black sneakers, just like his. "These are your Chucks. Guard them with your life."

I almost laugh, but the look he gives stops me. "Why not shiny shoes? Wouldn't that be better?"

Nico pushes the Chucks toward me. "We're not exactly the most conventional hotel. Sometimes we have to do a lot of walking in strange places." He taps the sole of his sneakers. "These are tailored to get you there and back, and they can be washed with the linens."

I pull the Chucks on. They're way more comfortable than the formal shoes Oma makes me wear sometimes.

"How does the Hotel get its guests, anyway?" I ask. "I've never heard of it."

"It's kinda hard to explain." He shrugs. "They say the Hotel 'calls' you. Like, through your dreams or something. It does all the work—tells the Business Office who to send brochures to, guides the doormen on which doors to bind, lets us bellmen hear the knocks of those it wants. You don't choose it, it chooses you."

I watch his face, trying to decide if he's telling me the truth. "Did it 'call' you?"

He grins. "Those secrets aren't mine to give."

I start to argue, but I realize that's what happened to me with the dreams, and the door in the strip mall. Maybe the Hotel was calling me, too. But why would it do that, if I'm only here to find my dad? Besides, it wasn't the Hotel that let me in; it was Nico, and Stripe.

"Oh! Almost forgot." Nico digs into his pocket and produces a coin—*his* coin, from before. "Keep it in your pocks."

I hold up the coin Agapios gave me. "I have my own. And Dad's. I don't need three."

"Mine is different," he says, pressing his coin into my palm. "See, the brokers set up these vacations—best vacations ever—for people the Hotel invites. But if our guests left here remembering the magic that runs the Hotel, they'd drive themselves crazy searching for it. Or worse . . . they might find a different sort of magic. The Hotel coins let guests use the map-boards and pass through the doors, but they also bind all the memories those guests make so they don't remember all the logistical details when they leave. Keeps things from getting messy, you know. They return their coin, and we keep those memories."

"That's dumb. Why go on a vacation you can't remember?"

"It doesn't take *everything*. Impressions of those memories still hang out in your subconscious. Guests relive their experiences in their dreams."

"Okay," I say, clutching my necklace. "So how come I can see *Dad's* memories if I didn't experience them?"

"A few reasons—because he's family and family bindings are some of the strongest, because you're wearing it, and because the hotel's magic is releasing more of the coin's bound memories to you the longer you're here." Nico points to his coin in my other hand. "Go ahead, put that one in your pock."

He's got that mischievous look in his eye—one I know is sure to get me in trouble. But I obey anyway, sliding both his coin and my own into my left pants pocket. Or pock. Whatever.

"My coin's bond with me is stronger than the others." He pats his pocket and pulls out two coins. "See? Mine always comes back to me."

I check my pocket to find both coins gone. He took them without even being near me. "How'd you do that?"

"Modified it with a little magic we call 'tailoring.'" He rolls the coins between his fingers. "Magic's good for more than just doors. This coin does all the same things as the others, but it also creates a little space around it that I can reach into. It'll always return to me when I call it."

"But . . . how do you keep getting the coin *into* my pocket?" I ask.

"That's just sleight of hand. You get pretty good at slipping things into people's pocks when you've got something that'll always come back. I've been working on a way to send it places, too, but no luck yet."

Our first job is what Nico calls Breakfast Service.

He leads me through dirty, underground back halls to an

enormous kitchen with a wall of windows that look out on the Eiffel Tower in France. The kitchen staff is also all around my age and a little older, just like the porters and ballroom servants I saw last night. A girl with long, black braids chops veggies. A pink-faced boy cleans a copper pot in a sink. Another arranges fruit in a big bowl. They all wear the same white jackets and ballooning white hats as the bearded chef who's issuing them orders.

I jog past a row of trays piled with all manner of pastries and quiches to line up next to Nico. "Where did all these kids come from?"

"Everywhere," Nico says, pushing one of the carts into a back hall. Every plate it carries is a tiny work of art. Sauces swizzle back and forth over cheesy breakfast crepes sprinkled with parsley and chives. Piles of fruit are chopped into smiling starbursts. There's even a pineapple cut and dusted with some red spice to look like flames. "Our staff hails from every country in the world. At least, the ones the Hotel can reach."

"But *why* do they work here? What's in it for them?"

"The Hotel chooses them; that's all I can say. I already got in trouble for sharing Hotel secrets with you. Not taking any more risks than I have to."

He inserts his coin into a slot on the back of the cart and heads down the hall. Before he's two paces ahead, the cart sparkles with an amber shimmer and starts following him on its own, as if he's dragging it with an invisible rope.

"That's . . . " I trail off, not quite believing what I'm seeing.

"That's simple binding. The coin connects me to the cart, and the cart does what I want. You'll see more of it all over the Hotel, if you look closely." He checks his pocket watch. "Now come on. We've got to get to work if you wanna stick around long enough to find out what happened to your dad.

9

War in a Room

The guests we serve breakfast to aren't very friendly. There's a sheik who grouses about the noise (which Nico points out is just the waves of the Indian Ocean lapping outside his window), a couple shouting at each other in German (words I'm pretty sure I should never repeat), and an Ethiopian lord who almost chases us out of his room with a stick (why he has a stick, I'll probably never know).

Nico handles it all very professionally, though. I do my best to match his calm, unflappable attitude, but every stop makes me more and more uncomfortable with my decision to work here, no matter how long.

"I can't believe anyone would want to serve these people," I say as we head to the next floor by way of the service elevator.

Nico shrugs. "Not all the guests are bad. The Hotel's meant to change people."

"Into jerks?"

He laughs. "Pretty sure those people were jerks before they

came here. There are plenty of good guests, too. They just don't need as much attention."

"Are the guests the ones Stripe wants to stop? Or the staff?"

Nico glances nervously around the hall. "I told you, be careful what you say about him here. The Hotel's always listening."

When breakfast service is done, I want to get to work on searching for my dad, but Nico says we first have to check in with the Maid Commander in what he calls the War Room.

We pass through a humid, seventh-floor walkway overlooking a beach with an endless teal ocean and a sky spotted with gulls. The bell-like hum of steel drums floats through the air. Little thatched-roof pagodas litter the sand; wooden masks hang from timbers painted to look like tribal spears.

"Well, if you can't tell me about . . . you-know-who," I say, "can you at least tell me why the Hotel has something called a War Room?"

"Why *wouldn't* the Hotel have a War Room?" Nico replies, as if it's the dumbest question in the world.

Beyond the next threshold, the temperature drops, sending goose bumps up my forearms. I breathe in hot, leather-smelling air from a nearby vent in the plank wall. Moose heads and bear rugs and hunting rifles hang everywhere. In a nearby window, mountains crest the horizon like the skeleton of an ancient dragon.

"It's a hotel, not a country," I say. "Hotels don't go to war." I adjust my jaw and another pop resonates in my eardrum.

"Ears popping?"

"Yeah. It's annoying."

"Altitude change," he says. "Moving to places at different heights changes the pressure in your ears. Also, you should know that if you hang around in a mountainous area for too long, you'll get the alti-tooties, too. Be careful of that. Don't want you farting in front of the guests." He presses the call button on the elevator. "And as for the War Room: This is a *magic* hotel. The Hotel's agenda has made it lots of enemies."

"Like you? And Mr.—"

He gives a warning look. "This House hasn't always been a hotel. That's just what it's currently posing as. The facade, remember? This place has been around a long, long time, and it's been lots of things over the years. A palace. A library. A military command center." He raises an eyebrow. "Imagine what a country could do with the power to travel the world in an instant. What an *army* could do."

"They could take over the world," I say, gripping Dad's coin.

Nico grunts approvingly. "Our *friend* wants to keep the Hotel from being too powerful—to keep everything in balance. That means keeping tabs on what the Hotel does and taking whatever artifacts we can get our hands on." He smiles. "Stop worrying about all that, though. Knowing all the binds and tailors of the Hotel will just make your job harder. Let Sev and me do the dirty work."

"That's easy for you to say."

He pulls me away from the elevator doors. "It's not just maids and the Old Man you have to worry about," he whispers. "The

Hotel itself knows the hearts of the people inside it. If it starts to think you're against it, we're gonna have a problem."

"But aren't you against it?"

"It's more complicated than that. Sev and I know how to stay on the Hotel's good side. And one of those rules is not to talk about all this stuff in here."

The elevator doors slide open, revealing a girl with tight, beaded braids and a nose ring. She's dressed in the uniform Nico wore when I first met him. She looks familiar—I think she's the girl I saw behind the counter when Nico let me peek through the Dallas Door.

"Well, well." The girl smiles wide. "Nico, the demoted."

"Shut up, Elizabeth." Nico steps onto the elevator, and I'm so glad it's one of the guest boxes. The walls in this one reveal a beach under the stars, an icy cave, and a city with even taller skyscrapers than the previous one.

"Is this the new boy?" Elizabeth shoots out a hand as I step on.

I nod and shake it. "Cam."

"Mistah Cam." Her accent reminds me of voices I overhear on the Congo show Cass likes watching—round and breathy.

Nico nods to the console. "War Room, please."

"War Room, War Room. Everyone to the War Room," she says, pressing a button.

"You're an aviator this morning?" Nico asks as the elevator starts up.

Elizabeth smiles and shakes her head. The beads in her braids clack together. "Fillin' in for Audrey while she's doing an errand in Australia for me. I'd ratha fly the lift than deal with those humungous spiders any day." The accent's strong, but her English is perfect.

Nico leans in. "Aviators are lift operators," he tells me. "But that's not Elizabeth's day job, is it?"

"Betta not be. Else someone's gonna pay."

"Wouldn't want to have a debt with you, Itsy-Beth."

She grins.

The way Nico does that—pretending to be everyone's friend while secrets hide behind his smile—makes my chest cold. I'm glad *I* know his secret, though. Or at least I'm in on this one. It's nice to have someone I can trust in this mess with me.

The elevator stops.

"Here you go," Elizabeth says. "Try not to get knocked down any lower, or you're gonna find yourself back on the streets of Berlin." She gives Nico a wink as the doors close behind us.

"Berlin?"

Nico shrugs. "I'm from all over. When I first came to the Hotel, they brought me in through the Berlin Door." He starts down the creamy white hall, tracing the copper-trimmed wainscoting as he walks. "The world's not as divided as you think. Nations like their borders, but the Hotel exists between those boundaries. Borders don't define us. I've met Asian families from France and Middle-Easterners from Canada and white folks from Africa. In the end, people are just people, no matter where they're from or what they look like. It's how they treat one another that matters."

He stops at a shiny, sleek metal door with the words WAR ROOM laser-etched across it.

"Now," Nico says, "what'd I say earlier?"

I shoot him a playful glare. "That you're in charge."

He sweeps the fallen strands of his gelled hair back into place. "That's right. Let me handle it," he says, and opens the door with a flourish.

We enter into what looks like the inside of a giant, glowing orb. The domed ceiling is a brilliant cascade of colored glass cut into the jagged, unruly shapes of countries. Crisscrossing lines of latitude and longitude reach toward us over the sky-blue oceans between continents.

"Wow."

"Yeah." Nico keeps walking. Asia and Australia hang on the edge of the room opposite us, lit from behind with a single bright light. "The light tracks with the sun so we always know what time it is across the globe."

Beneath the domed map stands a circular, high-tech command center. Giant computer screens wrap around the edge of the room, displaying rosters and lists of names and security camera footage. On one screen I see the lobby with the Dallas Door. On another, I recognize the ballroom where I met Sev.

There are no tables or chairs—everyone in the War Room stands with perfect posture at their stations. I quickly see why. The massive floor is taken up by a different map—an old, parchment-colored monstrosity—drawn in the same flowing, inky lines as the map-boards. Only this map is far more intricate, and doesn't make sense to me at all. Glittering ink curls under our feet in flourishes, drawing rooms and halls that connect at odd angles, overlapping where they shouldn't.

There are markings, too. Words, in swirling script.

"The Map Floor tracks the coins of our hotel staff and guests," Nico whispers. He points to little circles with names like "Malana Bustamante" and "Eric Frösche" and "Ylin Patel." "The artificers created it after some bad stuff happened years ago. Map-boards only show you what you need to know, but the Map *Floor* tracks everything. The Hotel's always watching."

I search the map for anything that looks remotely like this room, and find it slightly to the right of center. I recognize the names "Nico Flores" and "Cameron Jones," alongside others I don't know.

And one I do. The name "Reinhart Kuhn" curls across a banner beside my own fake name. But the ink fades and disappears almost as suddenly as I see it, as if someone took an eraser to it.

The floor must have detected Dad's coin. But why did his name vanish when all the others are still there? Did anyone else see it? Do they know who the coin belonged to? Or maybe I just imagined it.

"Here comes the MC," Nico murmurs.

Across the command center, the Maid Commander marches toward us.

Nico's expression tightens. "Great. Rahki's with her."

The girl from last night keeps pace with the MC, clipboard clutched in her arms, squinting at us with a wrinkled brow.

"I see you've brought my new recruit." The Maid Commander stops a couple of feet away, hands fisted, looking down her sharp nose at us. A giant, multicolored Europe shines behind her. "Mr. Cameron, was it?"

"Yes ma'am," I say. "I'm here to work."

"Well if you're not, you won't last long," Her tone is piercing. "It is our tireless duty to ensure the security and pleasure of our guests, as well as the safety of the Hotel's mission. Anything less will not be tolerated. Fail me, and I'll be rid of you before the sun hits the east."

I look up at the light streaming through North America. "But I thought my agreement was with Agapios," I blurt. "He said he determines when I leave."

Her nostrils flare. Nico's eyes widen. Rahki shakes her head.

Stupid, stupid Cam. Why can't I keep my mouth shut?

"The Old Man doesn't have a say in this, boy." Her voice snaps, and I picture her words flinging past and shattering the Pacific Ocean into a million pieces.

She snatches Rahki's clipboard and flips through it.

"Ms. Rahkaiah," the MC says, "take Mr. Cameron with you on the Hungary mission. See how he fares. And remember what we discussed."

"Yes ma'am." Rahki shoots me a scowl.

The MC turns to Nico. "It's throne patrol for you."

What? No! She can't take Nico away from me.

"Toilet duty?" Nico crosses his arms. "I'm a bellman, ma'am. I don't do dirties."

"A thorn in my side is what you are." She snorts. The Maid Commander *would* be a person who snorts. "We all pay our price for breaking the rules."

Nico rolls his eyes and places a hand on my shoulder. "Looks like you're on your own."

"Wait," I say, "you can't leave."

"He can, and must." The MC's posture stiffens, if that's even possible. I imagine her raising her voice and bringing the whole glass ceiling down on our heads. Death by falling country.

"Don't worry," Nico says, flicking me his coin, which had been in my pocket only moments ago. "We'll catch up later." His smile falters when he looks toward Rahki. "Just don't let this one get in your head."

He marches out of the War Room grumbling about how his lot in life is to be abused by the system.

"Now," the MC looks to Rahki, "you know what to do. Bring back the package for placement, and get the boy up to speed." She curls her nose at me. "We'll see what Mr. Cameron is really here for."

10

The Lights of Budapest

Rahki takes me down to the Lobby Level, the outermost ring of the Hotel.

I breathe a sigh of relief as we step from the Elevator Bank ring into the North American Lobby. Finally, a place I recognize. The sputtering fountain, the crystal chandelier, the twisting marble staircase with its cascading scarlet carpet—this is the place that convinced me magic might be real.

Only now I'm at the back of the lobby, past the couches and cushy chairs, facing the row of polished doors that line the far wall. Each bears a shiny bronze sign: WASHINGTON, D.C.; CHICAGO, IL.; VANCOUVER, CA.

DALLAS, TX.

Rahki speeds off to one side toward a drawn velvet curtain under a two-story granite moose. I have to dodge a magically mobile luggage rack being led by a young porter just to keep up.

"Where are we going?"

"Eastern European Lobby," Rahki barks. "Budapest."

We pass through the curtain into a similar, yet different, lobby.

The layout is the same, but this lobby features colorful stucco walls and potted trees trimmed with lights. An enormous stone bird spreads its red and yellow wings over the room. The statue seems to watch me as we pass beneath it.

What Nico said before skitters over my arms. The Hotel's watching. It knows what's in my heart. What does that even mean? Is it going to try and stop me?

"This is the South American Lobby," Rahki says. "Next up: Western Europe."

"How many lobbies does this place have?"

"Eight," she says. "Though if you'd come in the way you were supposed to and gotten the tour, you'd know that, wouldn't you?"

I suddenly understand Nico's urge to stick his tongue out at her.

We pass through the next curtain and enter a vestibule decorated with wrought-iron statues, huge portraits, and lots and lots of gold.

"So here's the quick version," she says. "Each lobby is dedicated to a particular region." She points to the row of doors marked with the names of European places. "The knockers—doors that lead out of the Hotel—run along the outer wall of the lobby ring." She nods to the grand staircase that leads to the upper level. "Up there, where we just came from, is the Elevator Bank, and beyond that is the Mezz, with—"

"Nico explained all that to me. But where's the Shaft fit in?"

"Doesn't work like that. The Shaft's just the Shaft. It's like . . . glue holding everything together. What's important are the four main rings that make up the trunk—Lobby Level, Elevator Bank, Mezzanine,

Courtyard. Everything else branches off those by way of turners, which is just what we call doors binding one part of the Hotel to another."

"Like branches of a tree," I say, picturing the recurring symbol.

She nods. "Turners and knockers are in all the great Houses. Just remember that the turners bind the insides, and the knockers connect to the outside."

After a quick detour to grab fur-lined coats from a closet, Rahki heads for the Budapest Door.

"One more thing," she says before opening the knocker. "If we get separated, don't panic."

My skin prickles. "Why would we get separated?" I'm not at all interested in getting lost forever in Hungary.

"It happens. But if something does go wrong, your coin will want to come back. The coin binds you to the Hotel—it always wants to bring you and the Hotel back together. As long as you have it, it will guide you to the door. Knock at the knocker, and someone will let you in. Here at the Hotel, a knocked door is always opened."

She glances to the landing atop the grand staircase and purses her lips. Agapios stands above us, hands clasped behind him, staring down at me. The grave look in his eyes sends a chill straight up my spine.

"Come on," Rahki says, opening the door and letting the snow billow through. "Welcome to Budapest."

The Budapest Door leads us into a wide-open town square.

"Wow," I say. It's the only word I can form.

All around us, tall glass-and-stone buildings drip with light.

Carved granite arches glow as the sun sets beyond them. Warm, yellow strings of incandescent bulbs drape from pop-up tents scattered throughout the square. Tree branches twist and curl, carrying the lights into the sky like the fiery breath of a dragon.

Rahki crouches down to retie her Chucks. "Vörösmarty tér," she says, pulling the knot. "The Eastern Orthodox countries really make a splash this time of year."

"It's . . . "

"Budapest at Christmastime is one of my favorites."

I shoot her a confused look. "Don't you . . . ?" I nod to her headscarf.

"Just because I don't celebrate the holiday doesn't mean I can't appreciate its festivities. Beautiful things are always beautiful. It's how we perceive them that makes us think they're not."

She turns to me, and I notice the long wooden baton hanging from her belt under her coat. It's sanded as smooth as its satin holster, with a flared, splintery end at the top.

"It's a duster," she explains when she sees me looking. "Maid Service weapon of choice."

She strikes a gloved finger up the wood.

"Maid Service gloves are rough, like sandpaper," she says, rubbing her fingers together. "The gloves shave off the topmost layer of our dusters to give us binding dust." She holds out her hand, her index finger glittering with powder from the baton.

"What's it do?"

She smiles. "Give me your hand."

I hesitate, but eventually give in.

Rahki runs her dusted fingertip along my index and middle fingers, then squeezes them together. "The dust binds. That's all. Go ahead; pull them apart."

At first I'm not sure what she means, but when I try to wiggle my fingers, I can't. At least, not the two she bound with the glitter-dust. "It's like they're superglued together." I try to shake it off, but no matter what I do, I can't separate my fingers. "How do you undo it?"

"It'll wear off eventually."

"Eventually?!"

"Calm down," she says, still smiling. "You're way better off than Nico was when I showed him." She snickers. "Bound that stupid bowler hat to his face. Used a little too much dust, but it was worth it. He was pretty much blind for a whole day." She narrows her eyes. "But you should know that if you get out of line, my dusting can get pretty creative."

It's totally a threat. She trusts me about as far as I trust her, which is pretty much not at all.

Rahki points to one of the glass buildings strung with lights wound in giant balls, and I can barely make out the head of a statue over the tents. "Our contact is meeting us behind the statue of Míhaly. Let's hurry."

"So, you fight with those duster things?" I ask, still struggling to force my fingers apart as she marches ahead of me.

"Dusters are good for fighting, but they have lots of other uses too. Binding people's hands, setting traps, mending doors—you can do a lot with a good duster, as long as you're willing to spend the dust."

I try spitting on my hand and using the spittle to rub my fingers free, but it doesn't work. I already wasn't a fan of Rahki after she turned us in, but this is downright insulting.

As we weave through the crowded square, I turn my attention to the cedar-posted tents that line the street. Each kiosk is wrapped in green garland and twinkling lights. The smell of smoked meats and honey and fir trees and cinnamon makes me feel like I'm *inside* the very essence of Christmas. Rahki's right. This is cool. I have to stay focused, though. We don't like her. She turned us in, bound my fingers. She's a maid, and Nico said maids are the enemy.

But she doesn't seem like an enemy.

Rahki passes a bill to a vendor and takes a jelly-filled donut in return.

"You just happen to have their kind of money?"

"Hotel bills are bound," she says. "Our money's universal, tailored to pass as whatever kind of cash we need it to be."

"Won't they notice it's . . . different?"

"They don't notice the doors, do they?" She shrugs. "There's a different kind of magic involved—one that distorts the reality of what people see. But no, those we give Hotel bills to don't notice right away. Before they figure out the money's not real, our Business Office calls it back and replaces it with whatever it should be."

"I'd think you'd be able to just . . . magically . . . you know?"

She looks confused.

"You know. Change it to whatever you want."

"You're talking about shaping, and it doesn't work like that. There are rules to this stuff." She takes a bite and looks me up and down. "All right, your turn. What's the deal with you? Why are you here?"

"Why does it matter?"

Rahki eyes me suspiciously. "Fine. Don't tell me. But I know you want something." She sinks her teeth into the pastry and continues down the row.

I struggle to keep up, pressing through the crowd. Coin or no coin, I do *not* want to get lost. "How do you know I want something? What if I just want to see the world?"

She stops, and I almost run into her. "See the world? Really? Because you look absolutely terrified out here."

My hands clench into fists. Truth is, I *am* terrified. My brain has already conjured fifteen different ways this trip could get me killed—everything from catching a Hungarian virus to getting mugged in a back alley. But I can't let her know that.

"The Hotel doesn't appear for just anyone," she says. "It invites those who are searching. People who need something they can't get anywhere else. So spill it."

I don't answer.

She glances up at a clock on one of the buildings and groans. "We need to pick up the pace. Got a schedule to keep to. But if you want to stick around, you're going to have to give me something."

We pass a heavenly smelling tent with cooked meats hanging from the supports. The barbecue smell reminds me of home: of Oma, and Cass, and backyard dinners. I miss them, especially Oma. Her not knowing where I went is probably worrying her to death. And I haven't been in touch with them yet; I'm a terrible brother and grandson.

I spy a rack of postcards at one of the vendors, and remember Oma's stacks and stacks of cards from Dad. "If I wanted to send someone something . . . "

Rahki understands right away, and passes me one of the bound bills. "Go get a postcard, and you can send it through the mail room."

She watches carefully as I purchase a card with the words *"Üdvözöljük Magyarország"* written in flourishing letters over a building dotted with domes and spires. I don't like the way she looks at me as I make my purchase. It's like she already knows the secret fears boiling inside me.

"Our contact will be over here," she says when I come back, then disappears through a group of laughing teens.

I start to follow, but something catches my eye. A man, dressed in a pinstriped suit and squatty straw hat, ordering a cone of candied nuts.

Mr. Stripe glances over, tips his boater hat with his cane, and winks.

Why's he here?

"Cam?" Rahki calls from the other side of the lane. "Where'd you go?"

Stripe waves me on and turns back to the vendor. I swallow the questions gurgling in my throat and hurry to join her.

A large stone man rises over us, glowing under the lit trees. He sits confidently on his bench as chiseled children peek out from under his feet. The statue almost reminds me of the Old Man, with his stern face and dark, empty eyes. Is that what the concierge feels like, with all those kids serving under him?

But the kids in the statue don't look scared. They look safe, as if the man's protecting them. I've always yearned for that. To feel safe. Protected. To be just as carefree as all the other kids I know. Oma takes good care of us, but it seems like it's different for the kids with parents. They all seem so . . . confident.

I glance back to where I saw Stripe, but he's not there. Maybe he has something to tell me. Maybe we can get Dad back a different way. But how'd he find me?

Rahki scans the crowd. "Where is he?"

"I'm here."

A pale-faced boy walks around the statue, wearing a heavy, navy trenchcoat with silver buttons. Curly black hair poofs out from under a rounded bowler like mine, and furry patches stick out on his face.

It takes a moment to figure out why he looks so familiar.

"*Szia*, Orban," Rahki says.

"*Szia*." He shakes her hand.

It's Orban . . . the one who was with Stripe in the Corridor. He looks so loose and casual. Back with Stripe, he'd been formal and deadpan.

Our eyes meet, and Orban smiles. "I don't believe we've met."

Wait . . . but he *has* met me! I want to correct him, but then I understand. He's only *pretending* not to know me.

"Cameron's new," Rahki says. "I'm showing him around."

"Good to meet you, Mr. Cameron," Orban says, rolling his Rs. He gives me a subtle bow. I shake his meaty hand, trying not to stare at the patches of fur on his face. The one under his eye looks like a boot, and another along his jaw could easily be a map of California. An extremely hairy map.

"Orban's one of our suppliers," Rahki says. "Not exactly staff, but he might as well be."

"Suppliers?" I ask.

"The Hotel traffics in very particular goods and services." Orban levels his gaze at me. "As long as everyone does their job, everything will be fine."

It's a message especially for me. Stripe, telling me this whole situation's under control.

But Rahki misses it. "Where's the pickup?"

"Always to business, this Rahki." Orban motions to the festivities, and pulls a cookie from his coat. "Have you enjoyed our treats? Vörösmarty has the very best."

Rahki's eyes widen. "Are those honey cookies?"

"Indeed. And they are halal!" Orban follows with an exclamation—something in Hungarian—and Rahki laughs. They seem so casual, as if this whole thing is no big deal. Maybe it's not. Maybe this "mission" thing is something they do all the time.

Their conversation continues without me, and I take in the twisting metal lampposts and snow-topped stonework. I'm in Hungary. And it's not as bad as I thought it'd be. Traveling. Being somewhere that's not home. It's almost . . . exciting.

Almost.

My attention turns back to the crowd, and the man in the pinstriped suit standing at the edge of the square. Stripe dips his fingers into the bag of candied nuts, watching us out of the corner of his eye. I need to talk to him, to get him to tell me what to do now that the Hotel knows I'm there, and with my Dad's coin, no less. I start to break away—Rahki and Orban are so deep in conversation that they probably wouldn't notice—but Stripe shakes his head. A serious look in his eye tells me to wait.

Orban leads us down an alley off the main square. Whereas Vörösmarty tér was clear and clean for the festival, the side streets are blanketed in dirty, gray snow. Long shadows from the coach lights grope down the alley. The noise of the festival dwindles to a dreadful silence.

Rahki and Orban continue their conversation as I trail behind them. Orban talks fast—too fast, I think, like he's nervous—but Rahki fills me in with a translation here and there.

" . . . he says they were in a sweatshop upriver . . . "

" . . . hadn't been fed well . . . "

" . . . they'll need some care before placement . . . "

I stop her. "Wait, are you talking about people?"

Rahki screws up her face. "Not just people. The mission."

Orban stops at a door behind a building just off the Danube River. Huge barges full of lit windows creak in the waves. I can smell the wet rocks from here.

He unlocks the door, revealing a dark hallway. The floor beyond is polished concrete, the walls a drab grayish-blue.

Rahki heads inside first. "Once we're done here we'll grab them some honey cookies. You're welcome to come too," she tells him.

Orban glances back the way we came. He keeps doing that—as though he's afraid of something. But there's nothing out there to be afraid of. At least not from what I can see. Just the crowd, the vendors, and Stripe.

"What's wrong?" I ask.

He touches a warning finger to his lips, and leads me through the door, out of the shadows and the cold and the smell of candied nuts.

It's a hotel. The rows of numbered doors, the smell of disinfectant . . . But it's not *the* Hotel. These doors are locked with keycards, not skeleton screws, which means they aren't bound like the Hotel's turners. And my ears didn't crackle when we crossed the threshold.

I hang back a little. Orban keeps giving me weird glances, and he's stopped speaking. I can't quit thinking about that look on Stripe's face. I should be okay with this—Orban's my ally, after all—but every danger sensor in my brain is going off.

Orban swipes a keycard to one of the rooms, and I catch a glimpse of something poking out of his deep pocket. It looks almost like . . . a knife? When he sees me looking, he tries to cover it.

I grab Rahki before she can step through. "Let me go first."

Rahki tilts her head. "Why?"

Because all of this feels wrong. Because if something bad's going to happen, it needs to happen to me first. That's my job. I protect others from the bad things. Cass. Oma. Everyone.

"I just want to see," I tell her, and push through the cracked door.

But I'm not prepared for what's waiting on the other side.

"They're kids," I say. Five of them—all under the age of eight—with worried expressions.

Oma's stories about evil spirits race through my head again. Spirits are greedy. They'd possess the world if they could. She always said children are hard to own; that's why the spirits want them so much. Kids don't do what they're told, don't obey the rules, so the craftiest spirits steal into people's homes and suck the joy out of their children. They ruin them.

These kids look like they've had more than just joy sucked out of them, though. Their eyes are bulbous and hollow. Their skin stretches tight across their faces, their arms, their ribs. Clothes hang off them like they're nothing more than hangers in a closet.

Rahki rushes forward with open arms and squats in the middle of them. "Come here, little ones."

The girls lean into her. The boys step back, watching with cautious eyes.

Many enter those doors, but not all return. Was Stripe talking about kids like these? Is Agapios one of Oma's greedy spirits? Is the Hotel stealing their joy? Or is it something else?

"What . . . happened to them?"

No one answers me. Rahki's busy comforting the children, and Orban's still standing outside the door.

I watch the kids. The looks in their eyes make me miss my sister, my home, more than I ever thought I could. Are they looking for me? Did they call the police? Will I just vanish?

Out of the corner of my eye, I see Orban take a step back and grab the door handle. Our eyes lock, and I don't like what his say.

"Orban?"

Orban pulls the knife from his overcoat and points it at me. Only it's not a knife. At least, not any kind of knife I've ever seen. The whole thing is wood, grip to tip—a sharp spike no bigger around than a pencil, but twice as long.

He jabs it toward me, warning me to stay back. "I won't be unbound," he says, his voice creaking. His next words are almost a whisper, directed straight at me: "Get out."

Rahki turns as he slams the door shut.

I reach for the handle to throw it open, but miss. I grab again, but my fingers find nothing but air.

There *is* no handle.

My arms tingle. My ears pound.

Orban says something in Hungarian from the other side of the door, and his footsteps scurry away.

I look to Rahki to translate.

She blinks. "He said . . . a debt was owed."

11

Dust to Dust

Rahki pulls the scared children close.

I won't be unbound.

Get out.

"What's going on?" I ask, but deep down I already know. Trouble. I can't tell what the trouble is, or what I'm supposed to be worried about, but that doesn't prevent me from running calculations.

Forty percent chance someone's coming to kill us with a chainsaw.

Twenty-three percent chance the walls are about to close in.

Sixteen percent chance we'll be drowned in toxic goop.

Ten percent chance the floor's going to open up and feed us to hungry sharks.

Seven percent chance a bunch of Budapestian spiders are going to wrap us in death cocoons, suck out our blood, and leave our shriveled-up bodies for the police to find.

And . . . I don't know what that leaves. I'm not a math person, so . . . maybe, like, four percent chance it'll be okay. I don't like those odds, especially since I'm pretty sure they don't add up.

Orban's supposed to be on my side, though. So why would he lock me in here?

Rahki watches the door like she expects it to open on its own. "That weapon . . . Orban had a sliver. He's with the Competition."

"The who?"

She stands, glaring at me, and then . . . she strikes a hand up her duster. Shimmering fingers flying toward my face. My cheek smashes into the wall. . . .

And I'm stuck.

"What did you—?"

"Quiet!" she shouts. "I need to think."

Meanwhile, my cheek is glued to the wall with Rahki's magic dust. I can't pull away, can't slide, can't even begin to peel myself loose. "Let me go!"

"I said quiet!" She hoists her duster menacingly.

"Okay, okay!" I turn to face her the best I can with my jaw currently in use as a wall fixture. "Just one itty-bitty question. Why'd you bind *me* to the wall?"

She runs a hand along the doorframe, searching for something. "Because you might be one of them."

I swallow hard and scramble for something to say—anything that'll prove I'm not . . . whatever she thinks I am. The children whimper behind me. I can't turn to see them. They must be so scared. "One of who?"

"The Competition," Rahki says, prying at the door.

"Will you please tell me what's going on?" I ask, giving in to my superglued fate.

Her gaze lingers where the hinges should be, but they're on the other side, unreachable. "The Competition are people who want to break up the Hotel. They're our enemy, and they've just caught us in one of their traps."

Stripe. Nico and Sev. Orban. Are they the Competition? Am I?

Rahki searches every corner, window, and drywall imperfection in the room.

"What are you doing?"

"Looking for a way out," she says.

Not being able to turn my head really stinks. "My neck's starting to hurt. And my shoulder is going numb."

"Deal with it." Rahki returns to the door and pounds a fist against it. "I need a hinge. They cleared out all the furniture, barred the windows . . . even took the bathroom door."

"Listen," I tell her, "I don't know what this is all about. If you let me loose, maybe I could help."

She gives me a quizzical look. "You really *don't* know what's going on, do you?"

"Promise." I hold my hands up. Though, hanging by my cheek as I am, I'm pretty sure it looks more like some lame chicken dance than surrender. "I'd never heard of the Competition before you mentioned them just now. I don't know why you've got these kids, or why Orban locked us in here."

Rahki twists her lips to the side, then pulls her duster from its holster and raises it.

I wince. "Please don't hit me."

"I'm not going to hit you, dummy. Hold still." She pushes the skinny end of her duster under my cheek and spins it. "The binding between the dust and the duster is stronger than the binding between you and the wall. Dust to dust, and . . . "

She pulls back on the duster, and my face peels free, sending me sprawling.

One of the girls gives a little giggle.

"You like that, huh?" I say, brushing myself off. "It'll be a week before my face goes back to normal."

The girl says something in Hungarian, and smiles.

I give her a funny, stretched-out expression. "Does it look all right?"

She laughs, but the girl beside her scoots away, fear in her eyes. Probably shouldn't joke with scary faces right now.

I scramble over and rest my hand on the frightened girl's shoulder, like I do when Cass is scared, and give it a reassuring squeeze. "It's going to be all right."

When we were younger, Oma used to tell me how vulnerable Cass was. She said some people need a little more attention than others, and that it was my job to care for and protect Cass. Cass isn't all that weak these days—the younger years for kids with spina bifida are always the worst. She still has her moments, like the other afternoon, but she's smart, more independent than ever, and hopeful.

These girls remind me of how Cass used to be.

When I look up, Rahki's watching me. "You're good at that."

"Lots of practice." I wipe away a tear from the scared girl's eyes and wink at the one who laughed.

"Okay." Rahki pulls a wooden pin from the pin-sleeves on her shirt. "This hinge-pin is bound to the Hotel. But the Competition knew I'd have one for emergencies, and therefore, no hinges."

I close my eyes and focus. This is another locker. Lockers have releases. There has to be a way out. No matter how hard Rahki looks, a hinge isn't going to just magically materialize. That means all we've got to work with are these kids, and the stuff we came here with. There's Rahki's duster, and the pin she pulled from her pin-sleeve, and . . .

Wait a minute . . . "Is there any magic in the hinge, or is it just the pin?" I ask.

"All in the pin. The hinge just keeps the pin connected to the doorframe."

"So . . . all you have to do is connect the two, and the pin will bind the door to the Hotel?"

"Something like that. But like I said, there are no hinges."

"There are no hinges *yet*."

Her eyes narrow. "What are you getting at?"

"What if we made our own?" I stick my finger in one of the empty pin-sleeves on my shirt and pull. The threads snap one-by-one as I rip the rectangular piece of fabric loose and hand it to her.

"Here. Use that dust stuff to glue the material to the door and the frame, and we can slide the pin in between, creating a new hinge on our side."

She hesitates, examining the strip of fabric.

"Will that not work?" I ask.

"Not sure," she says. "In theory, maybe. It might even separate this side of the door from the hinges on the other side."

"Only one way to find out, right?"

She grins. "All right, let's see what happens." Rahki strikes her duster and attaches the pin-sleeve where the hinge should be.

As she sticks the last bit to the door, a knock makes her jump back in alarm.

"*Helló?*" A man's voice. "*Ez senkit nem?*"

"Who is it?" I whisper.

"I don't know." Rahki lifts her head and replies to the man on the other side in Hungarian.

"You speak English?" the man says. A pause. "I saw a young man running away. He looked up to no good."

"That would be Orban the Traitor, escaping," Rahki mumbles.

"Think it's the Competition?" I ask.

She shakes her head. "Doubtful. They wouldn't be talking to us like this. They'd just come on in and take what they wanted, I think."

"You don't know?"

"I've never encountered the suits myself. Maid Commander just recently started sending me on the more dangerous missions."

Another knock. "Is everything all right in there?"

"Bind the door," I tell her. "Let's just see if we can get out of here."

Rahki inserts her pin into the makeshift fabric hinge. There's a crackle as the binding takes hold. "I think it worked," she says.

The door cracks open, and I catch the faintest scent of blueberry pie. We did it! We can—

But before it can open fully, there's a ripping sound. A pop. A glimmering wave of light as the fabric of the pin-sleeve tears and the door falls toward me. The pins that had held the door in place on the outside clatter to the ground.

Rahki helps me guide the door into the room and to the floor, then retrieves the pin that freed us.

When I stand back up and look through the open doorway, The Hotel Between isn't on the other side. But it's not the "where" of what I see that bothers me. It's the "who."

Mr. Stripe stands in the threshold, munching on his bag of candied nuts. "Well," he says, "after seeing the guilty look on that boy's face, I thought someone might need help. Looks like I was wrong."

My mind races, struggling to figure out what's going on. Why is Stripe still here? Did he conspire to lock us in this room?

"Since that's sorted, I guess I'll be going." Stripe tips his hat and shakes my hand vigorously. "You all have a happy holiday."

He saunters down the hall, leaning on his cane the whole way.

I feel something, like a folded piece of paper, in my palm; Stripe left it behind when he shook my hand.

A note.

12

Pinched

The Maid Commander is waiting for us in the Eastern European Lobby with her staff when we get back. The maids all wear slacks and flat-front button-downs under a vest just like Rahki's, and carry the same kind of wooden duster shaved down to various lengths. The MC scowls, indignant, like I put gum in her hair.

"Here comes the Maid Service," Rahki announces.

"The dusters were a dead giveaway," I whisper. "I'm going to have nightmares about having my face superglued to a moving car for months."

She chuckles. "I'll take it from here. Make sure you report to Nico for your afternoon errands. We'll talk later." She starts to go, but pauses. "And great job out there. Maybe when your trial period's over, the Hotel will let you join the maids with me."

Rahki leads the children forward, and the Maid Commander ushers them up the stairs to the Elevator Bank. I wonder where they're taking those kids, and whether anyone will see them again. The possibility that I may have helped this place disappear a few more children sours my stomach. But I don't know for sure that's what's happening. I need to find out more, and quickly.

The MC stops at the top of the stairs to look down at me, hand on the hilt of her sword, then turns on her heel, leaving me alone in the Hotel for the first time.

Though I'm not really alone. The lobbies are full of guests coming and going through the turners to other parts of the Hotel, staff answering the knockers to allow those who've been on excursions back inside. The giant bull statues flanking the grand staircase to the Elevator Bank stare me down. A man plays a jig on an accordion in the corner, though the music seems to come from everywhere. It's as if his instrument is bound to the entire room, and the walls are playing along.

But the warm light of the Hotel isn't so warm anymore. It feels alien without someone to guide me through it. Maybe it *is* alien, and Agapios is the alien king, and they're harvesting kids for experiments, and . . .

No, I'm pretty sure the Old Man and the MC aren't aliens. Of course, two days ago I was certain magic doors weren't a thing, either. And the closest I ever had to an enemy was the class bully who thought it was funny to wipe boogers on me when he passed by in school.

Orban's words echo like some awful pop song full of doo-wops and nonsense words. *I won't be unbound. Get out.*

I sit on one of the floral-painted benches and dig in my pocket for the note Stripe slipped to me when he shook my hand. The words are written in flowing black script, only slightly more legible than Agapios's.

Dear Cameron,

Forgive my little farce with Orban. When Nico informed me that you would be accompanying the maid sent to steal those children, I saw an opportunity to strengthen support for you within the Hotel ranks. Our little act may have revealed Orban as one of our own, but the Hotel staff will be far more likely to trust you now that they've seen you as vulnerable as they are.

I'm so pleased you managed to find a place at the Hotel. This will really help us locate your father and free him from whatever fate has kept you apart these twelve years. Wonderful, wonderful job. But now that you are in the Hotel, dangers lurk around every corner. I'm sure our encounter in Budapest has shown how deeply deceived the Hotel staff are concerning their so-called "mission."

It's this mission that I and your new friends have worked so diligently to stop. Agapios has convinced everyone that what the Hotel does is for the benefit of the children, but it is theft, plain and simple. Those stolen children have no idea what's in store for them.

Try not to trouble yourself with these things, though, else the Hotel may begin to sense your intentions. Set your sights on unlocking the secrets hidden in Reinhart's coin, and the Hotel will not fault you for it. Focus only on him, and you will find what you've always longed for.

Reinhart would be proud.

Stripe

I read it over again and again, lingering each time on those final words.

Reinhart would be proud.

So the Hotel *is* stealing kids, and Rahki's bought some lie that they're doing it for a good cause. That's why Nico views her as the enemy. She seems like a really good person, though, even if she threw me under the bus when I first arrived; I'm sure she just doesn't know the truth.

Stripe said they revealed Orban as one of their own. That could mean Stripe and the people working with him really are the Competition, and that the Competition's job is to stop the Hotel from taking these kids.

I gotta quit thinking about it, or it'll make me angry and tip off the Hotel heart-readers or whatever it is that can sense people's intentions. If Dad was working with Stripe to stop the Hotel, then he must have discovered something important that could help. Maybe in finding him, we could also help the children.

Unfortunately, I don't know how, and I don't have long to learn before my time here runs out.

The hubbub of the lobby swirls around me. People knocking at the doors, bellhops coining luggage carts, kids laughing and running around statues.

I stand up, close my eyes, and breathe in the Hotel's air, waiting for something. Anything. *Lead me, O great coin.*

Nothing.

So I walk the lobbies. Maybe if I retrace Dad's steps, the coin will . . . I dunno . . . float? Shine? I'd take anything to point me in the right direction.

As I explore, I notice differences between some of the lobby knockers. Many doors on the outer wall have signs that read OUT OF ORDER instead of the location they're bound to. Those knockers look darker, dingier, as if the color's been sucked out of them.

Between the Eastern European Lobby and the Asiatic Lobby, I find a display covered in brochures. Mixed in with rows and rows of see-the-sights-ofs and enjoy-the-luxuriousnesses stands a row of safety pamphlets. There's nothing I love more than a good safety pamphlet. The doctors have sent all sorts of guidebooks and diagrams home with Cass over the years to make sure we know what to do in case of emergency. I've read them all.

I thumb through one of the foldouts titled "In Case of Pin-Failure."

> 1. In the event of a failed hinge-pin, Hotel staff must evacuate all guests to the Mezzanine. Locate your nearest map-board and follow the instructions.
>
> 2. If you find yourself at the location of the pin emergency, do not panic. Notify the nearest doorman immediately. Again, ushering guests to the Mezzanine remains first priority.
>
> 3. If a doorman cannot be found, please contact the facilities workshop to notify them of the pin emergency.
>
> 4. If you find yourself trapped in the pin emergency, do not panic. Locate your nearest map-board, and follow the designated path. . . .

Whatever this pin-failure thing is, it sounds terrible. I pocket the pamphlet to read more thoroughly later, and continue through to the Asiatic Lobby.

I run my fingers around the granite pillar at the end of the staircase, taking in the pearl inlay in the tile. Red satin falls in waves from the ceiling. The hanging lanterns, the woman plucking out a soothing song on an unfamiliar instrument as people laugh and talk . . . it all seems unreal. Amazing. It's easy to forget that dirty secrets lie hidden behind all this glamour.

I insert my coin into the slot on the nearby map-board, and the gleaming ink curls and twists, drawing the framework of the Hotel. A shimmering line weaves between the doors, showing where I've been, and forming a banner across the top with the words, "Find Your Destination."

But the ink doesn't stop there. Intricate embellishments swirl in from the corners. Sharp lines and cross-hatching form a face. A man's face.

I start to pull back, but something about that face stops me. I know those eyes. I've seen them in the mirror when I'm brushing my teeth, and in the pictures I keep under my bed.

It's Dad.

I trace his jawline with my finger. Nico said the map-boards sense where I want to go. . . .

The board draws another face on the opposite edge, this time with a body to match. It's Cass. Only she's not in her wheelchair. She's walking, redrawn frame-by-frame, putting one foot in front of the other. She looks so healthy, spirited in the ink. It's strange, seeing her like this. Even after the surgeries to straighten her clubbed foot, she's never been able to walk. I know she's happy, but I've always selfishly wished she could run and play like I can.

More images pop across the page, but I can't stop looking between these two. This is why I'm here. My "destination."

And the Hotel knows it.

I yank my coin from the slot and step back. Everyone keeps saying the Hotel has a will of its own. Using the coin let it see what I want . . . who I am. Does the Hotel really know why I'm here? No, that's ridiculous. It's just a place.

Get out.

I glance up to see the security cameras in the corners of the lobby. The maids are watching. Tracking me. Rahki bound my face to the wall on the slightest suspicion I might be with the Competition. What will they do when they find out who I really am, and why I'm here?

I get my chance to ask my mounting questions later, when we meet back in Sev's room on the twenty-first floor. The barn-like smell of wood shavings and Sev's jars and jars of dust makes me sneeze as I fill him and Nico in on what happened in Budapest, and Stripe's note.

"Binding a door with a pin-sleeve," Nico says, shuffling a deck of cards on Sev's bed. The snow-dusted cathedral fills the window behind him. "Now there's something I've never seen. Good thinking. If you can get Rahki to trust you, your job'll be that much easier."

"Because she is *never* going to like Nico," Sev jokes.

Nico blows him a raspberry.

"So," I say, taking my time to find the right words, "does that mean you guys *are* the Competition?"

"Yep," Nico says.

I'm not sure whether his cool admission is comforting or troubling. "Rahki told me the Competition wants to stop the Hotel. She thinks you're bad."

Sev hmphs.

Nico scowls at him. "We're here to *protect* people, whatever the cost."

But that sounds exactly like what Rahki wants to do. "Where does the Maid Service take those kids?" I ask. "What do they want with them?"

"You do not want the answer to that question," Sev says, focused on the small stick he's whittling with his knife.

"Yes I do. Come on! Is this your task? Stopping the Hotel from stealing kids?"

"Shh." Nico shakes his head.

I'm getting tired of being shushed, though. "Just tell me. Did my dad know what the Hotel was up to? Did he figure out a way to stop them?"

"You'd have to ask him," Nico says. "Finding him is your only job here. If you do that, you're doing more to stop them than any-one else."

It's a dodge, but at least I know who's who now. It seems Dad trusted Stripe, and that's enough for me. When I find him, he'll be able to tell me all the things no one else is willing to. *If* I find him.

Sev gives Nico a side-glance, and returns to his whittling. He's so laid-back, working the wood as if it's the most natural thing in the world. With every swipe of his knife I can't help picturing what would happen if he missed and sent the blade through his finger. Every once in a while he rubs dirt from a nearby jar into the wood, which soaks the soil up like a sponge.

"Rahki said the magic's in the pin," I say, when I realize he's carving another one.

"Magic is in *life*," Sev says. "In the life of many things. Earth. Plants. Blood. Nico explains better. He is more sensitive to the binding than anyone I have met."

Nico leans back and shuffles the deck into the air. "Binding *comes* from life," he says. "It's a strong connection tethering one thing to another. Not many sources of binding are strong enough to feel it, though. You find it a lot in people, especially families— the magic of trust and dependence binds us together."

I point at the pin Sev's sanding. "But that's not a person."

Nico fans the cards and twists the deck like a master magician. "To make the doors work, you need something more than just natural binding between people. Trying to get that much magic out of a person is . . . dangerous."

"It is evil," Sev corrects, staring him down.

I swallow. Is the Hotel making pins out of kids?

But Nico waves Sev off. "Point is, getting enough magic out of a person to bind a door would make that person . . . less than themselves." He drops the deck and holds up a block of old, gray wood. "So we use this instead."

"This wood is special." Sev runs the sandpaper gently over the pin's smooth surface. "From special tree. Its magic winds through the Hotel like tree roots."

Like the tree from my dreams. And the symbol that's all over the Hotel. Only this wood's gray, like Cass's coin.

"Too bad the tree's lost," Nico adds. "All we have now are these old remnants."

"What happened to it?" I ask. "Did it die?"

"It got pinched."

I give Nico a confused look.

"You know. Pinched." He sighs. "Filched, swiped, stolen, whatever you want to call it. Someone took the whole Greenhouse over a decade ago, and the Vesima tree with it. Apparently the Hotel's been going downhill ever since."

"You can't just *steal* a place."

"You can if the only way to reach it is through the binding." Sev eyes down the length of his pin. "All you have to do is pop the pins."

"No," I say. "You could just go back to where the Greenhouse is in the real world and re-pin it. Right?"

Sev glances up. "Not if you do not know where to look. Some places are so hidden, the binding is the only way to reach them."

Nico checks his watch. "We gotta go, kiddo. Afternoon errands call."

"Before you leave . . . " Sev tosses him another secret look.

"Oh yeah," Nico says. "Almost forgot."

Sev pulls a long, needle-sharp stick from his desk drawer. "Let me see your hand, Cameron."

I scoot back. The way the pointed tip of the needle shimmers makes my shoulders itch. "Uhh, why?"

Nico rolls his eyes. "Just do it."

"Nuh-uh. Last time someone asked for my hand, they bound my fingers together."

"Pshh." Nico snags my wrist and holds my palm out to Sev, fingers spread.

My heart races. I try to break free, but Nico holds me firm. "Let go!"

"It's just a touch. Be still."

Sweat beads on my forehead. Sev's brown eyes darken. He focuses in on my finger and pricks the tip with the needle.

"There." Sev touches an eyedropper to the tiny bubble of blood that rises on my fingertip, and sucks a drop into the glass. "Done."

Nico releases me.

I rub my wrist. "What was that for?"

Sev holds out his open palm. "Hand me your father's coin, and I will show you."

I untie the necklace begrudgingly and hand it over. "You people are weird."

"I will consider that a compliment." Sev takes the coin and the eyedropper to his worktable. "The coin only wants to reveal its secrets to its true owner. This coin still knows it does not belong to you, so it is hiding all that it knows. We must strengthen the binding between you and the coin to speed up the process, and reveal those memories."

My binding. My blood. The stuff that connects me to Dad, and Cass, and Oma.

I rub my wet finger. "You could have asked."

"Where's the fun in that?" Nico winks.

Sev drips my blood onto the coin and rubs it with his finger. The back side of the disc sparkles like rubies, and I hear the crack of a door opening in my head as the glow fades.

"That's it?" I say, hanging Dad's coin back around my neck.

"Let's hope so."

"One more thing," Sev says as Nico pulls me toward the door. He hands me the pin he's been working on. "This is for you. It might get you out of trouble. *Iz dvukh zol vybirayut men'sheye.* If all options are bad, choose the one that hurts least."

The pin is perfect. Smooth. Exact. Just like the ones Nico and Rahki have.

"Don't I also need one of those little gun-thingies?"

Nico laughs. "The plugs aren't magic or anything. There are lots of ways to pin a door."

Sev grips my shoulders and looks me in the eye. "Do not use it unless you have to. Think of it as . . . a way out."

Orban's words reverberate in my head. *Get out. Get out.*

I nod, then slide the pin into the bottom pin-sleeve on my shirt as Nico drags me out to do more work.

13

To Your Statues!

I'm twisting and winding my way from the moss-covered rocks of Scotland to the crowded streets of Cuba. From Cuba to the temples of Laos. From Laos to the ancient stones of Israel, to the city-covered hills of Morocco. I know all these places, because I'm not me. I'm . . . someone else.

And I'm afraid.

I feel the coin in my pocket. I hate this coin. It's brought nothing but trouble. But soon I'll be free of it.

Every hall and door takes me further from who I want to be. These sparkling halls are claustrophobic. This is no longer my grand adventure. But I made a deal. All I have left is this one last job, and it'll be okay. Melissa will be okay.

I'm in a staff elevator, pressing the button for the fourth floor. Cold wind from the Shaft chills me to the core.

It's all happening so fast. Panic washes over me. Someone's with me. Her long, silky hair. Her scent—like blueberries. Beautiful Melissa, my light in this pit.

She's close, and then she isn't. She's being pulled away. Her face shrinks into the darkness.

A loud crack, and a burst of wind. Agapios stares back at me.

And the doors open.

I wake up groggy and exhausted. This could be from the endless list of errands Nico and I ran last night, or the weird dreams I've been having ever since Sev bound my blood to Dad's coin a few days ago, but my brain is spinning and I can barely open my eyes. I'm not even sure that I want to, because Mom's still hiding behind my eyelids. All of her this time . . . not just a picture. I drift in and out of consciousness, searching for her on the edge of sleep.

Nico's as chipper and loud as always when he shows up to help me get dressed, and I kinda hate him for it. Okay . . . maybe hate's a strong word, but I really, really dislike him right now.

"Hold your arms out," he says, draping the suspenders over my shoulders.

Even the Easter-colored Warsaw buildings outside my window make me yawn. "I don't wanna go. I wanna sleep."

Nico cinches the suspenders, and a shot of pain zips through my chest. "Not a chance. If you don't work, the Old Man will boot you, and you'll never find your dad. Only six days left, remember?"

But I can't do another day like yesterday. I won't survive it. I'll die of exhaustion, and Nico will have to cart my body back to Oma and tell her, "I'm sorry, but Mr. Cameron just couldn't cut it."

I glance over at my growing stack of postcards for Cass and Oma.

I'll have to send them this afternoon, before I get too many more. Either that, or stop getting them everywhere our errands take us. It's nice to be able to let them know I'm okay and haven't run away or been kidnapped, but I wish I could hear from them in return.

Last night Nico and I bought chocolate from a shop in Brussels that looked like Willy Wonka's dream world. We purchased Broadway tickets under the flashing screens of Times Square in New York, and picked up a box of cigars in Havana at a sweet-smelling shop full of wood and leather (Nico tried to get me to open the box, but Oma would absolutely kill me if I went anywhere near something like that). We even arranged a gondola ride through Venice. I still have a bad taste in my mouth from that one, since Nico tried to push me into the canal as a joke.

My feet moan as I slip my Chucks on. "What's on the fourth floor?" I ask through another yawn.

Nico stops. "Why?"

I haven't told him about my dreams yet, despite having every opportunity. Work at the Hotel these past few days has been grueling, but whenever we're not working Nico and I are usually hanging out. I'm glad for the time with him. He's got so many stories, and he always seems like he enjoys hanging out with me. With *me*! The boy no one wanted to hang out with. I'm even starting to get used to his pranks. He still refuses to talk about his task, though.

"Sounds like binding your dad's coin really worked," he says after I relate three days' worth of sleeps. "The coin would reveal the strongest and more recent memories first, so maybe what you saw has something to do with his disappearance." He stops to think. "But I don't know what's on the fourth floor. . . ."

"Why not?"

"Because it's out of order. Has been for as long as I've worked here. It'd take a topscrew to get in."

"A what?"

"Topscrew. A master key, like the ones the MC and the Old Man have. Topscrews open any door bound to the House." He watches my face, squinting as if he's thinking through a difficult math problem. "Hmm. I've got an idea. It'd be dangerous though."

Whenever Nico starts talking about danger, I know I need to tread carefully. "Dangerous, how?"

He shrugs. "All you need to do is nab a topscrew. So it's simple really."

"Yeah, but it's not like I can just take one from the Maid Commander."

"Not the MC." He grins with mischief. "The Old Man. He's got an extra pearl topscrew in his key cupboard. And you're gonna steal it."

Nico and I use breakfast service as a planning session, discussing our options between guest deliveries in Dubai. I keep telling him he should be the one to pinch the key—I mean, topscrew—but he won't hear of it.

"You've got to learn to take risks, kiddo," he says after our final stop. "This is the only way."

"Fine." Arguing with him is like trying to stop a runaway train. "So then . . . you and Sev will create a distraction—but you won't tell me what that is—and I'm supposed to . . . what? Sneak down to the sub-level, break into Agapios' office, and steal the key? By myself?"

"That's about it." Nico removes his coin from the breakfast cart, and the magic drains from it with a honey-colored shimmer. "The Old Man will never notice. I'll talk to Sev about setting something up. Make sure you're ready."

The thought of creeping through the submarine that leads to the Concierge Retreat makes my arms itch. My WWTD list doesn't even begin to cover the things Agapios could do to me if he finds out. "How will I know it's time?"

"Trust me," Nico says. "You'll know."

We head to the War Room for the day's assignments, and the MC once again puts me on a mission with Rahki—this time to the Democratic Republic of Congo.

Elizabeth groans when Rahki tells her on the service elevator where we're headed.

"Please take me with you. Please." The fact that Elizabeth actually *wants* to help the Hotel with its "mission" forms a bubble in my stomach. Or maybe it's just gas.

"Sorry," Rahki says, licking her pen and scribbling something on her pad in Arabic. The words disappear into the page. Today's the first time I've seen her use it. She said earlier that the pad is bound to a notebook she keeps in her room, but I can't help wondering what she's writing. "It's only an in-and-out. I'll let the MC know you want to join us next time."

Elizabeth sighs and gets off at Lobby Level.

I start to follow, but Rahki grabs my suspenders and pulls me back.

"Need transport where we're going." She hits the elevator button marked MP.

I gaze out over the Shaft as we continue our descent, watching the elevators travel up and down and side-to-side on their rails. The memory of Mom's face being dragged into a black abyss rises to the surface. In my dream it felt like some dark, clawed beast was ripping her away from me.

Not from me. From Dad.

I distract myself by running a finger down the steel plate of the elevator console. It's got all the normal buttons for guest floors and staff dormitories, but there are others, too: MS, MP, ACCO, MEZZ. Some I've been to. Most I haven't.

I trace the keyhole next to a button marked BO. "Body odor?"

Rahki laughs. "Business Office." She points to the next one, marked MS. "And that's Maid Service level."

A bunch of buttons are dimmed out—they look like the out-of-order doors in the lobbies.

I point to the button for floor four. "Why does the Hotel have these floors if they're not accessible?"

She shrugs. "Some are just off-limits. The rest? I think they're holding out hope we'll reopen them one day. That's unlikely, though, without the Greenhouse." The elevator halts its down-ward motion and shifts sideways. Rahki scrawls something else on her pad, and the words vanish. Are they notes for the MC? Notes about me?

"Nico and Sev were talking about the Greenhouse," I tell her. "Something about a tree?"

"The Vesima. I don't know the whole story. It happened a while ago. All I know is it came unbound from the Hotel, and without the tree, doors will continue to fail."

"Because the pins get old?"

"It's more than that. When we bind a door with Vesima wood, it's like grafting that door onto the tree itself. It's all connected, like invisible branches. If you break those branches from the roots that feed them—"

"They die."

Rahki nods. "The connection between the Vesima and the doors is weakened from being so distant for so long. The magic feeding the doors is slipping away." She sighs. "If that keeps on, we'll eventually lose the Hotel altogether."

She leans against the cage and watches the elevators travel along their sparkling rails. There's a sadness in her eyes that makes me want to tell her everything, but I resist. I don't want my secrets vanishing into her magic paper.

The elevator dings, and the doors beyond the cage slide open.

"Motor Pool," Rahki says, brightening a little. "Let's grab a ride."

The Hotel Motor Pool is the biggest parking garage I've ever seen. Shiny, sealed concrete floors reflect amber lights, lined with rows and rows and rows of cars: long black limos, boxy pastel buses, half a dozen ambulances. I imagine the Lamborghini purring at me, begging to be driven. It doesn't matter that I'm too young, or that car accidents are near the tippy-top of the WWTD—I want to smell the interior, feel the high-performance engine, experience all that horsepower.

The whirr of machine tools shocks me back to reality. I rush to follow Rahki behind the freestanding elevator.

The garage extends this way, too, but it's different. Rather than rows of vehicles, the back half of the Motor Pool is a giant mechanics' shop. Hydraulic power tools hang from the ceiling, lit by fluorescent lights. A bunch of old cars are up on lifts, and a horde of kids in coveralls drill and crank and socket beneath them. I breathe in the overpowering smell of oil.

Rahki winds her way through the bays. I struggle to keep up, unsuccessfully dodging toolboxes and tires and mechanics. She stops at one of the back bays and calls out, "Sana, we're here!"

A girl crouched at a toolbox stands and greets us with a big, brown-eyed smile. Streaks of oil smear her cheeks, and a shiny black braid curls down the front of her coveralls.

"Hi Rahki." She wipes her forehead, spreading even more grease, and slides a wrench into the pocket of a long leather tool belt draped around her like an Indian sari. The leather creaks as she moves. "I checked those icons for you. You should both have strong bonds."

Rahki nods. "Sana, this is Cameron."

I blink as Sana presses her hands together in front of her. Her fingers and wrists are covered in math equations, stained into her skin with some kind of dye. She gives a slight bow, and says, "Namaste."

"Uhh . . . " I look to Rahki, who rolls her eyes. "Namaste?" I say back, mimicking Sana's gesture.

"Awesome." Sana winks, and tosses her hand up in a flourish. "To your statues!"

Sana leads us through the bays, past the elevator, back to the rows of vehicles. She points out her favorite makes and models as we go. We pass shiny cars, rusty cars, strange cars with no wheels. And then come the tanks . . . heavy, powerful-looking machines. Sana knows more about war machines than I thought possible. She talks about them with the same enthusiasm Cass has for her travel shows. I wish she was here to experience this with me.

Eventually the military vehicles give way to statues. Sandstone camels. Onyx horses. Jade lions with stone saddles. A huge, twisting dragon with one clawed foot perched on a burnished cow.

"They're called icons," Rahki tells me.

They're freaky is what they are. The so-called icons watch me with lifeless, wooden eyes. They remind me of the statues scattered throughout the lobbies.

"These look good," Rahki says when we come to a pair of granite elephants.

"What are we supposed to do with them?" I ask.

Sana clasps her hands in front of her. "Has Mr. Cameron not been icon-bound before?"

"No." Rahki pats her stone elephant's backside. "Can you take care of him?"

"Sure." Sana bobbles her head and waves me to her. "Do you have your coin?"

I fish my coin from my right pocket—Nico's is still in my left, where he keeps sneaking it—and hand it to her.

"This won't hurt much," she says, taking my hand and pulling a needle from her tool-sari.

I pull back. "You're going to prick me again?"

"Again?" She scrunches her brow.

Rahki stops and watches me. Not good. I forgot that what Nico, Sev, and I do behind closed doors needs to stay secret.

"Of course I'm not going to prick you." Sana hands me the needle, which I realize now isn't a needle at all. It's an ink pen, shaped like the Hotel pins. Only it's got no ink.

"What's this for?"

"Icon-bindings are temporary," she says. "Touch the pen to your tongue—to wet it—and write your name on your coin. Your saliva, and your name, will strengthen the binding for a short time, connecting the icon to you."

I glance to Rahki, who's back to examining her elephant. "Like the dust."

"Yeah." Rahki pats the duster at her hip.

I lick the pen tip, and it zaps me with a tingly, metallic burn, like licking a nine-volt battery. This is temporary, I remind myself. Nothing to worry about. I write my name on the coin with my spit, and smile when an electric pop sounds in my ears.

Sana takes the pen back. "That should last a while. If the binding fails, you need only do that again with Rahki's pen. Now, hop on."

She motions to a rolling staircase next to one of the stone elephants. Rahki's already seated on hers, sliding her coin into a slot at the back of the statue's neck. A wave of color flushes across its surface, the hard stone softens, and it shifts. Spiderweb cracks spread down its legs, transforming the stone into tough, leathery skin.

Rahki's elephant shakes its head, and its long, floppy ears send a cloud of granite dust into the air.

It's alive. It's like the breakfast tray, and the luggage carts. I scan the other statues throughout the Motor Pool, and my gaze lands on the giant dragon that towers above the rest. "Can they all do this?"

"Mostly."

I climb the stairs—struggling not to think about all the ways giant stone elephants could result in my untimely demise—and have a seat in a saddle that's way too big for one person. The slot in the elephant's neck stares back at me. I'm about to take a ride on a magic stone elephant. Cass would be so jealous.

Rahki kicks the sides of her elephant, and it lumbers forward. "Any day now."

"Be easy on him," Sana chides. "We must all come to the binding in our own way."

I take a breath, and shove my coin into the slot.

A glimmer of light shines outward. The elephant shifts under me.

I grab tight to the saddle to keep from falling. "Where are the reins?"

"Don't need them." Rahki nods to the coin slot. "It'll do what you want."

My elephant takes a step, the cold stone now warm and squishy and alive. My weight shifts as the monstrous creature backs out of the bay.

"Calm yourself," Sana says, her voice smooth like a song. "The icon fears because you fear. Be strong. Confident."

I'm anything *but* confident. But I have to be if I'm going to survive this Hotel and find Dad.

The elephant slows.

"Good." Sana pulls a thick wooden rod from her tool-sari and heads for an enormous cedar arch.

"Just keep thinking about sticking with me," Rahki says. "The icon will follow as long as you want it to."

Sana removes a stick from a hinge in the arch frame, and slides the new peg in. A rippling wave of green trees and gray skies bursts between the beams. "Enjoy your first trip to the Congo."

14

Trust on Rocky Ground

I'm sweating almost as soon as our elephants barge through the Congo arch. The wet air sticks to my forehead, and to the big-leafed plants everywhere, collecting in muddy puddles that reflect the stormy sky.

A cloud of bugs whirls around me. I try to fight them off, but one flies up my nose, forcing me to cough. My elephant lurches forward, and I hold tight to the saddle, eyes watering, fighting to stay on.

"Shut the gate," Rahki calls back to Sana. "No bugs."

The Motor Pool disappears as soon as Sana pulls the enormous pin.

I slap a mosquito that's making me its lunch. "Shouldn't I have gotten a shot or something before heading to *Africa*? My immunizations aren't up-to-date." The "exotic diseases" section of the WWTD list goes on and on.

"The Hotel protects us from disease." She urges her elephant forward. "Takes forever to get bugs out of the lobbies, though. Mosquitoes are the worst."

My icon lumbers after her, and I start to slide off. I grab at anything I can to keep from falling into a puddle. "The Hotel prevents disease?" I ask, pretending to have a handle on this whole living statue thing.

Rahki's already five elephant paces ahead of me, riding past a series of straw huts. "More like it protects its guests," she says. "The Hotel can even extend a person's life, if their bond is strong enough. Though, with the wood getting older, that's questionable these days."

I wonder if it can cure conditions like Cass's, too. It's another example of just how much I don't know about this place, even after these past few days on staff. I need to find out more. And quickly.

Maybe Rahki can help me fill in some gaps. "Are we grafted into the tree, too? Like the doors?"

"It's different with people. The doors are just doors. No door binding is stronger than any other. But people can be bound to different degrees. The strength of a person's binding determines what magic they can draw from it. Since Agapios founded the Hotel ages ago, his bind is strongest, and he can do the most with it."

That still doesn't tell me why he's taking those kids.

My elephant's foot lands in a puddle and it shakes its head, spraying dirt and water everywhere.

Rahki laughs as I regain my balance and wipe mud from my face. "Need me to bind you to the saddle?"

"No!" I blurt. I'm not at all interested in having my butt superglued to a plodding stone pachyderm.

We ride on, the canopy above so dense I can't see the sky. Insects chitter in the branches. All these disease-ridden bugs and poisonous tree frogs and venomous snakes . . . I am not a fan of the Congo.

Though, it gets me thinking . . . I wonder if Mom and Dad ever got to see the tree before it disappeared. "How can the Old Man be so sure there's not another Vesima tree hiding in a jungle somewhere?"

"Don't you think they would have replaced it if there were?"

You never know.

The path opens into a clearing lined with huts. A woman carrying a plastic water jug watches me from the corner of her eye. In fact, lots of people are watching us. Eyes, everywhere, following the two fancy-dressed elephant riders clomping down the path. Do they know we're here to "pick up" more children? Do they secretly hate us for it?

"If there were any other way to save the Hotel, Agapios would have done it," Rahki says.

I picture that bony, pale face staring back at me in Dad's dreams. "He looks so ancient."

"No one knows how long he's been around. The MC won't say how long she's been here either, but I did see a picture of the two of them once, standing in front a knocker from the thirties."

My elephant stops. "As in, the 1930s?"

She nods. "They looked the same as they do now. It's no wonder Agapios is looking for a Concierge-in-Training again."

That makes sense. Stripe runs his fight against the Hotel from a museum. He must have figured out what Agapios was up to by uncovering the Hotel's history. Nico said the hotel part was just the facade, and that it had been around in different forms much longer. But didn't Nico say Stripe was old too? And he doesn't look that different today than he did in the picture with Dad.

Rahki hops off her elephant and runs a gloved finger in the grooves of a plaque hanging from one of the huts. A carving of two keys crossed over a tree—the same as Agapios's cross-keys lapel pin.

"Here we are," she says, and pushes through the faded, patterned curtain. I scramble off my elephant to follow her.

Shafts of afternoon sunlight shine through the twiggy roof, illuminating a roomful of children. Just like the kids we picked up in Budapest. A few are bandaged—almost all are shirtless. One little boy sits on a bench, a wrapped knee hanging off the edge. But a knee is all he's got—everything from his calf down is missing. Another kid looks at me with dirty gauze wrapped over one eye.

I glance to the boy with the missing leg. He smiles at me, and I look away. I wish I knew what happens to them after we take them to the Hotel. I can't even talk to them, because none of the children I've encountered so far speak English.

A lanky man in a flowery shirt and thigh-length jeans shorts tosses his hands up with a smile. "Aye, Rahki! Glad to see you!"

"You too, Philippe," she says.

"And who's this?" Philippe asks in a booming, bass-y accent. "A new friend?"

Rahki introduces me, and I shake the man's thick, callused hand.

"Cameron Jones?" he says. "My goodness, you look familiar. And that name . . . Cameron. You're not related to Melissa and Reinhart Kuhn, are you?"

Rahki shoots me a confused look, and I freeze. What do I do? This guy knows my parents.

"Of course you are!" Philippe laughs. "Jones was Reinhart's mother's name, way back when, wasn't it? You're Reinhart's boy! Cameron and . . . oh, what was your twin sister's name?"

I swallow. "Ca-Cassia."

"That's it!" He slaps me on the back, almost knocking me over. "Jones, ha! Can't pull the wool over these eyes. You're a Kuhn if I ever saw one. Old Reinhart—now there's a man you couldn't keep down." He leans in and whispers. "Did they ever find the Greenhouse?"

It's like all the heat leaves my arms, my legs, even my chest, and floods to my cheeks instead. My ears go numb. My head tingles. This guy knew my parents, and he's still working with the Hotel. What's worse, he's giving kids to them. He has to know what's going on. All these years . . . could he have been the reason Dad went on the run? Could this happy, smiling man have been the one who killed Mom?

Rahki steps closer. "Reinhart? The Green . . . what are you talking about?"

"Did he not tell you?" Philippe fixes his eyes on me. "Or do you not know?"

I clasp Dad's coin through my button-down collar. I've got to keep it together. Maybe this Philippe guy is like Rahki, and doesn't know the Hotel's secrets. But if he couldn't uncover them after all this time, how am I supposed to figure it out in only six more days?

"I . . . uh . . . I don't know what happened to my dad," I say, struggling to hide the panic in my voice. "I never knew him."

"Ahhh." Philippe's tone changes. "So sorry. And your sister? Does she still have that . . . what was it?"

"Spina bifida," I offer.

He snaps a finger. "That's it! What a shame the Hotel couldn't heal her. Reinhart was so shaken when he found out your sister would have to deal with that. Always hard when it's someone close." He glances back at the children. "But everyone's got something hard, no?"

"They do." Rahki stares at me like I'm some kind of freak.

I clench my jaw. How am I going to explain all this to Rahki? I want to drill Philippe more, to find out what he knows, but I can't. Who knows what Rahki's relaying back to the Maid Commander via that magic pad? And now she's got my name.

"On to business, then?" Philippe pulls a toothpick from his teeth and points to the kids. "Today's crop got pulled from the conflicts. They'll need some time before placement."

"I'll let the MC know," Rahki says.

"Good, good." Philippe waves his arms at the children and they all stand, except for the boy with the missing leg, who won't stop looking at me. "Goodbye, children."

Rahki gives Philippe a goodbye wave as she lines the kids up. "Hope you find your destination."

"Aye." Philippe lets out a booming laugh, and points at me. "You watch that one. If he's anything like his father, he's gonna be trouble."

I can't get out of Philippe's hut fast enough. My feet pound the wet earth, fists balled, the weight in my chest growing every second.

Trouble? *Trouble?* I'll show him trouble. If he had anything to do with Mom and Dad . . .

I stop my pacing and close my eyes. All I know for sure is that Philippe knew them. Knew Dad, specifically. That doesn't mean he's the reason I grew up without any parents.

Ugh. I want to go back in there and ask so many questions. Maybe he knows something that can help me. And he asked about the Greenhouse. Did Dad have something to do with its disappearance? Does Philippe know why? Everything's just getting more and more complicated. My one goal is branching off into many.

Rahki comes marching out of the hut, carrying the boy with the missing leg on her hip. The others trail behind her. Her eyes are bulging, nostrils flaring—she's upset. Probably at me.

"Hey," I say, hoping to mitigate some of the damage.

But she flashes a hand to stop me. "Not now, Mr. *Kuhn,*" she says, an edge to her voice. "We still have a job to do."

The rest of the mission goes smoothly, though much too quietly. The elephants carry the little ones on their backs with us. The boy with the bandaged leg rides behind me, squeezing my torso and pressing his face against my back.

Rahki keeps shooting me suspicious glances as she plays with the girls' braided hair. I wish I knew what she was thinking.

She binds a door in a hut on the edge of the forest, and knocks. Almost immediately Elizabeth opens up with a beaming smile and tons of questions before the MC and her maids show up. The MC takes the children to the Elevator Bank while two of the maids ride the stone elephants back the way we came, leaving just Rahki and myself in the African Lobby.

Rahki rounds on me. Here it comes. "Kuhn?! Your name isn't Jones? And your parents *worked* here?"

"I didn't know what to say when I came here. I never knew my parents."

She throws her hands up. "I've been trying to figure out who you are and why you had that coin, and all this time you were someone's kid."

"You've been . . . what?"

"The MC's had me watching you—evaluating you to make sure you don't pose a risk—and now it turns out you belonged here all along." Her tone's not at all what I expected. She sounds almost amused by it all.

"So wait," I say, "you're not mad at me?"

She shakes her head. "You're Melissa's son. I mean, yeah, it's annoying that I've been keeping tabs on you for no good reason, but at least now we know. If you'd just told them, I'm sure Agapios and the MC would've been happy to have you here." She pauses. "Wait till they find out who you really are."

My stomach clenches as she starts toward the curtain to the next lobby. She's going to tell them what she knows. If they don't already know, this could be the end of everything.

"Don't!" I say.

Rahki stops at the threshold.

I search for words that will keep her from telling the MC or Agapios anything else without causing her to reevaluate her trust in me. "Please . . . don't tell them."

She cocks her head. "Why not?"

I chew my lip. I want to trust her. If she only knew why I'm here, I'm sure she'd want to help. But Nico's warning about her hangs between us like an ancient stone wall.

"You didn't tell the MC that Sev was hiding me outside his window that first night," I say. "Just . . . do the same for me. Don't tell anyone about this."

Her eyes narrow. "You *are* hiding something."

I don't respond.

"Fine," she says. "But now you know." She glances up at the cameras. "The Old Man and the Maid Commander are watching you. *I'm* watching you."

She leaves me with a sick feeling in my gut.

Days at the Hotel pass faster than I can count. It's hard to gauge, since we jump time zones so much. The only way I can keep track is by my sleeps. Five so far, which means five to go before my trial period runs out.

The nights keep getting more and more tiring with each passing dream, too. Hiking the Alps with supplies strapped to my back. Cutting through overgrown jungles with a machete. Hailing taxis with a two-fingered whistle in towering concrete jungles. And every time I end up back in the Elevator Shaft, staring into that blackness. It feels like I'm running missions and hopping doors twenty-four hours a day. And I still don't understand how any of these memories will help me.

Unless they've already given me the answer. Nico says he and Sev can't promise when their distraction to get me onto the fourth floor will come . . . just that it will, soon, and I need to be ready when it does.

I head to the mailroom after morning errands to send more postcards through the brass-and-glass vacuum chutes. Oma and Cass are probably so worried by now. These postcards might be making me feel better, but they're probably just upsetting my grandma and sister more.

Just like Dad did all those years ago, I leave the return address blank. I don't even know what address I'd give. *The Hotel Between, 1001 Everywhere Lane, Somewhere, World?*

I sign the card I bought in Rome this morning and send it through the chute with a *whoosh* before the mailroom guy points out that I have a message in my mailbox. I can't believe it—mail? I reach into my cubby and pull out the loose letter.

If you get this, swing by the Accommodation at the begin-
ning of fourth shift. I want to talk to you.
—Rahki

Great. Rahki probably wants to grill me some more about my
parents. That's not even the worst part—she wants to meet aboard
the Dining Ship. Ugh.

All major Hotel meals prepared by Chef Silva's kitchen crew are
served aboard the Dining Ship *Accommodation*, a cruise ship somewhere near the Antarctic that the Hotel has repurposed as a banquet
hall. I've been avoiding it as much as possible, because every time I go,
I end up seasick. Man was not meant to go from land to water so often.

I take one of the seasickness patches Elizabeth gave me and
stick it behind my ear before heading to the elevators.

When I step through the turner into the *Accommodation*, my
equilibrium slips. The grand chandeliers sway back and forth, casting shadows across the banquet hall. The dark gray horizon tilts
and bobs, up and down.

The *Accommodation* is bustling with hosts and kitchen staff
preparing for the next meal. L'Maitre—the prim and proper man
who runs the dining services—eyes me as I enter. I may or may
not have made a scene by blowing chunks all over the fruit buffet
earlier this week.

Rahki waves at me from the second level. I skirt past tall,
statue-stiff L'Maitre, doing my best not to stare at the curls of his
mustache, and climb the stairs.

"I got your note," I say, swallowing my breakfast back down as the ocean tries to shake it out of me.

Rahki motions for me to have a seat as the ship shifts. The gold leaves and jeweled fruit on the enormous tree centerpieces sprouting from the tables shimmer.

She pushes a bowl of smooth, round stones toward me. "Have you had Chef Silva's sweet yet?"

I shake my head. "His sweet what?"

"It's just called sweet." She picks one of the stones out of the bowl and forces it into my hand. "He binds these little river stones to some he keeps in a vat in the kitchens. Changes the recipe every day, and since it's basically a rock it never loses its flavor. Just don't bite into it or try to swallow it." She pops one into her mouth. "Mmm . . . cinnamon, with a hint of fried puff."

My stomach gurgles unhappily just thinking about sweets on this boat. "It looks like a choking hazard."

"Try it," she insists. "They're softer than they look."

I stick the small rock on my tongue, and recognize the flavor right away. "Oh wow, that's sopapilla. We get them at the Tex-Mex restaurant back home all the time. I love these." I pull the sweet out of my mouth and examine it. "That's so weird."

"It's good, right?" Rahki agrees. "Make sure you try it every day, so you don't miss a flavor."

I set the candy aside. "So, you wanted to talk to me about flavored rocks?"

"No, I wanted to talk to you about the children."

Children? "You mean, like the kids we pick up on missions?"

She nods. Finally, someone wants to give me answers! Though, if the staff are as deceived as Stripe says, I'm not sure I can believe everything she tells me. Maybe I can pick out the truth hidden beneath what she thinks she knows.

Rahki puts her sweet on the table and cups her mug. "I was one of them, you know."

"*You* were one of the kids we pick up?"

"In Syria," she says. "I was the oldest from our group. That mission was longer and more dangerous than our recent trips. The Maid Commander kept us safe all the way to the Damascus Door. That was the first time I saw her fight—that sword she carries isn't just for decoration. I helped out as much as I could, and when we got here she asked if I wanted to keep helping. I said yes."

I'm supposed to say something here, some encouragement maybe? Cass is so much better at this whole "people" thing. I'm struggling just to keep my breakfast down.

"It doesn't feel right," I say finally. "The Hotel shouldn't take kids like that."

She looks me straight in the eye, and for a moment my sloshing brain stills. "You're not hearing me, Cam. The Hotel saved me. I'm here because I want to be."

Perhaps I'm wrong about the Hotel.

I bite my lip. I can see why Stripe told me not to get lured in by the Hotel's sheen. I'm sure Rahki believes she's doing something good by staying here, but there's stuff she doesn't know. That no one knows.

Secrets. I'm certain Dad uncovered something, and once I figure out what it was, I'll prove it to her. She'll help us. I know she will.

"That's not the only reason I asked you here," she says. "I wanted to discuss what happened yesterday, too."

I put a hand to my head, trying to focus. "Okay, listen, that wasn't—"

She stops me. "You don't want to tell me why you're here. Fine. I can let that slide for now. But I did some digging."

"Digging?"

"Found some stuff in the Maid Service files. Did you know your mom and dad were both working here when the Greenhouse disappeared?"

"Is that important?"

She gives me a very big nod. "Oh yeah. Your dad disappeared and your mom died on the same night, right here in the Hotel. The night the Greenhouse was taken."

Rahki passes me a leather-bound folio with the tree symbol on the front. I scan the yellowed pages. Logs, notes, photographs of locations they went to in their search for Dad . . .

This is what led to Dad leaving us with Oma. Something terrible happened here in the Hotel, and Mom died. Was it him or someone else who took the Greenhouse? Maybe he's still searching for it? Or is he keeping it out of the Hotel's hands?

I flip the page and land on a picture of Mom. I keep seeing her in my dreams, but it's different looking at her now, in the Maid Commander's files.

I've never thought about Mom in the same way I did about Dad. She died when we were so young; I never had the chance to even consider looking for her. Oma said it was better to accept that she passed and move on. *Passed.* As if she decided she didn't want the green beans. *Life? Nah, I'll pass.* But Mom didn't "pass." She was taken from us too.

"The Maid Service allocated a lot of resources to finding your dad after he vanished," Rahki continues. "The MC thought your dad knew what happened to the Greenhouse, and how to get it back."

I turn the page to find a picture of Dad working in a sunny garden. His gloves and face are dirty, but he's smiling as brightly as Philippe was. "So they *don't* know what happened to him after she . . . ?"

"I don't think so. But they *definitely* know who you are." Rahki reaches across and flips to a page near the back, clean and white and newer than the rest, marked with the name "Cameron Kuhn."

I snatch the picture from the folio. "That's me." My scraggly hair, my awkward school-photo smile. A sticky note next to my face has the words "What does he know?" written in curling script.

The bobbing of the ocean presses in again, making me want to vomit.

"The Old Man is . . . interested in you," Rahki says. "He and the MC are—"

She looks like she's going to say more—and I want her to, desperately—but before she can, a porter bursts through the turners, red-faced and sweating.

"Maid Commander's calling all hands!" he shouts. "Everyone to the Mezz. It's a pin-failure!"

"Great," says one of the caterers stocking the buffet. "Another drill."

"This is not a drill!" the boy yells.

This is it. Nico and Sev's distraction. I have to get to the elevators and down to the Concierge Retreat to take that top-screw.

But Rahki grabs my arm. "Do you have a pin?"

"What?"

"A pin! Do you have a hinge-pin?"

I slide the pin Sev gave me out of its special sleeve on my shirt.

"Good," she says. "We've got to get ahead of this."

She drags me up from my seat and through the turners.

15

Failure in the Pins

*I*n the event of a failed hinge-pin, Hotel staff must evacuate all guests to the Mezzanine. Locate your nearest map-board and follow the instructions.

Rahki's fast. Too fast for me to keep up. Then again, she knows all the things I don't, like why we're running in the first place, and why this pin-failure is such a big deal.

I have to get away to get that topscrew, but Rahki keeps urging me onward. I don't know how long Nico and Sev's distraction will last, but I'm pretty sure if I don't break away soon I'm going to miss my chance.

She rounds the next corner and I slow, hoping she'll forget I was following so I can return to the business of figuring out what happened to my family.

Ten seconds. Fifteen. This could work. Now I'll just head to the elevators and—

"Cam!" She comes back around the corner, huffing. "What are you doing? We've got to get to the Mezz."

"Go without me. I'll just slow you down." Please, oh please don't let her see the guilt written all over my face.

She grabs my arm and drags me down a spiral staircase. "We need every pin we've got."

Ugh! This isn't working. She's not going to let me out of her sight.

I shout, pretending to trip on the stairs. "Ah! My foot!"

But Rahki sees through my excuses. She hoists her duster in one hand, and fans the gloved fingers of the other. "Get up, or I'm going to bind your foot to your forehead."

She drags me to my feet and through the door.

The open-air Mezzanine never goes dark. At least, that's what Nico said when he first showed it to me. The Mezz grounds form a donut about the size of two football fields between the Elevator Bank that makes up the outer ring and the Courtyard, which serves as the hole in the donut. Ornate fountains and landscaped river features wind through carpeted groves of potted trees and decorative boulders.

But what always impresses me the most about the Mezz is the sun-windows. The rock cliffs that separate the Mezzanine from the outside world are topped with giant, wood-framed portals that hang at an angle over the grounds. Each is bound to a time zone that matches the Sundial Courtyard at the Mezz's center, and provides a view of the sky from a different corner of the globe. Whenever one frame shows night, the open window across from it shines with daylight, creating a weird kind of perpetual twilight over the Mezz. Even now, though it's nighttime in the sky overhead, more than half the frames shine like stadium lights across the carpeted floor.

"Good," Rahki says, "they've started."

Across the Mezz, staff frantically roll in tables and kiosks, transforming the grounds into a kind of check-in center. Elizabeth and the clerks stand at semicircular desks, speaking in hushed voices to calm the panicking guests. Off-duty porters direct the crowd pouring through the doors on all sides.

And at the center of it all stands Agapios—the man who's "interested" in me. Tall, bony shoulders, skeletal fingers pointing this way and that, his croaking accent calling out orders. Whatever the distraction is, it worked. The Old Man's out of his office. Now I just have to get down to his Retreat before this whole thing turns into a WWTD list entry.

"Do you see the Maid Commander?" Rahki asks.

I scan the grounds. Nico and some staffers I haven't met yet direct guests out of the potted grove on the far side. Sana's setting up a kiosk next to a waterfall that glistens with reflections of the sun- and star-lit skies overhead.

But no Maid Commander.

Nico catches my attention, points to Agapios, and mouths, "What are you doing?"

I motion to Rahki.

He taps his pocket watch. Yeah, no kidding.

"They're sorted here," Rahki says. "Let's get to the Elevator Bank."

Elevator Bank, perfect. I'll just take a different elevator from Rahki and head to the sub-level while she deals with this mess.

But the Bank ring is in complete disorder. Maids guard the elevators with dusters slung over their shoulders, barking commands at staff and guests alike. I'll never get through them. I have to find another way. Maybe one of the back halls?

"We're close," Rahki says, inserting her coin into the nearest map-board. Auburn ink spreads across the parchment, drawing the four rings of the Hotel trunk. Swirling lines curl away from the "You Are Here" marker toward a door leading off the Bank, guarded by maids.

If I could touch it without Rahki seeing, it might show me a path to get where I need to go. Then again, it might sense my intentions, too. The last thing I need is to have the building fight back against me, if that's even possible. But if I can figure out what's wrong up here, maybe that'll lead me to a way down.

I grab Rahki's attention. "What's going on?"

"One of the pins failed," she says. "It's leaking binding magic, putting stress on the other doors. If we don't stop it . . . "

"Bad news." That much I can understand.

I take in the shouting guests and militant maids. . . . All this fuss, just so I can get my hands on a key? Maybe we're going about this the wrong way.

A splitting sound echoes through the hall, and everyone goes silent.

The noise comes again—like splintering wood—followed by

a sound like someone popping the top on a shaken soda bottle. The maids back away from one of the elevators as its doors open, revealing . . .

Nothing. A dark, cold emptiness. The elevator's just gone, replaced by what looks like the deepest reaches of space, where even stars don't shine.

"Get back!" one of the maids yells, pushing guests away with his duster. "The pins binding the elevators are failing. The elevators are no longer safe. Staff, please lead guests directly to the Mezzanine."

The emptiness beyond those sliding doors makes me dizzy. It's like the elevator inside never existed. Swallowed up. I could have been on that elevator, headed for the Concierge Retreat. Suddenly making my way down to the sub-level doesn't seem like such a grand idea.

When Nico said they'd plan a distraction, I never imagined it would be something that would make everyone panic like this.

I'll stick with Rahki for now. If it's as bad as it seems, she might need my help. I don't want anyone getting hurt because of me.

We move into an offshoot hallway. Sev is at the end of the next hall crouched down in a circle with others bearing the maroon sash of the doormen. The stucco walls are lined with more doors to nothing.

I'm thankful to see Sev—he'll know what to do. But when he looks up at me, the fearful glimmer in his eyes makes my heart race. This "distraction" has definitely gone too far. Time to forget about the topscrew and focus on what's happening here.

Rahki ducks under swaths of purple fabric to meet him. "Status?"

"It is not a snap," Sev says. "Not yet. If we find and replace the cracked pin, we might get some failed doors back." He glances at the other doormen. "But we are out."

A roll of black canvas lies in the center of the group, sewn with dozens of empty pin-sleeves like the ones on my shirt.

"Why don't you just try the same pin in each hinge?" I ask.

"When one fails, all pins are weaker. More than one pin may be cracked by now. If the stress continues—"

"We won't let it get as far as a snap." Rahki pulls two more pins from her shirt. "I've got these. Cam's got another." She turns and shouts to the staffers gathering behind us. "Everyone have your pins ready, and do exactly what the doormen tell you."

Sev directs me to one of the vacant doors near the end of the hall, between two other determined staffers.

I step up and stare into the abyss, Sev's pin in hand. My vision tunnels. The cold darkness draws me forward. I want to know what lies at the end of all that black.

The girl next to me lines up her plug on the middle hinge of her door and flicks the trigger. The plug pops the old pin out like toast from a toaster, and she shoves her new pin into the hole.

There's another crack, another fizz. It didn't work.

I focus on my hinge and align the spring-loaded plug Sev gave me. The tool taps the pin up and out of the hole. The pin clatters to the floor. So far, so good. I slide my new pin into place, using the plug to snap it down tight.

Nothing. No crack, no fizz, no change in the landscape behind the door. It's like staring into insanity. Now that I've re-pinned it, this door should lead to Sev's room, but Sev's room isn't there.

I wonder what it would be like to step through into that endless black. Would I die from lack of oxygen? If it really is space, I could freeze to death, and my arms and legs and eyeballs would crack and shatter into a million pieces. Or maybe the lack of pressure would make me go boom, WWTD number 313-style.

Another staffer hammers his pin into place and exclaims, "I got it!" as a wave of light bursts down the hall.

But I don't turn to look, because the nothingness on the other side of my door is changing. Shapes begin to form. A bed. A dresser covered in knick-knacks. Safety posters and foldouts. It's my bedroom. At home. The pin Sev gave me isn't bound to his room—it's bound to Oma's house.

The weight of all the frustration and intrigue and danger of the Hotel comes crashing down on me. I don't want to be here. I belong at home, taking care of Cass—not breaking into offices and being trapped in foreign countries and stopping magic doors from tearing holes in space-time.

So I step through and close the door behind me.

16

Like Branches on a Tree

I'm back. My clothes are in the dresser. My squeaky bed invites me to lie down and forget all the chaos and magic of the Hotel.

It's like waking from a dream.

I glance back at my bedroom door, now bound to the Hotel instead of the hall leading to the living room. Bound to bizarre people, and places unknown, to doors all over the world and . . .

I don't want to think about it.

I pull my chest of drawers away from the wall and slide it in front of my door—blocking Rahki and Sev on the other side. I sit on the edge of my bed, wringing my hands. I failed. My one chance at stealing into the Old Man's office, and I blew it. I'm back where I started, sitting in Oma's house with no hope of finding Dad and less than five days to do it.

Oma. I wonder if she's here. She'd know what to say to make me feel better. I miss her, and Cass. Are they okay? Was Cass able to come home from the hospital yet? They're going to have so many questions. But if Sev or Rahki come through that door, they'll talk me into going back. I don't know what to do.

So I pace. Back and forth. In a circle. Clenching and unclenching my fists. My posters and junk remind me of who I am. I'm not staff at a magic Hotel. I'm Cam, the boy who locks himself in lockers and hides in his room and collects safety guides. The kid who dreamed of finding his parents but never knew where to look for them. Who takes care of his sister the way no one else can. It was dumb of me to leave in the first place.

Knock-knock. "Cam?" Cass's voice filters through the wall. "Is that you?"

I stop. The pin and my dresser are all that stand between us. Should I answer? The door jiggles, and I'm not sure whether it's coming from the hall or the Hotel, or even if Cass can get through while the door is bound. I'd have to un-pin it, wouldn't I? I'm not sure how it all works. But it's Cass! She's okay! She's back home, and well enough to be rolling around the house. At least that's a relief.

I sit against the dresser and put my head in my hands.

"Cam, let me in."

"I can't," I say. Now she knows I'm here.

"Where've you been? Why'd you leave?"

"I—I wanted to fix everything. But I messed it up."

"What? Let me in," she says. "I want to see you."

I fidget with my necklace, feeling the contours of Dad's coin. "I can't," I say again. And it's not because I don't want to. If I unbind that door, if I move that chest, I'll never finish my mission to help her and Oma. I still want that, even if I'm afraid of failing. They deserve it. . . . No, *we* deserve it.

"This isn't funny," Cass says. "You shouldn't have run away. Oma called the cops. And all those stupid postcards—"

"I didn't run away," I say. "I went to get help."

"You need to be home, with us, where it's safe."

Safe. I want to be safe. But in order to be safe, something has to change.

The Hotel can keep its mission; I have my own. I *will* find a way to help our family.

"I'll see you soon, Cass," I say, and start to pull the chest away from the door.

But when I do, I see a flash of something. A scene bubbling to the surface of my mind—another fleeting memory, only this time it's outside of my dreams.

A stone wall. A door. My hands pushing a big cedar armoire in front of it. And a tree. Enormous branches blocking out the sky. Shafts of sunlight streaming through the canopy. Roots as thick as my whole body curling through the grassy earth.

I back away from my bedroom door, trying to shake off the image.

Cold stone. The smell of dust. The double-doored armoire. The door behind it, and the looming tree beyond it, and dreadful sadness that surrounds it. Grief, like I lost something, or I myself am lost.

Oma's voice drags me back. "Cammy?"

I'll figure out what the memory means later. Now, I have to go.

"I'll be back," I say. "I'll bring him back."

I pull the dresser away from the door and step through, closing it and leaving home behind once more.

The staff is much calmer when I reenter the Hotel. I'm glad. . . .
I don't think I could handle any more panicky stuff right now.

Rahki stares me down. "Where did you go? You can't run off
like that. We've got things to do."

"I'm sorry," I say, though it feels more like I'm apologizing to
Cass than to Rahki.

"Hang out here. We still need to talk."

Talk. Right. About Agapios and all the horrible things the
Hotel doesn't want anyone to know about. I blow a puff of air.

Rahki goes back to shouting instructions to the staff. When
I'm certain she's not looking, I pop the pin Sev gave me out
of the hinge and slide it into my pin-sleeve. I only worry for a
moment that removing it might set off another nuclear melt-
down, but I need to keep this pin. The plug he handed me
before I went through, too. Even though technically I don't
need it, the plug definitely makes using the pins easier. With it,
I can keep Cass and Oma close. They're the reason I'm doing
this.

But that memory—*Dad's* memory . . . it felt important. His
thoughts were so strong.

I need to see what's behind that armoire.

Even though it feels like Dad wanted to leave it behind.

Rahki heads to the Maids' Wing to update the MC, and Sev and I
go to the Courtyard to wait by the fountain.

Sev's not saying anything. Probably because I never made it

down to Agapios's office. He must be disappointed in me, after he and Nico set up such a grand distraction.

"I'm sorry I failed," I say after a few minutes. "You gave me the opportunity, and I blew it."

Sev sighs. "There will be more."

The sun is rising over the Courtyard and the Mezz above, mixing with the out-of-place daylight from the sun-windows and casting a yellow-pink haze over the grounds. We sit in silence, watching the stars wink out.

I think back to the first sunrise I remember watching like this. It was only a few years ago . . . when I was eight, maybe. I've never been one to rise early. Cass had just been through another surgery—one of her biggest. In preparation, the surgeon went through all the possible complications with us before making Oma sign a release. The surgery could collapse Cass's lungs. She could lose her ability to swallow. Her heart might stop because of the anesthesia. Blood clots. Staph infection. So many things could go wrong. Oma kept saying Cass would be all right, but that didn't keep me from freaking out.

That was when I realized how many ways there were for her to die. My list has been growing ever since.

But when the sun came up, so did Cass. The doctor returned, smiling and promising us that everything would be okay. Sunrises are like that. They smile at you in the dark and promise that something good can still happen.

I glance up at the watery branches of the marble tree in the fountain, remembering the images that flashed back in my bedroom. The fountain tree looks similar to the one in Dad's memory, but like a miniature version. The other one was so big.

"You used the pin I gave you," Sev says, breaking my train of thought. "You left."

I pull the pin from its sleeve. It feels so light, so smooth. "It didn't go to your room."

"I never said it would," he replies with a hint of a smile. "I thought you would like a way out."

"How?" Then I remember. "The dirt Nico took from Oma's garden."

Sev nods. "Soil is how we bind doors to specific places. The dirt contains the binding of the earth—location data. The wood from the Vesima absorbs that binding the same as tree roots consume nutrients from soil. This is why we use Vesima wood for pins and coins." He points to the pin in my hand. "That pin absorbed the soil Nico brought from your home. Your attachment to your bedroom directed the magic to that door over all others in your house."

"But why? Why make this pin for me?"

He watches the grass. "Because bad things happen in the Hotel. *Slavny bubny za gorami*. You cannot trust everyone."

Quiet creeps back in between us. Who *can* I trust? I'd assumed Sev's pin went to his room, just like I assume he and Nico and Stripe are on my side. What if I'm wrong?

I have to trust someone, though. I can't do this alone. I only hope they're the right ones.

"Did you cause the pin-failure?" I ask.

Sev gazes up at the pink sky on the edge of the portico. "The wood goes bad over time. Imperfections form in the pins because they are old, and their connection to the Vesima is weak. To find one ready to crack is much too easy these days. Though I fear our plan got out of hand. We went too far."

I smile at hearing the ease with which he admits it. At least I know Sev won't lie to me. "You said the binding comes from life."

Sev grunts. "The doors are bound to their places, but also grafted invisibly into each other. They draw life from one another, depend on each other, like people."

"So all those doors failed because of one pin." I run my finger along the soft wood. "Why not replace them?"

"As I said, there is not enough wood."

"Because the Hotel doesn't have the tree." I glance back up at the stone branches spraying water in the fountain. Because . . . someone took it.

"I saw it," I tell him. "The Vesima tree. At least . . . I think it was the tree."

"How?"

I touch Dad's coin. "It was a memory. But I have a feeling . . . I think Dad took it. He's the one who stole the Greenhouse."

Sev raises an eyebrow.

I struggle to piece it together. "In all these memories, I'm worried. Like I'm going to get caught. And Mom's there, but something happens to her, and then Agapios, and something about the fourth floor." I pause. "You think that's where it is?"

"It is possible." Sev's voice turns somber. "No one knows what happened to the Greenhouse. It, like the Mezzanine, could only be reached through the doors. But if Reinhart re-bound a door somewhere in the Hotel after he unbound the others, it could still be here, hidden."

I start to ask more, but Sev looks past me. At Nico, who's bopping across the Courtyard toward us.

"Hey guys!" Nico says, smiling his outrageous smile as if he just got off a ride at the fair. "That was fun, wasn't it?"

Sev scowls at him. "We do not know the damage yet. It may take weeks to repair."

"Eh, you doormen got this." Nico gives me a slap on the back. "So, Mr. Cam, did you make it?"

My shoulders slump. "Your distraction was for nothing."

"Not for nothing. I mean, you survived your first pin drill, right?"

"I guess," I say, a little confused. I thought he'd be more irritated.

"This is cause for a celebration!" He claps his gloved hands. "I've got a surprise for you. What do you say?"

I look back to Sev, who gives us a weak smile. "Go on," he says. "I will tell Rahki you had business."

"Where are we headed?"

Nico's face brightens even more. "It's a surprise. Let's go get changed."

17

A Game in Central America

We go to Nico's room to change. I didn't grab any of my clothes when I pinned the door to Oma's—and going back now would be . . . well . . . stupid—so he lends me a pair of athletic shorts and a soccer jersey.

"*Fútbol* jersey," Nico corrects, spinning the soccer ball on his finger. The Sydney Opera House glows on the harbor outside his window. Gulls caw over the water. "You Americans and your soccer. Seriously, American football players barely use their feet at all."

He leads me to the Dallas Door, sticking his tongue out at Elizabeth as we pass the North American front desk. Nico's clothes are just a little too tight on me. The seam under my pits is totally going to cut off the blood flow to my arms. Wearing someone else's clothes is weird.

We emerge into the parking lot behind the 7-Eleven where I first met him, which seems like ages ago.

"Where are we going to play soccer in Dallas?"

"First off, I told you, it's *fútbol*. Second, who says we're playing in Dallas?"

I scrunch my eyebrows, and then it clicks. "We're taking Stripe's Corridor?"

"Yep."

"Why not use the Alcove Door in the back halls? It would've been faster."

"We don't use that door unless absolutely necessary." He bounces the ball on his knee as we walk. "Hidden doors have a way of being revealed."

A hidden door. Now that I've had time to learn more about how the Hotel works, something about the Alcove Door doesn't seem right. I've watched enough people use the map-boards to know that all the doors should be charted. It's as if the Hotel can sense where all its turners and knockers lead.

All, it seems . . . except the Alcove Door.

"How do you keep it hidden from the map-boards?" I ask as we head toward the hospital.

"Magic." He wiggles his fingers.

"I'm serious. Why don't the MC or Agapios know it's there?"

He shrugs. "Don't really know."

"You didn't bind it?"

"Nah."

"Did Stripe?"

Nico pauses to think. "I doubt it. Stripe doesn't really bother binding anything himself. He has other people do it for him. I'm not even sure he knows how."

"Wait, Stripe can't bind?" That's surprising.

"There are other kinds of magic than just binding." Nico goes back to juggling the ball. "And binding can take lots of forms, too. It's not just making pins."

The image of the door behind the armoire flashes again in my mind. "Could there be more hidden doors no one knows about?"

"Maybe." He snatches the ball and tucks it under his arm. "Why?"

"I dunno. I've got a feeling. . . ."

"Like"—he glances at my neck—"a coin kind of feeling?"

I take a breath. "In Dad's memories, I saw a door hidden behind some stuff. I think he may have bound a door somewhere on the fourth floor, but since we can't get in there, I can't check."

"Oh, I'll get you there," Nico says. "Don't you worry."

I study him as we walk. Nico always seems so sure of himself, like he knows things no one else does. Like he's got everything under control. He doesn't even seem bothered that I didn't swipe Agapios's topscrew. I wish I could be like that. Sure. Confident.

He notices me watching him. "What?"

"You're not mad at me."

Nico scoffs. "Of course I'm not mad. Why would I be mad?"

"Because I ruined our opportunity. I couldn't get the key."

"Nothing's *ruined*," he says with a laugh. "And what kind of friend would I be if I got upset about little stuff like that?"

The walk to the hospital where Nico bound the Corridor is

almost as familiar as my walk to school. But the path feels different knowing Cass is at home.

"Have you been back to see her?" Nico asks, nodding in the direction of our house.

"No." I'm pretty sure what happened with Sev's pin doesn't count, since I didn't actually *see* her.

"Why not?"

I don't know how to answer. Because I've been too busy? Because I know if I go back and spend time with her I won't want to come back? Because my time is almost up and I still don't know anything to help me find my dad? So I focus on the lines in the concrete instead.

"I think it's cool how you care for her." Nico scans the hospital ahead. "Family's important. The family you're born with, and the family you choose."

I furrow my brow. "The family you choose?"

"Well, like me. . . . I don't know who my parents are. I don't have any brothers or sisters that I know of. The only family I have are the people I've chosen to treat that way." He grins. "Good people. Like you."

When we reach the door behind the hospital, Nico has to jigger the magical lock to make his silver key work. The flashing lights of an ambulance cause my body to tense. "So, what do the keys do, exactly?"

"Keys use a different kind of binding." His key finally clicks.

"Deeper. It's harder to make a key than a pin. And in the right hands, they're way more dangerous."

"More dangerous than pins?" The void behind those failed doors itches in my mind.

"Pins just connect one place to another, but keys can do lots of things." He holds up his silver key. "Stripe gave me this one. It locks and unlocks bound doors so people don't accidentally stumble upon them." His eyes darken as he opens the door. "I've even heard of one that has the power to completely unbind whatever it's used on."

"That doesn't sound so bad."

"Yeah, until you imagine what it would be like to unbind a person." He stares intently at me. "All those atoms and things inside you just . . . loose. Undone. Falling apart." He shudders. "It ain't pretty."

"Oh." I immediately think back to what Orban said. *I won't be unbound.* The idea of Agapios carrying a key like that makes me want to hug myself.

The Corridor lights flicker on. It looks just like we left it: checkerboard tile extending in both directions, lined with simple wood doors. The Hotel at one end, Stripe's Museum at the other.

As we pass through this time, I pay closer attention to all the little details in the Corridor. The doors are old. Very old. The jots and tittles around the blocky letters on the nameplates look like something from the History Channel. And there's a musty smell, like old books.

"Stripe gave me my key when he showed me this Corridor, and the Alcove Door," Nico says. "It's my way back to him, if things at the Hotel ever go sideways."

A way out, like the pin Sev gave me. "You've known Stripe a long time."

"All my life. He's pretty much the only father figure I had growing up. But then . . . " Nico turns the crystal handle on one of the doors, and the muggy scent of rain and mud washes into the hall. "Well, I've got some people to introduce you to."

Beyond the door, a field slopes up to some woods. Trees cover a round-top mountain that partially blocks the low sun. Insects trill in the thick air. This side of the door barely hangs from its hinges on a small, cinderblock building. A rusted tricycle lies buried in the weeds next to it, along with old shovels, trowels, and sledgehammers.

I wipe a bubble of sweat from my forehead. "Where are we?"

"Honduras. A little community you've never heard of."

As we climb the muddy road, I take in the scenery. Painted square houses. Yards wrapped in chain-link fences, littered with broken toys. Shirtless old men watch from behind cracked windows. A woman wrings blue dye from a pair of pants and hangs them from a drooping power line to dry.

A tiny girl in an oversize T-shirt plays with a doll next to the road. The doll's hair is faded, and it's got no clothes on, but still I recognize it. Cass had one, but she threw it away years ago. This little girl hugs the doll as if it's her best friend.

Most of our errands have taken place in big cities, but there've been a few places like this, where the people live off leftovers. Left-over toys sent from countries with more money than they know what to do with. Leftover clothes people got tired of.

"Most of the world does not live with the same luxuries as you, my friend," Nico says, catching me midstare. "Don't you pity them. These folks are happier than most people you know."

The road breaks left to an open soccer—I mean *fútbol*—field, full of guys and girls around our age. One of the girls notices Nico and shouts to the others. The game pauses as the whole group runs toward us.

"They know you."

"Of course they do," he says. "They're my family."

Nico spends the next few minutes introducing the Jimenez family. There are at least ten kids, all uniquely different.

"I told them you're my friend," he says after giving me more names than I'll ever remember.

I grin hearing him call me his friend.

"They're all adopted," Nico tells me as some race back to their game. "*Mami* and *Papi* took me in a while back, along with all these other fantastic *locos*. Nothing official . . . they just welcomed me into their home."

"But you live at the Hotel. And didn't you say you were raised by Stripe?"

He shrugs. "I get around."

"Nico don't stay," one of the brothers shouts in broken English. "*¿A donde fué esta vez?*"

Nico answers with a long string of Spanish. I sit back and listen. Nico has a family. I never even thought to ask him about that. A family he left.

And he can still go back to them.

After their happy reunion, it's time to play.

Now I understand why they don't call it soccer. This game feels like a completely different sport. I mean, the rules are the same, but these kids dance around me like I'm an elephant statue with no coin. They don't make fun of me, though. At school, sports almost always end with the others roasting me. Nico's family makes me feel like I'm one of them—even though I can't understand anything they're telling me.

We go to their house at the top of the hill after the game. Mr. and Mrs. Jimenez have some spicy dishes prepared. The meal is simple and the place settings are sparse, but everyone laughs and eats like it's the full-on buffet served aboard the *Accommodation*. Afterward, we hang out on the uneven back porch as the sun drops behind the mountain. One of the brothers plays mariachi music on a guitar.

I never knew family could be like this. All they're doing is hanging out together, but it's different from me and Cass and Oma. They're so loud, and happy. There's so many of them to support and watch out for each other. To be honest, I'm kinda jealous.

A couple of Nico's siblings have disabilities, too. He pays particular attention to a girl with withered hands that curl inward, giving her a stuffed doll with slick black horsehair and a beaded dress. She curls up in his arms, watching him with big brown eyes as he chatters on in Spanish. Every once in a while, I hear the name of a place I recognize. He's telling them about his travels.

Before we leave, I catch Nico secretly giving his papi a bundle of bills. It's the tips he's been collecting from the breakfast service. He gives it all to his family.

Back home it's just the three of us. Oma works so hard to provide that she's not around for every meal, and when she is home, she's exhausted. I know she loves us, but our house ends up so quiet. Compared to this, our family feels broken.

It's almost dark when Nico and I head back to the Corridor.

"Have fun?" he asks.

I feel a pinch on my neck, and swat away another bloodsucker making a meal out of me. "Yeah." Though I can't stop thinking about how Nico's family is so unlike my own.

"What's wrong? Are you mad?"

"I don't know." I didn't think I was, but maybe I am.

"Why?"

"I don't know!" I glance ahead to the door to Stripe's Corridor. "It's just . . . you keep all these secrets. So does Sev. It's not right, asking me to help take those kids without telling me why, or what happens to them." I pause. Is this what I'm really upset about? Maybe. All I know is these are the only words I can find.

The sky's getting darker now. A smattering of stars pricks into view.

"At least tell me why you're working with Stripe."

"I thought I made that clear tonight." Nico looks back down the road. "I'm doing it for my family."

Another nonanswer.

He lowers his gaze. "For you, helping Stripe is all about finding out what happened to your dad. If you find him, you get to go home, and that's it. For me it's . . . different. I don't get to go home. I'm bound to the people here, but I've got other bindings too. Responsibilities. Everything I do is for them. To keep them safe."

"Safe from what, though?"

"Just safe. The binding comes from life, yeah? Well . . . there's power in a person's life, and in the relationships we have. And there are people out there who collect others in order to collect power." He pauses, and slaps a mosquito. "I don't want *anyone* collecting my family."

"Is that what's going on? Is Agapios collecting kids to gain power?"

Nico twists his lips. "I wish I could say, Cam. I really do. But those secrets . . . they're not mine to tell."

I growl under my breath. "Everyone keeps saying that."

"You know why, right? Why we can't tell you?"

I pause for a second. Oma, Nico, Sev, even Rahki—they wouldn't all say the same thing unless there was a reason. Maybe even . . . a magical reason.

Then it hits me. "Your lips are bound. You really can't tell me, can you?"

"At last, he gets it." Nico squeezes my shoulder. "Some secrets protect themselves, and some truths only reveal themselves when they're ready. Like the Hotel not calling you until you were old enough to work here. But I can tell you this: I don't want something bad to happen to you, either. We'll find your dad, and when we do, this'll all be over."

"But what if—"

"No." He looks me in the eye. "I promise. I won't let anyone collect you."

He's serious. Nico's never serious. He makes jokes out of everything.

"There's a bit of binding people tend to forget," he says, "but I want to do it with you. Maybe this way, you'll understand me better. Where I come from, and where I'm going."

He reaches to his side and pulls out a little knife. No, not a knife—a sliver, like the one Orban had in Budapest. It's sharp along one edge, with a grip at the bottom, and comes to an extreme point at the tip. All wood.

"I want to be your blood-brother," he says. "It's a kind of binding between equals, friends. A promise that binds me to you as a brother, forever."

A brother. I've never had someone choose to be that close to me. I've had friends, sure, but no one who wanted to keep me around when school was out. I mean, there's Cass of course, but she's . . . well . . . Cass. My sister.

"Will you do it?"

"Umm, I guess," I say, but part of me is screaming *yes!* I've always wanted to belong to a big family, like the Jimenezes. To have people who choose me. People who want to stick around.

Nico pulls out his handkerchief. "We need a contract."

"Why?"

"It's just the way things are done." He bends over, holding the sliver like he would a pen, and scribbles with it on the cloth from his pocket.

"The sliver writes?"

"Burns," Nico clarifies, still writing. "But yeah, most slivers can double as a pen. Pins, too. Contracts are important in binding."

He finishes, blows on the handkerchief, and hands it to me.

> I, Nico Flores, bind myself as blood-brother to Cameron Kuhn. I promise to do everything in my power to find and protect his family. What's bound to me is bound to him, everything I have, forever in perpetuity.

"Perpetuity?"

"It means it lasts forever and ever. Even after this is all over and you go home."

I narrow my eyes. "Why would you do this?"

"Remember when I told you I was going to be master of my own House?" He glances back down the path again. "If I'm going to protect my family, I need power too. The Hotel's got it. If I can become Concierge—master of Agapios's House—I'll be able to take care of my family forever."

"I thought Agapios demoted you."

"A temporary setback." He smiles. "And there are other great Houses, too. Like the Museum. If I can become master of any of the Houses, I'll be set, and so will my family. But I need people I can trust to help me get there. People who trust *me*, no matter what happens. And with this, you'll be my family too."

It's strange, having someone tell me they trust me like that after only knowing me a week. But it's Nico, the guy I followed out of the hospital to start this journey.

"Do you trust me?" he says, as if reading my mind.

I nod, though part of me is still hesitant. I think through all the people Nico's lied to. He hasn't lied to me, though. Not as far as I can tell. And the thought of being a part of his family . . . wouldn't that be worth a little risk?

"Then give me your hand." He opens my palm and holds the sliver like Sev held the needle back in his room. "Be still. Don't want it going too deep, or we'll activate the sliver's binding, and we *don't* want that."

"Why not?"

"Let's just say that if I poke you with this, it'll hurt. A lot."

Nico draws the sharp edge of the sliver across the muscle at the bottom of my thumb. It stings, but I don't pull back. A tiny line of red bubbles up along the cut.

He does the same to his own palm.

"Do we sign somewhere?"

"Signing is good, but this is better. Stronger." He places the handkerchief over his palm and holds his hand out toward me. "A contract between us. What's bound to me is bound to you. Everything we have, forever in perpetuity."

He grips my hand through the fabric. I grip back. The warm liquid sticks our palms together, the handkerchief contract between us, and I can almost hear the sound of a door opening in my head. I feel stronger, gripping his hand, as if his confidence is bleeding into me.

"Now," he says, "let's find your dad."

18

Still Waters Run Deep

I'm walking through the Mezzanine in my tailcoat, wringing my gloved hands. I try not to look at the night-windows on the cliffs—the ones that show a starry twilight even though the sky over the Mezz is bright and sunny. Those pitch-dark windows remind me too much of the darkness that hides in the spaces between doors. And I can't think about that now. I've got a job to do.

I climb the stairs to the Elevator Bank, slipping a hand around the key in my pocket. This is for the best. We'll be okay. Cassia, Cameron, Melissa . . . we'll be safe.

I press the button and wait for the elevator to take me to floor four.

Someone's coming. Running. A hand stops the closing doors. Another slaps my cheek.

It's happening again. Melissa's face zooming away into the black. A loud snap, like something breaking inside me. Leaves fluttering from an enormous tree in the sunlight. The door behind the armoire, the pearl key in my hand, and a pale, lifeless face staring back at me. I know that face. I hate that face.

And I'm so, so sad.

• • •

I open my eyes, struggling to figure out where I am. *Who* I am. I'm me, right? I'm not someone else. I'm . . . Cameron.

And I'm cold.

I glance down to see Dad's coin hanging against my bare chest. I'm dressed for bed, but I'm not in my room. I'm in the elevator, my finger outstretched toward the button for the fourth floor.

A burst of cold whips through the cage from the Shaft below, making even my goose bumps ache. This can't be real. I'm dreaming again, the one where I'm standing naked in front of all those kids at the overnighter and everyone laughs. Only this is no dream. I'm really standing in the service elevator, in my underwear.

The elevator dings and the doors slide open, revealing a girl with two long black braids, dressed in the white uniform of the kitchen staff. She stares at me, and I stare back in horror.

This is *not* happening.

Mercifully, she backs away and lets the doors close. I can't press the button for the seventeenth floor fast enough.

I must have been sleepwalking. But I've never sleepwalked before. Maybe the coin was finally taking me to Dad, to my destination, only I woke up too soon.

Another cold gust cuts through me. The Shaft is always in Dad's dreams. Something important happened here. Something cold and dark and sad. A memory even the coin doesn't want me to see, like the reason Dad was in the elevator, and the face I can't quite remember.

One thing's for certain, though: From now on I'm wearing pajamas to bed.

The day after the pin-failure, everything about the Hotel feels different. The doormen hang more OUT OF ORDER signs. Many guests head home, fearful another pin-emergency will strand them in some far-flung corner of the world. Everyone's saying it was sabotage. Maids patrol the halls. The Hotel's on high alert, and I have less than four days before my trial period expires.

At an all-staff meeting in the ballroom, Agapios updates us on the Hotel's situation and offers a reward for information about who caused the pin-failure. The whole time he's at the podium, my mind keeps flashing back to the Shaft, and Mom, and Agapios's old, bony face gazing into my soul. Though something inside me doesn't feel as scared of him as I once did. Instead, there's a sense of challenge . . . like he's a foe I need to trick. An obstacle in my way.

Then come the checks. Nico and I spend the entire fifth shift delivering payments to people the Hotel rents its rooms from. Shoring up alliances, Nico says.

We turn on to a street in Manila with more cars than I've ever seen in one place. Everyone's honking and shouting. Filipino pedestrians cut through traffic as if they're strolling through the park.

Nico steps in front of a multicolored bus, leaving me no choice but to brave the busy street to keep up. He's been acting strangely toward me ever since Honduras. Colder. I'm not sure why, though.

"Are you upset with me?" I ask, dodging a car as it surges forward to fill a gap.

"No," he says.

"What's up then? You seem angry, or worried. Different, somehow."

Nico sighs and pulls me into an alley to block out the noise. "We're both different," he says. "We're blood-bound now." He leans against the dirty wall. "Though I didn't think it would be like this."

"I-I don't understand."

He runs a hand through his hair. "There are different kinds of binding between people. People who are bound naturally are drawn together, like you and your dad. People bound as servants are forced to follow their master. But those bound as equals share a piece of themselves with the one they're bound to. They change each other. And man, you worry a lot."

"You can feel my worry?"

"Everything we have, remember? You've got a bit of me, too. And we didn't seal it with a signature. We sealed it with *us*. Nothing held back. You change me, and I change you."

"I knew it sounded risky." Though, it's strange; I don't feel like I'm changing.

"I'm still glad I did it." Nico stands up straight. "Anyway, you fret too much about risks. It's exhausting."

"Sorry."

He laughs. "Listen, kiddo, you don't ever have to apologize to me. We're past that now. We're family."

Family. The word makes my lungs shrink.

"Hey," Nico says, clapping a hand on my shoulder, "don't look like that. We'll find him."

"Time's running out."

"I'm working on something that'll help." He winks. "I told you, I'm doing everything in my power. You'll have your dad back before you know it."

The following day, the Old Man announces the grand reopening of the Hotel pool to boost staff morale. It's apparently been closed for months now, for groundskeeper maintenance.

"This is fortunate," Sev says as he, Nico, and I hop onto the elevator in our swimsuits. This one's a guest lift displaying views of a geyser, and a mountain stream, and a town somewhere in what might be South Africa. "Stripe would like a meeting. He can join us at the pool."

"Won't people see us?" I ask. "See *him*?"

"We're meeting in the caves below." Nico shakes me by my shoulders. "Plus, hello! It's a pool! You're going to love it. The water's warmed through geothermal rock in Yosemite."

I rub the waterproof bandage on my hand. The cut from Nico's sliver still stings. "Shouldn't we be looking for a way onto the fourth floor instead?"

Nico shakes his head. "Trust me. We've still got time."

The doors open, and we step onto a boardwalk dividing two completely different locations.

On our right, a white sand beach rolls down to a crystal-clear ocean. One of the European staffers stands on a ladder, using binding dust on a giant sandcastle to hold it together. Guests sip colorful drinks and eat clam-shaped cakes. A few adventurous surfers brave the waves.

But the landscape to our left is something else entirely. The board-walk drops into a glassy lake full of fishing boats, surrounded by moun-tains. The smell of fir trees and spring water mixes with the salty breeze, all under a sky split right down the middle between sunrise and sunset.

I smile, feeling the warmth on my face. "There's two suns!"

"Only one sun," Nico says. "You're just seeing it from two different angles."

"The boardwalk binds lake and ocean shore together," Sev explains. "As soon as you step off the boards, you enter fully into one or the other."

I scan the seam in the sky over the boardwalk, where sunset pink and sunrise yellow blend together. "I thought binding places only worked with a door, or a frame like the sun-windows?"

"This is old binding. The boardwalk has absorbed both locations over time, distorting the land itself and connecting the two places without the need of a frame."

A glint of light lakeside draws my gaze. An enormous stone finger rises from the lake shore on the opposite side and protrudes out at an angle over the center of the lake, with a waterfall—a huge, foamy wall of white water—exploding from a pair of ancient doors at its tip high above.

"The Giant's Finger," Sev says. "Another marvel of the Hotel."

The statue's as tall as the surrounding mountains. I trace the path of the water, expecting to see the cloud of spray where the waterfall meets the lake, but the falls don't crash *into* the water below—they go *through* it.

"There's a hole," I say. "A hole . . . in the lake." A square, wooden portal, built just under the water's surface. Calm lake water rolls softly over the edges into the darkness below, but the waterfall roars like TV static through the center, never disturbing the lake's smooth, glassy surface.

"The doormen put a frame under the water to make the water-fall taller," Nico explains. "It's bound to the Pool grotto, so the falls drop into the caves below. Or . . . wherever the grotto is."

I lean over the rail, straining to see into the enormous hole. "There are caves down there?"

"Yep." Nico's tone bounces with excitement. For once he seems as impressed as I am. "The water falls from the Finger, through the frame, into the grotto. From there, it filters through the under-ground river—to keep it clean, you know—and back through doors bound to those big ones on top of the Finger, where it becomes the waterfall again. Over and over. It's like a fountain . . . a really, really *big* fountain."

"It's beautiful."

Sev sees Rahki on the beach and breaks off to follow her and

Sana with a wave and a reminder not to miss our meeting.

I stick with Nico, scanning the doorless frames that line the boardwalk. They're shortcuts, I realize . . . bound to other frames scattered all over the area. A kid I recognize from the mailroom jumps through one frame and flies out a different one atop a boulder in the lake. Another frame shows kids climbing damp, dripping rocks, and yet another leads right to the edge of the ocean. Granite mer-people statues—icons, like the ones in the Motor Pool—stand guard near each frame with obsidian tridents and catfish-faced lizard-beasts on leashes. They turn their heads to watch the people as they pass. The sights make my heart race, but it's a different kind of feeling than I'm used to. A strange, unfamiliar sense of . . . anticipation. Eagerness. Even . . . mischief?

"Hurry!" Nico calls from a frame farther down. "Let's ride the waterfall!"

The frame takes us into a grand cavern that curves over a blue-green pool.

"Grotto," he reminds me. "Somewhere in the Bermuda Triangle." He points to the mouth-shaped opening at the far end that's flooding the chamber with early twilight. The hanging stalactites shimmer. It's like being in the belly of a giant rock-fish. WWTD number 975: grotto indigestion, yum. My feet slip on moss as we slide down the rocks to the water's edge.

"How on earth are we supposed to 'ride' *that*?" The Giant's Finger waterfall pours through the frame in the cavernous ceiling that must be bound to the one Nico pointed out in the lake above. Amazing, how it's all connected: So many different places smashed on top of one another to form one complete water park.

Nico points to a stream that splits off into a tunnel, yelling over the roar. "Just hop in! The current carries you through the underground river and spits you out at the fingertip. The rest is gravity!"

"Is that safe?"

"Who cares?" he shouts, and dives in.

I care. I care a lot. Or at least . . . I should. Surprisingly, though, I feel like I can handle it this time. Maybe it won't be so bad after all.

I take a gulp, clench my fists, and jump.

The current grabs me as soon as I swim near the tunnel. I struggle to keep control, but the stream flows so fast.

Nico floats in the current with his hands behind his head. "Don't fight it!"

He's totally going to get me killed.

Despite the anchor in my stomach, I let the current drag me along. In the tunnel, everything goes dark. I can't tell which way is left, right, forward, back . . . the shadows draw me in like the void behind the failed doors. The roar of water grows until it's all I can hear.

And then, light. Open air. Birds.

I've made a huge mistake.

I fly out of the doors atop the Giant's Fingertip and tumble toward the lake, reordering my list so "drowning" and "heights" take more prominent positions. Somewhere in all that falling and screaming, there's a split second where the pounding in my chest and the rush of blood almost feel good. Almost.

Maybe Nico's affecting me more than I thought.

But when I plunge through the hole in the lake, my world goes dark. Flashes of memory press in. I see Mom, rushing away so very fast. Falling, like I am, into a black pit.

My feet break into the water. The falls shove me deeper, faster, down, down, down. I try to swim, but with every push through the current I'm pushing the armoire instead. It's so heavy, but no one can ever see what's behind it. The door must stay hidden.

The crashing of the falls transforms into a low, gurgling grumble. I can't breathe. My chest tingles as I scramble for what I think is up. In my mind, I press the button for the fourth floor again and again. I struggle to pull the elevator doors open, to get out.

I break the surface and gasp as Dad's memory gives way to reality. I check to make sure I'm still a whole person. Arms? Check. Legs? Check. Sense of personal well-being? Working on it.

Mom's ghostly face haunts me. My heart clangs in my chest. Then it clicks.

She fell. She . . . fell.

My eyes burn as the terrible realization soaks into me.

"Woohoo! That was *awesome!*" Nico shouts, treading water nearby. His usually slick hair sticks to his face in curls. "Wanna go again?"

"No." All I want is to get out of this water and away from all those awful memories.

I swim toward the rocks.

Nico catches up in a few strokes. "Hey, wait. You okay?"

"I'm fine," I say, totally not fine at all.

He swims alongside me, voice full of concern. "Wanna talk about it?"

"No."

"Seriously, if something's up, you can tell me." He lifts his bandaged hand out of the water. "We're blood-bros, after all. That's kinda the point."

I finally look at him, glad to know he really does care. "I'll be fine," I say, and this time I mean it.

"Well, okay." He grins softly. "Sure you don't want to ride the falls again? It only gets better."

"No way." I glance back at the glassy tower of water. "Thanks, but I'm never doing that again."

Nico huffs. "Fine. Suit yourself. Just don't miss our appointment."

He swims back for the underground river, and I climb out of the water, dripping and cold, trying to calm my racing heart.

It takes a few minutes before I start to recover. The pit in my stomach is as deep as the Shaft itself. I saw it clearly this time. Mom fell. She wasn't being pulled away; she was falling, into that awful hole. Didn't Nico say he'd heard someone fell a long time ago? It was her. They caged in the service elevators because that's where Mom died.

I jump when I feel a hand on my shoulder, and turn to find Rahki standing behind me.

"Are you okay?"

"Yeah." I wipe my eyes, pretending my tears are just lake water. "I'm fine. Just don't like riding the waterfall."

"Who would?" Rahki sits beside the pool, spreading the cream-colored fabric of her outfit on the mossy rocks. Black leggings and a tight-sleeved shirt cover every inch of her from ankle to wrist. "Come. Sit with me."

I join her on the rocks, taking deep, slow breaths to calm the panic in my chest.

"The Hotel must really like you." She dips her toes in and out of the water.

"Agapios said the same thing when he brought me on," I tell her. "Creepy, if you ask me."

"It's not creepy. It's an honor," she says, her voice stern. "The Hotel's not just a place. Every part of it is bound to all the others. Those places have memories. Personality. Put the pieces together, you get something more. Something . . . alive."

I glimpse Nico and Sev heading for an offshoot tunnel near the back of the grotto. Nico sees me, and beckons me to follow.

The meeting is about to start. But I can't go with Rahki here. For all I know she's still reporting on what I do. This has to be why Agapios is letting me have free roam of the Hotel. He wants me to lead him to my secrets—to Stripe, or the Museum, or both.

I can't risk it. They'll have to meet Stripe without me.

Instead, I turn my attention back to Rahki. "You said before that the Hotel saved you. How?"

She watches the wall of water. "When my group of refugees

came through the Damascus Door, I was hurt. The Hotel took care of me. Healed me. Sev has a similar story."

"Wait . . . *our* Sev?" I thought he was against the Hotel.

"He had it worse than I did. There are bad people out there. The people the Hotel saved Sev from had put him in a rough situation, even convinced him he was so stupid that he could never escape. Can you imagine, Sev being considered stupid? The Hotel tended to him, provided him peace and books to enrich his mind. It showed him that those bad people did not determine what he could become. He wouldn't be who he is today if not for this place."

That doesn't make sense. Rahki and Sev spend a lot of time together, but he's always said it wasn't a good idea to tell her what we're here for. Maybe Sev lied to her about how he got here? "What about Nico?"

Rahki sighs. "My point is the mission is special. It saves and protects the people who need protecting. The Hotel sees us as who we could be, not as who we are, and helps us reach our potential. Nearly all of us on staff have benefitted from it one way or another. Agapios and the Maid Commander will do everything in their power to protect it."

"Agapios." His name tastes bitter on my tongue.

She takes my hand. Her fingers are soft, but marred by little white scars. And so warm. "Agapios isn't what you think."

I want to tell her *she's* the one who doesn't know who she's working for, but I can't. Not yet. Hopefully, soon.

"I just want you to understand why we're here," she says. "The

Hotel is not the people inside it. It's . . . something different. And I don't know why, but it trusts you. It knows who you are and why you're here, even if the rest of us don't, and it's letting you stay. If the Hotel can trust you, that means I trust you too." She stands. "If the MC or the Old Man ask, that's what I'll tell them."

"Where are you going?"

Rahki motions to the frame leading back to the boardwalk. "To my room. I'm not going to swim, and one can only sit in the dark for so long before it darkens them, too."

I grin. "You get that from Sev?"

She doesn't return the smile. "I know you're up to something, Cam." She glances at Dad's coin around my neck. "Just be careful."

With that, she leaves.

I chew my lip, briefly considering whether I should head for the caves to join the meeting with Stripe. But I can't risk it, even with Rahki gone. Any one of these people could be watching me. So I walk the beach instead.

Rahki really believes she's doing good by helping Agapios collect—or steal—those kids from all over the world. She even thinks Sev is grateful for the Hotel . . . as if it was the Hotel that saved him. But it wasn't the Hotel—it was Stripe. She doesn't realize that she's been collected too. Placed, to give Agapios power.

It's wrong to keep her in the dark like this. If she knew the truth, she could help. She deserves that chance.

I'm going to have to tell her.

Before it's too late.

19

Missing Pieces

Later that evening, a knock comes at my door.

Sev pushes past me when I answer it and starts pacing my hotel room, ducking to avoid hitting his head on the angled ceiling.

"I cannot do it," he says, wringing his hands. He's still wearing his swimsuit, though it's dry and looks like it has been for a while. "No more."

I've never seen him agitated like this. Sev is always the reasonable one in our little infiltration. "Okay, Sev, calm down."

"Why were you not there?" he says, a quaver in his voice. "Did Rahki stop you? Does she know?"

"No, I—"

"It does not matter." He stops midstride and tries to catch his breath. "It is too much."

"Sev, sit down."

He flops onto my bed, hands in his lap, and stares blankly at the floor.

"What's going on?"

Sev balls his calloused hands into fists. "Stripe had me stay, after Nico left. He wants me to do something. But what Stripe asks . . . I cannot do."

I sit awkwardly next to him. "What does Stripe want?"

He takes another breath, focusing on the carpet. "Have you ever felt . . . ?" He doesn't finish the thought.

I've got to do something. Cass gets frustrated like this sometimes, and I've grown pretty good at dragging the problem out of her, even when she doesn't know what it is.

I reach for a bag of Chef Silva's sweet on my bedside table and hand him one. "I thought Stripe saved you?"

Sev examines the candy slowly, as if he's unraveling the mysteries of the world, before popping it in his mouth.

"It is hard belonging to someone else," he says, rolling the pebble around on his tongue. "Who you are, who you were, is forfeit. You do things you do not want to do." He pauses for a long moment. "I should have stayed lost."

"I—"

"Cameron, you must listen to me." He looks up, eyes red and bloodshot. "Sometimes, when one is lost, it is better they stay lost. Better that everyone forget."

At first I don't understand, but then a tingle rushes through my arms. "Are . . . are you saying my dad should stay lost?"

He looks away.

Anger balloons in my throat. "Seriously?"

"You must understand. We—"

I stand to face him, gritting my teeth. "I've waited my whole life to find him. I'm so close!"

"You may not like what you find."

"Shut up!" I throw the bag of sweet at him.

Sev tries to dodge, but the bag hits him in the eye, scattering rock candy everywhere. "Cameron, please."

"Get out!"

"You must—"

I sweep a handful of rocks off the bed and chuck them at him. "Go!"

Sev hangs his head. "I am sorry."

He closes the door behind him, and I sit on my bed and cry.

It doesn't take long for me to regret my tantrum. Sev's one of the only people here who's befriended me. But I can't believe he'd try to talk me out of my search, after everything. It was Stripe who wanted me to find my dad in the first place. What could he have asked Sev to do that was so hard?

A thought whispers in my ear. Rahki said Agapios wasn't who I thought he was. What if . . . ?

No. Nico's the one who took me to Stripe. He's my blood-brother. I trust him.

The trial period is over in just three days—less than seventy-two hours—but this feels important. I need to make things right with Sev.

• • •

The next morning I head to the facilities workshop where the doormen do most of their work, looking to apologize. Only the other doormen haven't seen Sev since yesterday. He didn't come in to work. That's not like him.

I risk another bout of nausea by stopping at the *Accommodation* to see if maybe he's having a late breakfast, but he's not there either. No response when I knock on his door. And when I check the map-boards, his coin isn't tracking. The map-boards might not always show everyone, but they're at least supposed to show who you're looking for.

Which means even the Hotel doesn't know where he is. Now I'm really worried. Whatever Stripe said had scared him, and I let him go. I should have listened.

I take the staff elevator to Nico's floor, trying not to look out over the cavernous pit that swallowed Mom. Nico will think I'm crazy. He'll say I'm worried for nothing. But worrying is how I've made sure Cass survived this long. If I wasn't always looking out for the bad, things might be a lot worse.

That thought grinds in my chest. Cass has been without me for over a week now. I hope she's okay.

I race down the hall as soon as the elevator opens and pound on Nico's door. "Nico!" *Boom-boom-boom.* "Get out here!"

He opens up wearing shorts and a T-shirt, rubbing his eyes, hair sprigging up in all directions.

"Where's Sev?" I peek past him into his messy room.

He runs a hand through his hair and blinks away sleep boogers. "I don't know. Why?"

I tell him about the way Sev was acting last night, and how now I can't find him.

That seems to wake Nico up. "And his coin's not showing on the map-board?"

"No." I grit my teeth. "You should have seen him. He said Stripe asked him to do something. Something he couldn't—or wouldn't—do."

Nico's face goes slack. "No." Then louder, "NO!"

He takes off running down the hall.

20

Broken Bonds

"Crisis mode" is what happens when you go from worrying bad things are going to happen, to dealing with them when they do. Call nine-one-one. Turn Cass over so she doesn't choke. Stanch any bleeding.

Replace the pin to stop the failure. Follow Nico.

He bolts down the next hall as I'm rounding the previous corner. Nico's so fast, and I'm still sore from the game the other night. But when I see the door he takes in the Courtyard, I know where he's headed. The Alcove Door. Stripe's Corridor.

"What's all the commotion?" It's Rahki, sitting on one of the fountain benches with Sana.

"Nothing," I tell her. "We're just . . . playing a game."

I start to follow Nico into the back halls, but something stops me.

"Coins want to return to the person they're bound to, right?" I turn back and hold my Hotel coin out to Rahki. "If I don't come right back, use it to follow me."

As I hand her the coin, another memory flashes. An image of

Mom, a pair of coins, and a pearl skeleton key. Another flash, and I'm giving the coins to Oma, who's standing between two baby carriers.

No. Not now. I can't do anything about Dad's memories while I've got Nico to catch up with.

Rahki gives me a concerned look. "Cameron—"

"It's a touch," I say. "Nothing to worry about." And I head for the back halls, leaving my coin with her. Nico wouldn't approve, but I have to take the risk. That's what you do in crisis mode—take risks. The *right* risks.

When I reach the hidden hall under the stairs, the door at the end is already open. Nico would never leave it open like that unless something was really, *really* wrong. I hurry through, my Chucks squeaking on the checkered tile of Stripe's Corridor. Halfway down, dull gray light streams through another open door. I know that one too. Honduras. Nico's family.

I burst out into the rain and up the gravel path. The empty *fútbol* field makes my stomach clench.

When I finally reach the Jimenez's house, it's quiet. Dim light wafts through the curtains. Silence snakes around me.

"Nico?" I shout, but there's no answer.

The kitchen table is set, only the dishes have been overturned. A cup full of some red liquid has spilled. Toys lie scattered.

"They're gone," I realize. And not just gone.

Taken.

I find Nico on the other side of the table, his legs folded under him like another scattered toy. "He took them," he says. "He really took them."

A growl rises in my throat. "Agapios."

Nico wipes his tears and turns. "Not Agapios, you dummy. Stripe."

This is the secret Nico's been keeping from me. It's why he never wanted me asking questions about his task. The reason for all those looks between him and Sev.

Nico stands to face me, fists clenched. "Stripe took my family. Or he had Sev do it. Stripe never does his own dirty work."

That doesn't make sense. "Why would he do that?"

A voice answers from the hall. "To get what I want, of course."

Nico and I turn to find Stripe standing in the kitchen door.

"You!" Nico rushes toward the man in the pinstriped suit.

Stripe holds up a black, iron key, and Nico slides to a stop.

He pats Nico on the head. "Good boy. No need to pretend any longer."

"You . . . took them?" I say, still struggling to understand. Mr. Stripe's our friend—our ally. The only dad Nico ever knew, and the one who put me on this path to finding my own dad. "Why would you take Nico's family?"

"Because that's what Stripe does." Nico's lip curls. "Because he wants to *own* everything. He's not willing to share."

"Now, Nico, you know it's not that simple." Stripe pops his cane up into his hand. "You were merely taking too long. My patience is a limited resource. I figured if I took your family, you'd remember what's at stake."

Nico clenches his teeth. "You greedy, no-good—"

Stripe touches a finger to Nico's chest and leans close. "Oh, you haven't seen me be greedy."

I glance back and forth between them. "I don't get it."

"You're right, Mr. Cameron." Stripe flashes a grin. "Time is of the essence, so let's get to business. Nico and I have lied to you."

I look to Nico. "You . . . lied?"

"Terrible, isn't it?" Stripe says. "I'm sure young Nico's fed you all sorts of drivel about how he trusts you, and how you have to trust him, but it's all been a scam."

Nico hangs his shoulders.

"There, there." Stripe gives him a pat on the head. "It was his idea. He's quite the con artist when he wants to be."

It can't be true. All this time. All we've done. Joining the Hotel, hiding the truth from the staff. "What about my dad? I thought—"

"Oh, this is *all* about your father," Stripe says. "See, when Nico came to tell me about your situation, we both already knew who dear Reinhart was. It's Reinhart's fault we're in this mess in the first place. I considered simply taking what I wanted from you, but Nico convinced me we could *use* you instead."

"Use me, how?"

"To find the Greenhouse, of course. We've been searching such a long time now. And all along the secret's been hidden in that coin around your neck."

I grip my necklace. No. It's not possible. "You . . . betrayed me."

Stripe smiles, spinning the black key between his fingers. "Nico didn't exactly *betray* you. He was never your friend in the first place. Nico's my protégé. I've been training him for years to be master of the House I built for him. In order for Nico to come into his own, however, I must first acquire the means to start a new House."

Mr. Stripe touches a plate on the table with his black key. It explodes into a rain of tiny fragments. He taps a cup, too, and it bursts like a water balloon, sending red liquid and shards of plastic everywhere.

He continues around the kitchen table, tapping each dish as he passes. Cups, plates, even silverware—it all shatters in a storm of sharp, jagged pieces, spinning in the air. I cover my face as the swirling explosion of ceramic and plastic grows.

"You see," Stripe says as he taps the table and it, too, breaks down into individual slats of wood, "each great House must have a focus—a source from which every part flows. There are few sources left these days, so we have to acquire them by any means possible."

He inserts his black key into an invisible keyhole at the center of the cloud of boards and dish fragments. The key hangs in the air as the remnants of the Jimenez's dinner table gather around it to form the floating shape of a tree. White and silver dust from the shattered dishes and disintegrated forks glitter like leaves around the blocky branches, breaking into smaller and smaller pieces.

This magic feels different from the binding. It's hot. Burning, even. The dust around the misshapen branches ripples in fiery waves. It reminds me of what Nico said before about keys. *I've even heard of one that has the power to completely unbind whatever it's used on.* A key that destroys.

I gulp, remembering the look on Orban's face when he told me, *I won't be unbound. Get out.* Orban wasn't warning me to get out of the Hotel. He was warning me to get out of this business with Stripe.

"The Vesima is the focus for Agapios's House, which you know as The Hotel Between." Stripe wiggles his fingers like a teacher pointing at a visual aid, and the suspended key shimmers. The boards at the low end of the trunk shatter and spread apart to form roots reaching out of the kitchen. "The connections between the tree and the pins made from it supply the Hotel's magic. Your father supposedly stole the Greenhouse and its tree from the Hotel, but the Hotel's binding has only weakened, rather than disappear. That tells me he left at least one door leading to the Greenhouse bound somewhere in the Hotel. It must be well hidden if Agapios still hasn't found it."

The door behind the armoire. The fourth floor. "So you never cared about finding my Dad."

Stripe twirls his gloved fingers in the cloud of silver and white dust. "Such a brilliant boy. You've got your mother's mind."

I growl at his mention of Mom, but he doesn't seem to notice.

"The Greenhouse is mine by right," he says, toying with the upper branches of the floating tree. "I made a deal with your father, and that deal has yet to be fulfilled. I've tried extracting the location from Reinhart's empty head, but he's proven gloriously unhelpful. The magic binding his memories works too well."

I struggle to process what he's telling me, but one thought screams over all the others. "You . . . you know where he is."

"Of course! I've kept my finger on Reinhart all these years—hoping for what, I don't know." He nods to my necklace. "Now that we have you and that coin, however, we'll be able to finish what I started."

I glance back to Nico, anger roiling in my stomach. "You knew where my dad was all along, and you didn't tell me."

Nico flattens his lips. "We needed you to focus on finding the Greenhouse. If you'd thought there was any other way, you'd have been distracted." He pauses. "Sorry, Cam, but we've all got a job to do."

Stripe scoffs. "He's not sorry. Nico's getting what he always wanted out of this deal." He stops and turns his attention to the window. His eyes widen. "Oh, just wonderful . . ."

Nico rushes to the glass. "Did you tell anyone we were here?"

Rahki. I smile. "Maybe."

Stripe glares. "Don't be smug, boy. I still have your father."

My smile fades.

"It's Maid Service," Nico says.

"Well then, time to move this along." Stripe pulls his key from the invisible keyhole, and the fragmented tree crashes to the ground in clattering bits. "You'll want this."

He taps his rope-shaped cane and a small peg pops up from the top. Stripe hands me the smooth, wooden pin.

"Why?" I ask.

"Because you still have a job to do." He leans close, and I can smell his damp, moldy breath. "I'm not unreasonable. Return to the Hotel and find the Greenhouse. Bind a door near it with that pin. When you're gone, I'll come in secret and take what's mine." His back straightens. "If all goes well, I'll bring you your father, too."

"That's it?"

He claps the slivery dust from his gloves. "That's it. The Hotel already views the Greenhouse as lost, so it won't even matter. No one need ever know what you did, and you'll have your father back, safe and sound. It'll be our little secret." Stripe turns his black key in the door, then looks back to me. "Think about it, but not too long. Reinhart's *dying* to meet you."

21

A Wind in the Door

When Stripe closes the door behind him, it explodes into tiny fragments—just like the kitchen table and the dishes. I cover my head against the hail of wood.

My mind spins. Stripe has my dad. He wants to exchange him for the missing Greenhouse. He's been manipulating me all along. Him, and Sev . . .

. . . and Nico.

I round on my blood-brother. "You!"

Nico throws his hands up in surrender. "Calm down, kiddo."

"You lied to me! We made a contract! I . . . bound myself to you."

He shrugs. "I wouldn't exactly go around telling people that."

I glare at him, grinding my teeth.

"I know you're mad, but you don't have time to worry about that now." He points to the maids marching up the hill, led by Rahki and the Maid Commander. "We've got to figure out how to spin this."

"Spin this?" I shout. "You sold me out!"

"Cam, it's not that simple. Stripe took my family, too."

And I can't hold it in anymore. I ball my fist and swing at him.

Nico dodges. His hand zips to his pocket and pulls out the sliver he used to bind our blood-brother contract. "Stop, Cam. Think about it."

I leap forward, knocking him into the remains of the Jimenez's dining table.

"Let go," Nico grunts. He's strong, but I manage to pin him to the floor and grab the sliver with my bandaged hand.

"Get back!" I shout, jumping up and aiming the weapon at him.

Nico scrambles to his feet. "Cam, please."

Through the window I see Rahki and the MC drawing close. "Why even make that stupid blood-brother thing? Is the Greenhouse really that important?"

His eyes darken. "The Greenhouse is everything. You don't understand. Stripe raised me. I know who he is. What he can do. This was the only way things could play out."

The front door bursts open and before I can react, the Maid Commander unsheathes her sword and points it at me. "Drop it, Mr. Cameron."

"Nico's a traitor," I declare, not lowering the sliver an inch. He has to get what he deserves.

"Where did you get that sliver?" the MC asks.

"I-I don't know what it is." Which is true. For all I know, slivers shoot laser beams out of their tips. Number 751: Incineration by laser. Seems an appropriate way for Nico to die. "I took it from him.

He's the one who caused the pin-failure. Him and Sev. They've been working for the Competition."

Her eyes bore into me. "And what about you, Mr. Cameron?"

"I—" What do I say? That I was working with them too, but now I see who they really are? Pretty sure that won't go over well. And what about the Hotel? I thought I knew who *they* were, what they wanted.

I was wrong about them.

"I think they wanted me to do something," I say, still gripping the pin Stripe gave me in my other hand.

I'm about to tell her about the Greenhouse, but something stops me. If Stripe has my dad, and I tell the MC everything, that's it. I lose my chance to get him back, forever. Now I see why Nico and Sev kept telling me to focus only on finding him. The truth I now know—that the Hotel's good and I'm on the wrong side— complicates everything.

"Cameron's no docent," Rahki tells her, and gives me a long look. "I trust him."

I swallow a silent *thank you.*

The Maid Commander nods to her maids. "Take the other one, then."

"No!" Nico bolts for the back door.

But Rahki's too quick. In one swift movement she hoists her duster, drags her gloved fingers down its surface, and sweeps it under Nico's feet in a dive. He falls forward with a shout as Rahki binds his foot to the floor.

"You broke my ankle!" he screams, reaching for his bound foot.

The Maid Commander presses her sword against his neck. "Quiet, or I'm going to tailor you myself, suit." She lifts his chin with her blade. "Agapios should never have brought you through our doors."

Nico scowls up at her, clenching his teeth in pain. "Maybe not, but you still owe me my wages."

Rahki strikes her duster and slaps Nico's face, binding his lips shut.

"I've wanted to close that mouth for so long," she says, clapping the dust from her gloves.

She breaks one of the flared splinters off her duster and curls it around Nico's wrists. The wood shimmers as it tightens, binding him like handcuffs. I smile as Nico shouts another muffled insult. Serves him right.

The MC grins too. "Back to the Hotel. We will sort this out there."

The maids support Nico—one on either side—as we make our way back to the Corridor. A third maid carries the sliver in his belt, holstered beside his duster.

Nico winces with every limping step. His ankle might very well be broken, but I don't care. He betrayed me—I want him to suffer. Unfortunately, the binding between us causes my ankle to hurt a bit too. I find myself limping the closer we get to the Corridor.

"You okay?" Rahki asks.

"Yeah," I say, gritting my teeth. "I promise, I don't get in a lot of fights."

She chuckles and hands my coin back to me. "You did good."

I turn it over in my hand. It seems . . . heavier now. "I don't *feel* like I did good. I got played."

"We all did."

"You didn't. You knew he was up to something."

She twists her lips and stares off into the trees. "I didn't know Sev was a docent. I really believed him."

"Docents are people who work with the Competition?"

"That's just what we call them. There are different types of people who serve the Competition. Docents, suits . . . docents are people who've signed a contract that *requires* them to work for Stripe and the Museum. They're controlled, to a certain degree. That control can make them do things against their will, under certain circumstances. I think Sev was trying to tell me that was happening to him. But suits are different. They work with the Competition willingly."

"Why?"

"The Competition thinks of itself as a business empire. I don't know what their real goals are. I'm not even sure Agapios and the MC know. But when it comes down to it, they're all just empty people in nice suits." Her sad tone gives way to false happiness. "Anyway, Agapios is going to reward you for turning Nico in. You'll see."

She doesn't know the only reward I want is the one thing the Hotel can't give me.

"What's this hallway?" the MC asks, examining the pin binding the shack door to Stripe's Corridor.

"It belongs to the Competition," I tell her. "The Corridor's how Nico snuck me into the Hotel." I look away, ashamed.

She heaves a sigh. "I guess the truth comes better late than not at all."

My ears crackle as Rahki and I pass through the checkered Corridor. It seems so different now. Darker. Uglier. The MC's shoes echo down the hall behind us, all the way to the Alcove Door.

When we enter the back halls of the Hotel, the MC starts to say something. But as I turn to check on Nico—still in Stripe's Corridor behind us—his calculating eyes catch my attention. His gaze is locked on his sliver in the belt of the maid in front of him.

Then he looks up at me, and smirks.

Oh no. "He's about to—"

Nico throws his shoulder into one of the maids supporting him, knocking her back, and manages to slip the sliver out of the other maid's belt. He spins—hands now freed—and jabs the third maid with the pointy end of his weapon.

The woman cries out, but her scream is distorted. In fact, *she's* distorted. Shrinking. Bending. Crumpled into the tip of the sliver like a piece of paper sucked into a vacuum cleaner hose.

And then, she's gone.

Nico jukes away from the others and heads for us, limping

toward the door. I watch in utter shock as he draws closer. He made that woman disappear. Minutes ago, *I* was holding that sliver. Did it . . . did he . . . kill her?

The Maid Commander draws her sword, but I'm already moving, reaching for the open doorway to stop him. We come face to face at the threshold. I reach for his sliver, but he casts it aside and grabs the collar of my shirt.

"It's just a touch, brother," he whispers. "Trust me."

He gives me a shove and I tumble toward the ground. The MC catches me, but shoves me aside to pursue him. Nico's not running, though. He collapses to his knees at the threshold binding the Corridor to the Hotel, the glimmer of something shiny in his hand.

A plug.

Nico pops the pin halfway out of the hinge and snaps it off.

A clap, like thunder, as a wave of force bursts from the door, and I'm flying. Rolling. An electric current zips through my body as my face skids across the linoleum. Janitorial supplies rain around me. Everything hurts.

I struggle to sit up, but a weight holds me down. A metal shelf cuts into my back. My jacket tears as I push it off me.

The wind from the door whips old toiletries and moldy paper towels off the shelves and down the cramped hall. Cold air and dust stings my eyes.

He broke the pin in the hinge. Severed the binding. It's like the pin-failure, though I get the feeling this is worse. This pin wasn't just cracked—it was snapped in half. I read about this in the safety brochure. *In the event of pin-snap, do not panic.*

I steady myself as the tempest whips around me. The MC lies unconscious on the other side of the rubble. Rahki's pulling herself out from under a stack of chairs, but her leg's stuck.

Nico and the two remaining maids were still on the other side when he broke the pin, but they're gone now. And the one Nico pricked with the sliver . . .

"The hinge!" Rahki yells. "Stop the pin!"

I glance back at the door to nowhere, shielding my eyes against the gusts of icy nothing. If I don't stop it, the Hotel could lose another wing, or worse.

In the event of pin-snap, isolate and re-pin the broken door before the root system collapses.

I pull the pin Sev gave me from its sleeve and stand, bracing against the gale.

"Hurry!"

Gusts of cold, dusty air press me backwards and scrape past my face. Thank the binding we wear Chucks and not slippery formal shoes. The grip on my sneakers gives me traction enough to inch forward. Closer. Step by step. My face feels like it's being rubbed down with Sev's sandpaper, like bits of me are tearing loose and flying down the hall. Where does disintegration by magic wind fit on my list?

I grab the door and pull myself to the hinge. The broken pin is wedged in tight. I pull Sev's plug— the one I kept after the pin failure—from my jacket pocket. Slide it into place. *Pop.* The remnants of the broken pin fall to the floor.

But the wind keeps coming. In that cold, black darkness beyond the door, I can almost feel something watching me.

"Cameron!"

I slam my pin into place painfully with my bandaged palm.

The air stills.

I fall through the door and collapse to the floor on the other side. My muscles quiver. I did it. I stopped the pin-snap. *In the event of pin-snap, just don't die.*

The stillness of the room washes over me. Peaceful. Quiet.

Home.

"Cam?"

I look up to see my sister staring down at me from her wheel-chair. "Cass? What are you—" I scramble to my knees and whirl around to see the Hotel back halls through my bedroom door. Not the hall outside my bedroom, like it should be. I didn't have time to realize that re-pinning the door would also bind the Hotel to Oma's house.

Wonder practically drools down Cass's face as she gazes past the threshold. "What . . . is that?"

I bite my thumbnail. What was she doing in my room, anyway? I can't get out of this one. I remember what it was like for me the first time I saw something that didn't belong on the other side of a door. And Cass is *far* more curious than I am.

She rolls toward the devastated hallway.

I grab the handles of her chair to stop her. "You can't go in there." On the other side, Rahki shoves the chairs off herself, and the MC stirs.

Cass turns one of her killer stink-eyes on me. "Is that where you've been?"

I swallow, noticing the worn, gray coin hanging from her neck. There'll be no stopping her now. There are magics in the world, and she's just seen one.

She grits her teeth and punches me in the leg. "You left us! Just like Dad, you *left* us!"

"I-I can explain." Though I have no idea what I'd say. Angry Cass is a running theme throughout the WWTD list.

I reach up to touch Dad's coin at my neck for comfort, but it's not there.

My heart stops. I dig under my collar, frantically searching for the thing that's comforted me my whole life.

It's gone.

Then I remember Nico grabbing my collar. Pushing me back. *It's just a touch, brother.* He snatched Dad's coin when he grabbed me! Nico stole it.

My breath sticks in my throat. My arms tingle. Through bleary eyes, I catch a shadow of movement at the far end of the Hotel alcove as a tall, pale man rounds the corner.

Agapios.

"Not now," I whisper.

The Old Man floats through the wreckage on bony legs, his

hollow eyes sending sparks of electricity down my arms.

"Follow my lead," I tell Cass. "Don't say or do *anything* unless I tell you to. Just . . . be quiet."

"No one tells me who to be," she snaps.

"Listen to me!" I whisper-yell. "For once. Please."

"Mr. Cameron." Agapios steps into my bedroom and scans the safety posters on my walls. "Where are we?"

Cass tries to roll out of my grip toward him. "I don't know who you are, but you don't just waltz into my brother's room like that."

Great. Off to a bad start already.

"Ah. I wondered when we would get to meet your sister." Agapios strokes his knobby chin. "This is your home, then?" Behind him, Rahki helps the Maid Commander out of the rubble.

"My grandmother's house," I say. I've got to keep everything under control. Though I'm not sure what that looks like anymore.

Agapios studies the hinge. "Where did you get this pin?"

"From one of the doormen," I reply. "Sev. Vsevolod Pronichev. He told me it was a way out. I used it in the pin-failure a few days ago, too, but . . . I think he and Nico were the ones who caused that pin-failure."

"Ah." He nods as if it all makes sense.

But nothing makes sense. If Stripe and the others were lying to me, does that mean old death-face here is the good guy? I picture that maid being sucked into the sliver like a milkshake through a straw, and Nico snapping the pin as if it was nothing. I was helping them.

No, not helping. I was only trying to find Dad. I'm one of the good guys. I've got to be.

The Old Man glides around my room, investigating every- thing. My posters. The dusty bed. The cat statue with its ever- bobbing paw.

"What's going on?" Cass whispers.

"Quiet," I whisper back.

"Mr. Cameron has just saved a great many people." Agapios's angular cheekbones cast long shadows down his face. "Your brother is a hero."

A hero? I'm no hero.

"Saved who? From what?" Cass gestures to the door. "And what happened to our house?!"

Agapios turns to me. "Your sister does not know?"

I shake my head. "You said the secret of the Hotel wasn't mine to share."

He smiles. "So I did. Maybe it's time we broke that rule." Agapios kneels in front of Cass, taking her hand in his spindly fingers. "Ms. Cassia, I knew your mother and father. There is much to tell you. Would you join me for dinner?"

"Uh . . . y-yes?" Cass stutters. She never stutters.

"Perfect." Agapios stands and claps his hands once, raising his voice. "We welcome a new guest tonight." Then, taking her hand again and giving it a long kiss, he says, "Ms. Cassia, welcome to The Hotel Between."

22

Keys to the Kingdom

My stomach lurches at the thought of going back aboard the Dining Ship.

The past few hours have been a whirlwind. I haven't seen Cass since Agapios brought her in as his honored guest and instructed the staff to prepare us for dinner at the Concierge's Table. In the meantime, I got a haircut and a tuxedo, and even Rahki— invited at the MC's request—wears a snazzy new pantsuit for the occasion.

"What's keeping her?" I ask as we wait in the Pyramid Foyer reception area. "Shouldn't Cass be here already?"

"We're early," Rahki says, sitting on the embroidered formal couch.

I huff and flop down beside her. It's strange to think a few hours ago I would have been mortified at the idea of Cass alone with Agapios. Now I only wish I was with her, hearing whatever the Old Man's telling her.

My hand keeps reaching for my neck, where Dad's coin should be. Why would Nico take it, anyway? He can't use it. And Stripe still wants me to find the Greenhouse. I can't do that without the coin. Nothing makes sense.

Pretty soon guests start lining up outside the *Accommodation* turners. Breakfast, lunch, supper—meals aboard the *Accommodation* are always a big deal. But a message went out hours ago informing everyone that tonight's New Year's Eve dinner will be a formal affair. Glittery dresses, linen suits trimmed with brilliant colors . . . even in my tux, I feel underdressed.

I shove my hands in my pockets to keep from touching my collar, and feel the pin Stripe gave me. With Dad's coin, Nico could lead Stripe to the Greenhouse without me, and I'd never get the chance to exchange it for Dad. If only I could speak to Agapios, tell him everything. If I do that, though, I'm definitely not getting Dad back.

"Why didn't the Old Man want to talk to me?" I ask Rahki. "Did I do something wrong?"

She laughs. "No way. Though you probably should've been up front and told them you were Melissa and Reinhart's kid when you first arrived. Not saying anything made them suspicious. That doesn't change the fact you stopped a pin-snap, though."

"Was it that big of a deal?" I say, doubtfully. "We just had a pin-failure the other day."

"This was something else." She folds her hands in her lap. "Binding two places like we do puts a lot of magic tension on those pins. When they crack, the magic leaks. But when they *snap*, all that magic floods out like water from a busted hydrant. All the pins are weak right now, which means they could all snap under the pressure. Breaking the binding like Nico did could have dismantled the entire Hotel. But you stopped it. That's huge."

Rahki waves across the gathering crowd at Cass, who's being rolled through the doors by a steward I know as Mr. Sakamoto-san.

"Wow," Rahki says. "Your sister's stunning."

And she's not wrong. I've never seen Cass look so pretty. Decked out in a sparkly blue dress, hair in an up-do—even riding a brass wheelchair that sparkles under the pyramid's skylights.

"This place is awesome!" Cass says in her loud, outside-use-only voice as Sakamoto-san rolls her over. "I can't believe you tried to keep this to yourself, Cam. You are completely, totally selfish."

"What did he say?" I ask, ignoring her jab.

"The Old Man?" She rubs her hands maniacally. "Secrets."

I groan. "Come on."

"No. You kept this place from me, so I get to keep some things from you." Cass-logic: dense as a brick wall, and utterly unscalable. "So?" she says, raising her eyebrows impishly. "What are you two talking about?"

"The Old Man's going to honor Cameron," Rahki says.

I roll my eyes. "He's not."

"I guarantee he will," she replies. "I overheard him telling the MC you've got as much potential as your mother."

"What's that supposed to mean?"

Cass interrupts with a hearty laugh. "Yeah, right. Cam's got about as much potential as I have diamonds in my jewelry box."

SEAN EASLEY

I grumble. Cass doesn't have a jewelry box.

She gazes around the foyer, lost in the gold and blue decor and sandstone pharaohs. Cass still has no idea why I came here. And I can't tell her just yet. Especially when I don't know if I'll be able to get him back.

"What do slivers do?" I ask Rahki instead. "What did Nico do to that maid?"

Rahki frowns. "Slivers are like pins, only the Competition uses them on people, something that's strictly forbidden by the Embassy. They're bound to a place, and when you stick them in a person"—she swallows—"that person is transported to the bound location. Violently."

I remember the pained look on the maid's face when she was folded up and sucked inside. "Then . . . she's alive?"

"Probably. But slivers are crude and unpredictable. They don't always do what you want. And they hurt. A lot."

"Tell me more. What do you know about the Competition? Do they have any weaknesses? We have to stop them."

"Oh good grief," Cass says, sipping her flute. "You're always so worried."

I shoot her a nasty look. "Yeah, and for good reason. Did Agapios even tell you what goes on around here?"

"Did he tell *you*?" She lifts an infuriating eyebrow.

Before I can respond, L'Maitre—the tall, willowy master of the dining services—appears through one of the turners and clears his throat. "Follow me."

The *Accommodation* looks different for tonight's event. Each window around the cruise ship has been bound to a location—like the sun-windows in the Mezz, and the guest elevator walls—displaying rain forest rivers, packed downtown boroughs, a big-top circus show, the swirling winds of a desert. The chandeliers have been dimmed to allow the fireworks exploding in some of the windows to flash their own light across the banquet hall.

I can't believe it's New Year's already. Only two days left before my time runs out.

The Concierge's Table has sat empty since I first arrived at the Hotel, its cloth napkins folded into tall towers on the plates. Two-story gold tree centerpieces sprout from the tables, dripping with gemstone fruit over the seats. The metallic leaves shimmer as the ship rises and falls. The crown jewels of the *Accommodation*.

When I see them now, though, all I can think of is the harsh, jagged kitchen table tree Stripe conjured. He demolished everything as easily as he laughed. No pins. No dusters or slivers. Just a thought, and his black key.

The hosts seat us at our place settings, marked by cards with our names written in flowing script. Only two seats remain empty, with cards that read GRAND CONCIERGE, AGAPIOS PANOTIERRI and MAID COMMANDER, JEHANNA LA PUCELLE.

Cass leans over the arm of her wheelchair, giggling like a goober. If she knew what I know, she wouldn't be so flippant. Trouble's growing, alongside the seasickness in my stomach.

Around the hall, waiters take drink and dinner orders. Rahki and Cass talk and laugh about the places Rahki's been, but I can't laugh. Not as long as Stripe has Dad, and Nico has his coin.

At last, the intercom announces the arrival of the two missing leaders of the Hotel.

Everyone in the banquet hall rises as Agapios and the MC enter through the double doors atop the grand staircase. The Maid Commander glitters in a green dress embroidered with flowers, with long satin gloves almost to her shoulders. Her bobbed hair is spiked and feathered, held in place with a diamond-studded comb. If it weren't for the burn on her face, she would be unrecognizable. Descending the steps alongside her, Agapios wears a tux like mine, only slightly more formal than his usual getup. His knobby knees poke out of his slacks with every graceful step.

"Good evening, friends," Agapios says as we take our seats at the table and everyone in the hall goes back to their dinners. "A pleasure to dine with you."

"Thank you, sir," Rahki replies.

After everything with Stripe, I don't exactly feel up for conversation. Thankfully, Cass is a fountain of words, talking on and on about her travel shows, asking if what she's seen is anything like the real thing.

When the food comes, all I can do is pick at it. I imagine what Dad's been eating all these years, and whether Stripe's docents have infiltrated Chef Silva's kitchen. I wonder what poison smells like. Maybe I should have searched which poisons can be put in food, so I'd know what'll kill me and what won't. Poison is number 5 on my list, because there are so many, and the majority of them kill in really nasty ways. Oh, please don't let this food be poisoned. . . .

Agapios turns to me. "Is dinner not to your liking?"

I set my fork and knife down and stare at my surf and turf. My gut bobs with the ocean. "It's fancier than I'm used to."

Cass laughs. "At home he only eats Pop-Tarts and frozen waffles." She shovels another mouthful of the decadent meal the cooks prepared special for her. "Cam doesn't like change. He doesn't go places. He likes routine."

The MC lifts an eyebrow. "He came here, did he not? And Mr. Cameron's performed all the errands we've given."

"He does what he has to," Cass says, "but that's all. He doesn't take risks."

"Don't talk about me like I'm not here," I say.

"Quite right." Agapios dabs his lips. "However, I do wish you had taken the risk and told me the truth when you first came to the Hotel." He glances at the MC. "Your deception about who you were had Jehanna very worried about your intentions."

"I'm sorry," I say, avoiding his dark, sunken eyes. "I was . . . scared. I didn't know who to trust."

He waves my apology away. "No concern. The Curator is a very good liar."

"The Curator?" I ask. "You mean Mr. Stripe."

"This House has been at odds with him a long time." Agapios takes another careful bite.

I have to look away to keep from being sick. "Does Stripe really run a museum?"

The Maid Commander scoffs. "That's what he calls it."

Agapios shoots her a disapproving look, and then turns back to me. "The man you call Stripe is a collector, of sorts. Objects, people, anything with a binding he can add to his gallery."

"But why?" I ask. "What does he want?"

"Power. Stripe hungers for it, like a dog hungers for meat. The more he binds to himself and those under him, the stronger he grows."

"Stronger for what?"

The Old Man smiles. "Those secrets will reveal themselves to you in time, should you stay with us." A pause as he studies my face. "Your parents would be proud of you."

A flood of warmth momentarily calms my nauseated stomach.

Agapios raises his glass. "To Cameron and Cassia Kuhn, children of The Hotel Between." The others raise their drinks, echoing the toast.

"At least tell me this," I say as everyone sips their drinks. "Why'd you let me stay if you thought I was with the Competition?"

"Because they wanted to find the Greenhouse," Cass says, taking a mouthful of chicken. "Duh."

I sit back, shocked. "*You* know about the Greenhouse?"

"I told her," Agapios says. "Knowing who she was from the start, I told her more than I told you when we first met. And yes, it's true. We allowed you freedom to roam the hotel in hopes that your father's coin would lead you to our missing Greenhouse. I fear, however, that if Reinhart's coin held its location, you would have already found it."

A memory of pressing the fourth floor button flashes through me.

Agapios eyes me carefully. "Unless you have, and you have not told us. *Do* you know where your father hid the Greenhouse?"

My stomach lurches as everyone at the table turns to look at me. "No," I say.

"Pity." Agapios goes back to his pasta.

Why'd I lie like that? He needs to know how close Stripe is to finding it.

I finger the pin in my pocket again. "So, Stripe wants the Greenhouse . . . because he wants power?"

"He wants to stop us," the Old Man says. "Our mission threatens him. Should he break that last hidden connection between the Hotel and the Greenhouse, the Hotel will fall apart. Pin-failures are only the beginning. Once he has the binding of the Vesima tree . . . "

A hush falls over the table.

Stripe's going to find it. Nico's got Dad's coin, and he knows about the fourth floor. It's only a matter of time. And it's my fault. So why can't I bring myself to say anything?

I bet it's because of Nico. If he were here, he'd withhold as much information as possible to manipulate the situation. Could he be doing that now? Manipulating me through our contract? Making me think like him?

"Sir," Rahki says, breaking the silence, "did the pin-snap cause any further damage?"

Agapios grins at the Maid Commander. "Your protégé is very focused."

The MC smiles approvingly, but it looks weird on her. As if the knots in a tree grew a personality and are now trying to change shape to match.

"We have not re-bound the wings since the failure," Agapios says. "But we *have* rescued our stranded guests. They have been compensated and returned to their homes. As for the pin-snap, Cameron's quick thinking saved the Hotel from great catastrophe. We are ever in his debt."

My stomach groans.

"It is for this reason we honor you tonight, Cameron."

Agapios stands and waves to one of the hostesses, who presses a button on a column supporting the upper balconies. There's a click and a whirr as a shiny microphone lowers from the ceiling over Agapios's place setting.

"Guests and ambassadors." The concierge's amplified voice echoes. Fireworks explode in a few of the windows, flashing pink and green light across the banquet hall to celebrate the New Year. "Tonight is a special night. Tonight we honor one of our newest employees for his selfless service and dedication." He bows and holds out a hand. "Please welcome Mr. Cameron Kuhn."

L'Maitre appears behind me as applause ripples through the room. "Rise, and bow."

He pulls my chair out, and I stand to meet the ovation. I shove my hands in my pockets to steady myself, and wrap my fingers around Stripe's pin the way I used to clutch Dad's coin.

"In his short time with us," Agapios announces, "young Cameron has twice prevented failures of the magic that binds our beloved Hotel, foiled the plans of our Competition, and revealed traitors in our midst who sought to shut us down."

His smile turns my heart to stone. This honor . . . it isn't true. I mean—I did those things—but I was working with the enemy. I was a traitor too. Even now, with Stripe's pin in my palm, I know that if I still had the chance I'd do whatever it took to get Dad back.

But the applause feels good. No one's ever looked at me the way these people are right now. Even if they're going to forget it happened when they leave this place, it means something.

Flashes of blue burst over a distant cityscape and a smile curls up my face. This must be how Nico feels—so proud of himself. So powerful, with all his secrets. Can he feel my pride, in this moment? No. I can't let him influence me. I shouldn't be proud. Ugh, this is all so complicated.

Agapios continues. "Even more exciting for those who have been with us many years is the discovery that Cameron and his sister, Cassia, are the children of our own Reinhart and Melissa Kuhn."

A hush falls over the room, followed by an awkward round of applause from the older staff. Guests murmur to their neighbors, but I can't understand why. Did they know my parents too? Did they look up to them?

"Melissa was a singularly special servant of the Hotel. Years ago I selected her to be my Concierge-in-Training. If not for her untimely departure, she would likely have been the one addressing you tonight, instead of me."

Mom was . . . what?

I look to Cass, who's smiling like it's no big deal. Agapios must've told her. But what does that mean?

"More than any other member of our staff, Melissa had plans. Plans to thwart our Competition and expand the Hotel's mission far beyond these walls. Had those unfortunate events twelve years ago turned out differently, the threat of the Competition would be greatly diminished, and Cameron and Cassia would have grown up among us."

Mom had plans to stop Stripe. Dad must've been helping her. That's why it all happened the way it did. They were a threat to the Competition, and Stripe stopped them.

The boom and pop of the fireworks increases.

"Cameron's actions prove him as much a child of the Hotel as any," Agapios says. "Now, as a gesture of gratitude for his service and that of his mother, the Hotel wishes to present Cameron with his mother's key."

He pulls a shiny, pearl skeleton key from his inner jacket pocket. The detail and design glitters in the spotlight.

"Go to him," L'Maitre urges amid the applause.

My feet move on their own, heavy, as if caked with mud. The leaning of the ship makes me stumble.

Agapios hands me the pearl key, and a wave of new memories floods through me.

Standing in the spotlight aboard the Accommodation. *Guests applauding my appointment. Me, pulling this same key from a jacket pocket and inserting it into the elevator console. Pressing the button for the fourth floor.*

These are Mom's memories. *This* is the key from my dreams. The pearl topscrew Nico wanted me to steal, it's . . . Mom's.

"This great House requires more than knowledge of its workings to lead it. For many years, we have searched for Melissa's replacement, and now the Hotel informs me we have found it." The weight in my chest grows as Agapios pulls me to his side and wraps cold, skeletal fingers around my shoulder. "This key provides access to all areas of the Hotel. Mr. Cameron will need it in his new role as my Concierge-in-Training."

My stomach rolls—partly from the list of the ship, partly because I can't believe what I'm hearing. The twinkling explosions outside the windows quicken, illuminating the dining hall with an air of celebration.

The Old Man gazes down at me. "He who knows his master's will only fulfills his obligation. But he who does not know his master's will, and accomplishes it anyway, will be given much. This is only the beginning of Cameron's story, should he accept my offer and begin training to take over my role as Grand Concierge of The Hotel Between."

I'm so confused. The lights dazzle me as the fireworks reach their finale. The leaves hanging from the tree centerpieces shimmer and move, and I feel so very, very small and puny, yet big and important at the same time. And my stomach, it's . . . it's—

I fall to my knees and vomit all over the floor. It's like everything inside wants to get out, and everything outside wants to run away as fast as it can.

My face tingles when I pause. I gasp for air, and retch all over again.

I'm dying. I'm finally dying.

I slump to the floor and wait for the end.

23

The Fourth Floor

The hosts carry me to my Hotel room. Even after I'm back on land, the world keeps shifting. I lie on my bed in nauseated agony as rain falls in sheets outside my Warsaw window.

Rahki calls the room phone to tell me Cass is bunking with her for the night. Sana brings a brass plate with crackers, sliced sour apples, and a crystal cup of ginger ale. I'm dying, and she thinks snacks are going to help?

But an hour later I find myself still in bed, sucking on one of the apple slices. Not dead. And I do feel better . . . at least, a bit. I guess it was just seasickness.

The truth about my parents gnaws at my brain. *Munch-munch-munch.* Mom wasn't just staff, she was training to be Agapios's replacement. *Bite-bite-bite.* Dad stole the Greenhouse on the same night Mom died, and left the secret of its location with me. *Chew-chew-chew.* That secret is my only way of getting him back, and I've lost it.

Mom had a plan to stop Stripe, but Stripe was a step ahead of her. He killed her for it. Then Dad hid the Greenhouse, Cass, and me. He almost got away, but Stripe caught him.

I glance at the pearl key on my nightstand, and the crossed-keys lapel pin L'Maitre brought me later. Mom's topscrew. The key to all those locked doors. My key to the fourth floor.

Gnaw-gnaw-gnaw.

Dad must've known the plan. It's probably bound to his coin, but I don't have that anymore. I've got to find a way to get him back and to save the Hotel from whatever Stripe has planned.

Leaves rustling, branches creaking, the tree rises before me, waving in a wind I can't feel. The doors hanging from its boughs clap open and shut, but through their frames I no longer see the same worldly destinations they were once bound to. Now, all that lies beyond those doors is the cold, menacing darkness.

The door at the base of the tree opens, revealing a black, starry night.

A woman steps up to the threshold. She looks at me, her dark hair shimmering as it whips in the wind from the door. Mom. She's whispering something, her voice carried by the whoosh of the leaves.

Cameron . . .

I run for her, but she's falling now, into the emptiness behind the door. As I reach the doorway, I find myself back in the elevator. I lean over the edge and watch her drift into the black. Coins spill around her, floating, glistening as she falls.

The darkness has teeth. It's gobbling her up, devouring her and all her coins.

The invisible pin inside me snaps, and I turn to see the button for the fourth floor light up. And next to that, the Man in the Pinstriped Suit, looking back at me.

I wake up screaming Mom's name for the fourth time in just the past few hours.

Tonight's dreams don't make sense. They're not like the memories from Dad's coin. They're more like the beckoning dreams I had before I came here. One thing is clear, though: It wasn't Agapios's face Dad saw in that elevator—it was Stripe's. Stripe was there with them. He must've pushed Mom to her death. And if Stripe killed Mom, he'll kill Dad too.

There has to be a way to keep the Greenhouse away from Stripe and get Dad back at the same time. Before I can figure out what that is, though, I've got to find it.

So I call down to Rahki's room.

"Uh, *allō?*" she answers groggily.

"Get dressed and meet me on the Mezz." I pause. Do I really want to do this? "And bring Cass."

I grab Mom's topscrew from the bedside table before I leave. The pearl key fits my hand perfectly, like an extension of myself. Holding it makes me feel stronger, like I can actually do something to stop Stripe.

When I reach the sunny Courtyard, I instantly spot Rahki sitting on a bench in the shadow of the fountain-tree. Cass sits next to her in her normal, black wheelchair, wearing Hotel gift shop pajamas covered with cartoon keys and clutching a pillow to her chest.

"I told you to get dressed," I say.

"It's stupid o'clock in the morning," Cass whines. "I'm not getting dressed if I don't have to."

Rahki rubs her eyes. "What's going on?"

There's no going back. "I need to know what's on the fourth floor."

"Now?" Rahki says. "It's the middle of the night."

I look up at the bright sky over the Mezz. "It's daytime somewhere, right?" She crosses her arms, and I sigh. I have to tell her something to get her to go along with what I'm asking her to do. "I remember, Rahki."

She blinks. "You remem—" Then the light dawns in her eyes. "The Greenhouse?"

"I think I know where it is, but I want to make sure." I hold up Mom's topscrew. "Will you go with us to the fourth floor?"

"You *and* Cass?" Rahki tweaks her mouth. "It's not the easiest path."

"Hey!" Cass protests.

"Yes," I say. "Both of us. If this is the last thing Dad did before he disappeared, I want us both there to find out why."

That's not true. I just want Cass with me when Stripe gives us Dad back.

"That's settled," Cass says with a mischievous smile. "Let's go for a little walk, then. I really need to stretch my wheels."

• • •

Rahki pushes Cass's chair onto the service elevator. All three of us have donned the Hotel's heavy winter coats—a fourth floor necessity, Rahki says. I had no idea she knew so much about it.

I pause at the lift doors, fingering Stripe's pin in my pocket, right next to Mom's key. I'm still deceiving them. But it'll all be worth it. This is for the best.

"You coming?" Cass asks. "I could be sleeping, you know."

"Yeah." I slide Stripe's pin into the open pin-sleeve above the one to my bedroom, and step into the cage.

Rahki nods at the keyhole next to the button for the fourth floor. I trace it with my finger, take a deep breath, and turn the topscrew in the lock.

The elevator starts up with a clatter of gears and cables. Cool, musty air cuts through the cage, sending a tingle up my spine. Every time I blink, I see Mom's face and Stripe's sneer as she falls into the black.

"What do you remember, exactly?" Rahki asks as we ascend.

"Too much," I say. "And not enough. I know Dad came to the fourth floor, and that it was important. He had Mom's key. And . . . something happened."

Cass eyes me with suspicion, but I ignore the look.

"He bound a door somewhere on the fourth floor, and hid it from everyone. I know it."

"Hid it? How? Where?" Rahki asks.

"I'll know when I see it."

The elevator creaks to a stop, and the doors ding open to a stony mountain path. Icy wind whips into the Shaft, carrying a burst of snow with it and chilling me to the roots of my teeth.

Cass whistles at the grandness of the scene before us.

"*This* is the fourth floor?" I ask. "It's just . . . mountains."

"It's a buffer," Rahki says. "Protection."

"You've been here before?"

She nods and follows Cass out into the icy wind. "Fourth floor is where the Hotel keeps things safe," she says. "Its location is secret, but if I were to guess, I'd say we're somewhere in the Himalayas."

Cass practically squeals her excitement at the view. "Awesome."

Her reaction makes me smile. I always thought she was crazy for wanting to travel, but maybe I was wrong, like I've been wrong about everything else. With the right accommodations, like the Hotel, she could have her wish. She really could do all the things I thought she couldn't.

"The Monastery's up ahead," Rahki says. "It's a climb, but not too far." She guides Cass's chair around a boulder and up the rocky path, out of sight.

I squeeze my arms for warmth and scan the horizon. I can feel the path pulling me. Calling me forward.

It strikes me that my coin can still be tracked, even out here. Could the Competition use it to find me? That's a risk I can't take.

I turn back to the elevator and toss my coin onto the cage inside. No one can follow me now. Not even the Hotel.

I'm coming, Dad.

. . .

My footing slips as I shove Cass's chair up the steep mountain path. She doesn't typically like me pushing her—she's all about doing everything on her own—but whenever it's rocky I usually slip in without her having to say anything. This gravel is by far the hardest terrain we've faced, especially with this annoying pain still in my ankle. On one side of us, a cliff face rises into the sky. On the other, the ground drops away into clouds. We're so high even the weather can't reach us. My lungs ache from the lack of oxygen. Biting wind stings my cheeks.

Rahki swears we're not far from what she keeps calling the Monastery, but *not far* quickly turns into *really, really far* when you're pushing your sister's wheelchair up a steep, rocky incline.

I keep close watch on Cass, trying to make sure she's okay without actually asking. She hates when I fuss over her, but so many things could go wrong with her body at this altitude. And if something *did* go wrong, I'd never get her to a hospital in time.

"Whoa . . . ," Cass says as we round the next bend.

The path rises to an enormous structure carved into the cliffs. Blocky, gray stone walls jut from the rock face, dropping into the ravine below. Smoke curls from slitted windows. Strings of rectangular flags flutter in the wind.

"It's huge." Cass's voice shudders as her chair bounces over the rocks.

"It's a fortress," Rahki says. "Our safe place. Agapios uses it to protect the Hotel's most precious guests."

At last we reach a pair of arched doors.

The Monastery looms over us. Warrior statues on either side of the enormous gate seem to grip their spears tighter as we draw near.

"We made it," I say, unable to hide the genuine surprise in my voice.

"Shame you didn't slide off." Cass gives me an over-the-top wink. I roll my eyes.

"Hello?" I call out, trying not to look at the grotesque, tusked masks on the warrior icons' faces. The air is so thin I might pass out. "We need to come in!"

Rahki laughs. "Haven't you figured this stuff out yet? A knocked door . . . "

" . . . is always opened." Of course. I step forward and rap on the knocker.

The click of a lock and the squeal of hinges sound in the shadows to our left. A hooded head pops out of a smaller, hidden door and waves us inside.

The man—dressed in a robe tied at the waist with rope—ushers us into a small, cubby-lined room full of rolled coats and cloaks. He greets us in a language I don't recognize—long, wavy vowels and harsh, popping consonants. Rahki must understand, because she responds before translating.

"He's wondering why the Maid Commander didn't come." She nods to my lapel pin. "But he saw your cross-keys and figured out who we were. He says the children are waiting."

The kids? They're the Hotel's most precious guests?

The monk opens a door, and the sounds of children tumble into the hallway, all laughter and giggles. We step with a binding crackle into a warm, walled lawn. Painted stucco walls and lattice covered in honey-scented vines. Oversize half-man/half-horse statues playfully strum stone instruments. Soccer balls—I mean, *fútbols*—fly everywhere.

"This is where the Maid Service takes the kids we pick up," Rahki says. "The Monastery's a place of healing. All over the world—in every country, even yours—there are kids who've been taken, hurt, mistreated. Here, the Hotel hopes to undo the damage inflicted on them."

Kids grab drinks and snacks from long wooden tables, and a group on the far side plays some variety of tag I've never seen. The scared girl from our Budapest mission plays a hand game with others on a picnic blanket.

"What does the Hotel do with them after?" Cass asks.

"Depends on what the children want. The Hotel's job is to free them, heal them, and give them a choice."

Cass basks in the sunlight. "Can they stay if they want?"

Rahki grins. "I did. But some need the kind of care only a real family can bring. It's up to them where they end up. The Hotel lets them choose their own destination."

The boy from the Congo with the missing leg runs alongside the *fútbol* players. It takes a moment before I register what

I'm seeing. He's not just standing—he's *running*, fully upright, on a stone leg with a tiny, coin-size slot in the side. A prosthetic-leg icon, made just for him.

I finally understand. The mission, the guests . . . it's all about these children. The Hotel provides kids who've been hurt a home, and a chance for a better future. I can't betray this. Dad, Mom . . . they both did what they could to keep the Greenhouse out of Stripe's hands because they knew this was at stake.

There's got to be another way to get Dad back.

"We're not inside the Hotel here, are we?" I ask. "The path . . . the buffer . . . "

"It's still connected," Rahki says. "This place is protected by the same magic that keeps the Competition's suits and docents out of the Hotel. The only way our enemies can get in is if someone bound to the Hotel invites them in."

"And Nico? How'd he get into the Hotel?"

She twists her lips. "He was invited, just like all these kids were."

Cass scoffs. "Who made *that* mistake?"

Rahki shrugs. "I don't know. But he shouldn't be able to get in anymore. The Hotel severed his coin. Without it binding him to the Hotel, Nico's got no connection."

Thank goodness.

Cass's eyes glisten as she watches the kids play in the yard. When we get Dad back, hopefully, he'll want to stay here too. I can keep working with Agapios. Dad will fill me in on Mom's plan to stop Stripe. Maybe the Hotel's magic can even keep Cass healthy, and give her the opportunity to do all the things she couldn't before. And Oma can come, and we'll continue to save all these kids. Together.

Cameron . . .

I spin around to find the source of the voice from my dreams. It's louder than ever.

Through an ivy-covered arch on the far wall, I see . . . an illusion—like a shadowy figure waiting for me. Or maybe it's not an illusion. Maybe it's a memory.

"I'll be right back," I say.

Cass furrows her brow. "Where are you going?"

"Just . . . stay here. I want to check something." And I head through the arch.

My path is clear. I march through the stone Monastery halls, weaving through ancient passages, passing door after door. It's almost like I'm watching someone else navigate this maze instead of me.

Before long, I arrive in a dark cellar that smells of mold, facing a cedar armoire hidden in shadow. It's here. It's really here. And it's no wonder no one's found it—the cellar's full of cobweb-covered barrels and years of dust. It doesn't look like anyone's been down here in ages.

I peek behind the armoire, but it's so dark I can't see anything. I reach into the shadows, and my hand finds a door handle. Yes.

It takes all my strength to move the armoire. When I finally get it to slide, it leans. I try to steady it, to keep it upright, but it's too heavy.

The armoire crashes to the stone floor.

Wiping sweat from my brow, I take in the plain, rotting door behind it. I turn the knob, but nothing happens. Memories flood through me again. Glittery foam. A pearl key. A magic keyhole. This door was locked with Mom's topscrew, like Nico locked the Alcove Door. Is that why it doesn't show on the maps?

I pull out Mom's key and turn it in the wood with a shimmer of foam. The door opens, and sunlight and the smell of wet grass draw me into the bright green reeds beyond.

There it is. The Vesima.

The tree I've dreamed about for months stands atop a hill before me. I never could've believed it would be this grand. The trunk is as big around as Oma's house, taller than Cass's hospital. Twisting, leafy branches hide the sun, letting only a few dappled shafts of light through the canopy to shine patches on the waving grass. A glass dome curls up and over it, speckled with condensation. A wall of hedges forms a circle around the inside of the dome, with doors at the north, south, east, and west.

The tree looks slightly different from the one in my dreams—no doors hang from these branches, nor is there one in the massive trunk—but deep down I know this is it.

I can't let it stay hidden any longer. The Hotel needs this tree to continue its mission. I have to tell Agapios before Stripe—

"It's even more impressive in real life, isn't it?"

I whirl to find Nico, leaning heavily on a crutch in front of the doorway that leads out of the dome.

"Hey blood-bro," he says, with a twisted smile. "Looks like you did it. You found the thing everyone's been looking for, and with a day to spare."

A rush of adrenaline plows through my chest. "How did . . . what are you doing here?"

He shrugs. "I followed you."

"But I got rid of my coin. And the Hotel severed yours. You're not allowed to be here."

"You are, though. And I'm bound to you, blood-bro. Everything we have, remember? I sensed you were on the move, and so I followed our connection. As long as you're welcome in the Hotel, so am I."

The contract. He can still get in, because of me. "How'd you find me?"

Nico points to my pin-sleeves, and the pin Stripe gave me in Honduras. "You don't really think Stripe would give you a direct line back to him, do you?" He grins. "That's not a pin. But it did allow us to track you."

I slide Stripe's pin out of its sleeve and examine it. It looks just like all the others. How could I have been so stupid? "Dad's coin . . . "

"I never could access his memories, even after the contract. My binding's too far removed from his. But taking your dad's coin sure lit a fire under you to find this place fast."

My heart collapses. In looking for a way to stop them from

finding the Greenhouse, I led Nico right to it.

I rub my eyes with my palms, wishing I could rub Nico out of existence. "Why are you doing this? The Hotel's helping people. Why do you want to hurt them?"

"I don't want to *hurt* anyone." Nico pushes off the door and hobbles past me, gazing up at the enormous tree. "Everyone does what they think is right, Cam. I know what I'm doing. You have to trust me."

Trust. "I'll never be able to believe another word you say."

He sighs. "You're probably right. But I bet you'll believe me when I say you'd better hurry back, before all the action's over."

Action?

Cass! Rahki and the kids! If Nico's still connected to the Hotel, then he could invite Stripe—

I rush back through the door to the Monastery cellar, leaving Nico and the Greenhouse behind.

"I'm sorry!" he calls after me.

I clench my teeth as I run up the stone passages. If Stripe hurts Cass because of me, I'll never forgive myself.

24

Children of the Hotel

I burst through the door into the Monastery yard, and freeze at the sight before me.

"No, no, no."

A dozen men and women in sharp suits fill the lawn, each brandishing a long, wooden sliver. The children are running, struggling to get away from Stripe's docents. The monk who led us here is shouting, directing the children to flee, but they're not fast enough.

I watch in horror as a docent pokes his sliver into the arm of one of the girls from Budapest, and the girl is slurped into the sliver's tip like water through a drain.

"Stop!" I shout. "Leave them alone!"

But the docents keep pouring through a door on the far side.

A woman in an apron rushes across the yard, gathering children to her. Little ones cry as they run for safety. Bells chime overhead.

A team of monks appears in a far doorway, brandishing tall wooden staves that look like bigger versions of Rahki's duster. They face off against the docents nearest them, striking the tips of their staves across the lawn like matches being lit, sparking as they slam the glittering ends into the intruders to bind them to the ground.

But there are too many.

I find Cass with Rahki next to the refreshment tables. Rahki wields her duster like some ancient warrior, striking the baton with her gloved fingers to bind the enemies to the earth, the wall, even each other. She's protecting Cass, along with the few children who've taken shelter behind her.

"What can I do?" I ask.

Rahki binds a woman's face to the grass, kicks the sliver away, and shoots me a glare. "Someone invited the docents in. No way they could have reached the Monastery otherwise. Did you do this?"

"I-I—"

My hesitation is all the answer she needs.

Rahki skims her fingers down the baton, gathering a film of glittering dust, and then swings the duster under my legs, knocking me onto my butt. I scramble to get away, but she slaps my hand to the ground with her dusted glove, binding me in place.

"Traitor," she growls, yanking my pins from their pin-sleeves before rejoining the fight.

The battle rages across the lawn, docents slivering monks and kids alike, monks striking and binding alongside Rahki. It's far from a fair fight, though. The Competition outnumbers us, and their slivers swallow monk after monk, child after child, with a single prick, removing them from the fray and depositing them somewhere across the globe.

I struggle to free myself of Rahki's binding, but it's no use. Only she can release me before the dust wears off.

Behind her, a monk inserts his coin into one of the centaur statues and strikes an attack pose. The icon springs to life, mirroring the monk's stance. Lyre raised, teeth bared. The centaur rears up and races forward, but before it reaches its target the monk controlling it gets slivered away.

The centaur stills as the monk bound to it vanishes.

This Monastery was supposed to be a safe place. The children . . . they were protected. That's why Dad chose it as his hiding spot for the Greenhouse. It was the least likely place Stripe would find it. I'm a fool. A weak pin that's failed and is causing all the others to fail around me. I fell for another of Nico's tricks, and now everyone's going to pay the price.

Cass grabs my free hand. "What did you do, Cam?"

"I didn't . . . " I want to cover my face, but my other hand tingles with Rahki's binding. "This wasn't supposed to happen. I was trying to prevent this. All I wanted was to get Dad back."

"Dad?" Cass's tone flares with anger.

"They have him," I tell her. "Stripe said he'd give Dad back in exchange for the Greenhouse, but—"

A voice from the door stops me. "Well, this is a bit more chaotic than expected."

Stripe tips his flat straw hat in our direction. Nico hobbles on his crutch behind him. He looks so much like Stripe now, dressed in a similar suit, hair slicked to the side under his identical hat.

"Nico!" Rahki yells from across the yard.

She strikes her duster and dashes for him. Nico dodges her palm, slides a sliver from an inner jacket pocket, and sticks her with the pointy end.

"No!" I scream as Rahki balls up into the tip of Nico's weapon.

The lawn goes silent.

She's gone. Everyone from the Hotel is gone. The kids, the monks . . . all slivered away. I did this. I led him here. If I'd just thrown that pin away, if I hadn't entertained the idea of doing what Stripe asked. . . .

"You said it would be quiet!" I rage. "That no one had to know!"

Mr. Stripe adjusts his cufflinks. "It only counts if it's in writing. Besides, I decided if I'm going to take the Greenhouse, I might as well get back the other things the Hotel stole from me, too."

"They're not things!" Cass yells. "They're people! Children!"

He pops his cane into his hand and leans over her. "They're possessions, dear, like any other."

"What are you going to do with them?" I ask.

"I'll put them to good use." He gives me a wink. "People never understand the value of those around them until they're history. Like you. Was the hope of finding your father worth risking all those kids? Probably not." He taps his forehead with his cane. "But your mistake is my gain."

I gulp down the stone forming in my throat. "And what about us?"

"Dear boy"—Stripe cocks his head—"I couldn't have done this without you. I'll keep my end of the bargain." He nods to Nico, who, after a quick glance at me, limps back through the door on his crutch. "For your trouble, you'll get the man you always wanted. Unfortunately, he may not be all you hoped for."

Cass spits in the grass at Stripe's feet.

"Now that's plain rude." He stuffs his cane in the crook of his arm and pulls on his gloves. "We'll have to tell Reinhart to work some manners into your education."

Nico shuffles back through the door, followed by two docents dragging a man between them.

My blood freezes. My heart clangs in my chest, in my toes, in my fingers that are still bound to the earth. I'm shaking as the docents throw the haggard, bearded man to the ground at Cass's wheels.

"I told you I'd help you find him," Nico whispers, and tosses me the necklace with Dad's coin.

I've never felt such hatred toward anyone in my entire life.

"Thus concludes our business," Stripe says, patting the man on the head. "Goodbye, Reinhart. Shame Melissa died for nothing." He steps through the door and inserts his black iron key into the other side.

Nico gives me one last look, pats his pocket, and says, "Hope you find your destination," before following.

Stripe closes the door, and it explodes in a cloud of wood and metal.

When the dust settles, it's only Cass, me, and a man we've never met left in the empty yard.

25

What I Wanted

I stare at the shattered door, unable to look away. Unable to accept what just happened. I said I'd pay any price, and now I have.

Cass has her elbows on her knees. She's crying. I want to comfort her, to stroke her hair like Oma does and encourage her to face this with me. I struggle to pull my hand free from Rahki's binding to go to her, but it won't budge.

A tingle of fear buzzes through my body when I think about the man behind me. What if he doesn't want us? What if he hates me for what I did to get him back? He and Mom fought to keep the Greenhouse out of Stripe's hands, and I undid all that.

But this is what I've wanted for so long. I found him.

So I turn to see my end of the bargain.

The man sits cross-legged in the grass, a crumpled flap of cardboard pressed to his chest. Long, yellow toenails poke through the holes in his shoes. A once-puffy coat hangs off him in tatters. He sets his cardboard scrap aside, and I read the words scribbled on it in permanent marker: HOMELESS, COLD, ALONE,

HUNGRY. PLEASE HELP. What has Stripe done to him?

"Reinhart? Reinhart Kuhn?"

He looks up, glancing between Cass and me. His long, oily hair is so matted it doesn't look real. Even his facial hair looks like it was glued on. "How do you know my name?"

I breathe in a shudder. It's him.

Cass wipes her tears and scoots toward him. "It's us, Dad. Cassia"—she points at me—"and Cameron."

"Cameron?" His expression falters, like he's struggling to understand. "That name . . . no. I'm dreaming. You're not real. You can't . . . I don't . . . I can't remember."

"His coin, Cam," Cass says. "Agapios said his memories were bound."

I turn the necklace over in my free hand, feeling the smooth surface of the etchings worn down from years of me handling it.

I hold it out to him. "Take it."

He crawls toward me on all fours, reaching.

As he takes the wooden disc, a shock jumps from him to me. Memories flash through my mind, faster and more complete than ever before. Mom's face, and the lapel pin Agapios gave me. The memory of traveling through doors I've never seen, all over the world. Twin babies—one in Mom's arms, the other lying in a clear glass box, connected to a hospital machine.

The images of Dad's time at the Hotel scorch entire stories into my brain at once. Mom, carving coins. The joy in her smile. The unspeakable mystery of getting to know her, and loving her more than anything in the world. A wedding on an island beach, with the Old Man standing at the podium and the Maid Commander giving the wooden rings. The signing of the contract with all those beaming hotel faces watching.

But there are other stories, too. Stories of a man in dark alleys, wearing a pinstriped suit. Posh hallways lined with glassed-in boxes of a different sort. Museum exhibits, displaying conquests long past. Children, like the ones Stripe stole, all connected back to the Curator, who wants to make a deal.

And finally, a story that ends with a woman falling out of a service elevator. I see it clearly for the first time, as though Dad and I are the same person. I'm arguing with Mom. She's upset. And then, the argument stills. We're alone in the elevator, but a static-y, binding sound roars so loud that I can't make out what she's saying.

She slides her coin into my pocket. Gives me a kiss.

I reach for her.

She falls.

The crack of a pin and a blinding light. A clap like thunder. And when I look back at those elevator doors, the face I see isn't Stripe's, or Agapios's. It's my father's face, reflected in the steel.

I let go of the coin, and the memories drain away, becoming little more than dim, jumbled images. What I remember, though, makes me sick.

Tears boil up into my eyes. "It's your fault."

My father stares at me, mouth open, unblinking. The guilt on his face tells me he remembers now too.

I wipe my eyes and stand, Rahki's binding finally broken. My shoulders are electrified with anger. "It was you," I say, the knot in my chest a thousand times bigger and impossible to untie. "You loved her, and then you let her go."

He rises to his knees. "Cameron, you have to understand—"

"You were *working* for him!" Shadows of terrible things shift in my mind. "You knew what Stripe was. You'd seen the awful places where those kids ended up, and you helped him anyway, just like Nico. Stripe wanted you to steal the Greenhouse to stop Mom's plan, but she found out. She tried to stop you. And you . . . " I can't bring myself to say it again.

"It wasn't like that." He reaches for my hand.

But I yank it away. "I saw it! In *your* memories. All those kids— the ones the Hotel's trying to save—he takes them and binds them to serve terrible people. That's why Mom died. She was trying to stop what *you* started."

"I didn't intend for it to go like that."

"Did you not *intend* to work for Stripe? Did you *accidentally* steal Mom's topscrew?" I dig out the pearl key and chuck it at him. "Take it! You wanted it; you can have it. Just stay away."

A door down the yard bursts open, and the Maid Commander races through, sword drawn.

I kneel beside Cass as the maids position themselves between us and the man who should be our dad. "It's going to be okay," I whisper, wrapping my arm around Cass's shoulder.

She shoves me off and shoots me a scowl that says it's not okay.

It'll never be okay, because I traded a bunch of innocent kids for this. The man I was searching for all this time was a traitor. The villain responsible for our mother's death.

The father who abandoned us.

I got what I wanted. Only now I don't want it anymore.

I sit on the toppled armoire in the Monastery cellar, running my fingers through the mossy stones. Thinking. Hoping I haven't ruined everything, as bad as it seems, but knowing it couldn't possibly be worse.

The door in the shadows that had been bound to the Greenhouse now lies in a pile of broken fragments, just like everything else. Stripe destroyed it when he took what he came for.

The memories I saw through the coin are beginning to fade. The stories in my head don't make as much sense as they did when Dad and I both held it. *Reinhart*. Not Dad. I refuse to call that man "Dad" ever again after what he did, and what I did to save him.

The MC separated us as soon as she arrived. I haven't seen Cass for hours, and who knows where Rahki got slivered away to. I've messed it all up.

The latch clanks and slides, and the heavy door screeches open. It's Agapios. Not the Maid Commander. I'm not sure whether I've been delivered *from* the MC's wrath or *into* the hands of Death himself.

"You're very lucky," the Old Man says as the door locks behind him. He glides forward, bony cheeks curved in a slight, but false, smile. "You escaped the Competition. That is no easy feat."

"Stripe *let* me get away." The faces of all those poor, scared children rise up in my brain. "He said it was the deal. But I swear, I was trying to stop him."

"Is that why you brought a pin that belonged to him with you to the Monastery? To stop him?"

A tide of guilt rises in my throat. "I didn't realize what he was going to do. He said no one would know."

Agapios scratches his hooked nose and squats eye-level with me. "The Curator is, at his core, a thief. He promises people their desires in exchange for what he wants to add to his collection. However, none who enter an agreement with him ever get what they truly seek."

I close my eyes and fight to control the guilt bubbling inside me. "And Reinhart?"

Agapios breathes a raspy sigh. "Years ago, your father made such an agreement with Stripe. Many have paid for it since."

"I saw what happened," I say. "When I handed him his coin, it was like his memories . . ."

"A transaction," Agapios says. "You kept your father's coin so long, it had become bound to you, and you began to see his memories when you grew old enough. When your binding and your father's met, the coin and its memories transferred back to their original owner."

"So I won't dream anymore?"

"Not his dreams. From now on, your dreams will be your own."

I fix my gaze on the stones in the floor.

"The man you call Stripe has long sought a successor," Agapios says. "He believes that if he can create a willing copy of himself, he can grow his empire far beyond what he could otherwise. This is the agreement your father made: to become Stripe's . . . replacement."

"So Reinhart was like Nico."

"Yes. However, Reinhart's love for Melissa complicated matters."

"You don't do what he did to the people you love." I finger the carved wood of the armoire. "Reinhart betrayed the Hotel. Betrayed her. And . . . so did I."

"Your father had his reasons, just as you had yours."

My insides curl. "Mom was trying to overthrow Stripe for good, wasn't she? She had an idea. I saw her, carving coins."

Agapios sits down next to me. "Melissa was a remarkable woman. She believed in the mission of this ancient House more than most, because she knew the truth about the terrible people who do terrible things in hidden corners of the world. She wanted to use our doors to provide an escape not just for our guests, but for those the world has mistreated."

"The kids."

"Yes. The Hotel Between exists to serve those lost and forgotten children. It is why we charge so much for guests to use our doors. Most of these wealthy patrons are unaware that their money funds our mission."

My lip curls. "All those guests—"

"—are not who you think they are." He gives me a stern, bony stare. "Many of them are just as lost. Your mother saw this. She recognized that so many people live their lives never understanding—never even seeing—the misfortune of others. The world turns away from those who hurt, excusing themselves by saying that they 'could not possibly understand.'" He pauses. "You know this, yes?"

He means Cass. Kids at school make fun of me sometimes because I care about my sister so much, but they don't understand what it's like. They don't *want* to understand.

Agapios pulls a coin from his pocket. "Before your mother joined us, the Hotel was merely a front for our deeper mission. We hid our true purpose behind the shine of our doors. But she made the operation of our Hotel a *part* of the mission. Melissa created the coins to open the hearts of those who stay here. She believed if the Hotel could guide the dreams of our guests, they would carry our purpose beyond these walls, to the whole world. So she began the practice of binding a coin to each person who entered, and the Hotel in turn called those it believed could benefit."

"I thought the coins just bound memories?"

He shakes his head. "The coins bind the Hotel to the person as much as they bind the person to the Hotel. Once bound, a bit of our Hotel will always remain in them. Though the specific logistics of our guests' vacations are left behind when they return their coin, their binding with the Hotel will continue to remind them of what they've seen, and reveal to them through their dreams the world they haven't seen."

"She wasn't going to attack Stripe head on," I realize. "She was going to let the Hotel make people care."

"Yes. As the Hotel's influence spread, Stripe's empire began to shrink. He sent your father to steal the Greenhouse, knowing that without the Vesima tree, the Hotel's influence over those bound to it would wane, and Melissa's plan would fail."

In the memory, Mom put her coin into Reinhart's pocket. Was she performing some last-minute binding to stop him? To make him care?

I try to soak it all in. Dad being trained by Stripe. Mom, trained by Agapios. "How'd they end up together? Couldn't she see who Reinhart was?"

Agapios shakes his head. "We are never as simple as we appear. Every House contains both terrors and treasures."

I'm not sure what he means, but it sounds good.

"I don't know why, or how," Agapios continues, "but Reinhart left one connection binding the Hotel to the Greenhouse, and hid it from us." He motions to the shattered door. "Because of this, our Hotel has survived, barely. Now that the tree is fully gone, however . . . "

"The binding will fail."

"The Hotel and its doors will unravel. Pin-failures will increase, and we will be forced to abandon this House."

I hang my head. "I ruined everything."

Agapios wraps his arm around my shoulder. His touch feels different from Stripe's. The concierge's fingers are cold and sharp, but they hold no lies, no hidden message except to say *I'm here*.

"The Curator manipulates even the best of people with their own good intentions. You really are Melissa's son, as well as Reinhart's." He stands and moves to the door. "Jehanna will attend to you soon. You are no longer welcome in the Hotel, such as it is. You and your sister will return to Dallas."

"What about Reinhart?"

The Old Man scratches his bony cheek. "Your father stays. We must save what we can, and he has information we need." Agapios bows, and opens the door. "I hope you find your destination, Cameron Kuhn."

And with that, he leaves.

After everything, Cass and I will be going home empty-handed. I may be angry, but that doesn't change the facts. I found my father, only to lose him all over again.

26

Out of His Hands

Agapios isn't there to see us off when the Maid Commander kicks us out of the Hotel. He probably has bigger issues to deal with, like getting the kids back, along with the Greenhouse. There's a hole in my heart, knowing I disappointed him. Can you die from a hole in your heart?

The maids take all our coins, leaving me with only my dirty Chucks to serve as a souvenir of my time here. Without the coins, my memories of this place will soon fade into dreams. When I first came to the Hotel, all I wanted was to go home. But I made friends here. Rahki, Elizabeth, Sana. Even Sev and Nico. And once I got used to it, the whole traveling thing wasn't so bad, either. I don't want to forget.

The MC asks what happened to the pins I had, and I tell her how Rahki took them before she got slivered. I wish she'd tell me if Rahki's okay. I search for her face in the crowd as the maids escort us through the Dallas Door, but she's not there.

It's morning in Texas, but the kind of early morning that doesn't show any traces of sunlight on the horizon yet. I push Cass's chair all the way home, like the good brother I'm supposed to be. I don't feel like a good brother, though. I failed her. Failed everyone. This is why I don't do anything. I always screw things up. I get nervous. Freak out. I don't belong out there, traveling the world. I need to stay home, where I don't disappoint anyone, and where I can wish that things would happen, but they don't, and that people would come back, but I never have to deal with what happens when they do.

When I open the door to Oma's, the familiar smell of moth-balls and sweet tea washes over me.

"Oma!" Cass calls out as she rolls over the threshold. "We're back! You can call off the search party."

The house is quiet.

Cass turns on all the lights on her way to Oma's room.

I find the note Oma left on the kitchen table, and skim over it.

> Cass and Cammy,
> I've gone out to look for you.
> If you come home, I expect you to _STAY PUT_ and _CALL_
> _MY CELL IMMEDIATELY_.
> Love and kisses,
> Oma

Does Oma know about the Hotel? _Those secrets aren't mine to tell._ If she does, she'll be sorely disappointed when she finds it and we're not there. And that's if she's even able to find a knocker. I wouldn't want to be on Agapios's end when she finds him, though.

"She's not here," Cass calls from around the hall corner.

"I'm sure she'll be back soon," I shout in reply.

I fold the note so she won't see it, and then head for my room, close the door, and crawl into bed. I'll call Oma when the sun comes up. I'm not ready to answer her questions.

A few minutes later, there's a knock at my door.

"Go away." I wipe my face and bury my nose in the sheets.

The door squeaks as Cass rolls in. I peek over my pillow. She's got that you're-crazy look, but I don't care.

I turn over and face the wall. "It's not fair," I say.

"I know."

"It wasn't supposed to be like that. He was supposed to be . . . "

"Different," she says. And again, "I know."

Deep down, I know she does. All those years watching *National Geographic* and reading travel books—somehow I've always known she did it because she wanted to connect with our parents too. She just wouldn't admit it.

I roll over to look her in the eye. "Finding him was supposed to fix it."

Her eyes narrow. "Fix what?"

"Everything. Like you . . . "

"What about me?" she snaps, and I can tell I've insulted her.

"I-I didn't—"

She flicks her brake and scoots closer. "I'm fine."

"But your condi—"

"I'm exactly who I want to be," she says again, and if I try to say one more word about it I know she's going to punch me.

I've always struggled with understanding how she feels. After all these years, I still can't imagine what it's like for her. It's easy to forget that her chair isn't the burden I think it would be if I were trapped in it instead. I don't think I'll ever fully comprehend how she feels. I'm starting to get some of it, though. For her, it's not a trap at all. It's a door that takes her places she couldn't go otherwise.

It makes me realize how much better Cass is at being happy than I am. Like Nico said, she's stronger than I give her credit for. *I'm* the one who's always worried; she's just living her life.

"Well, I'm not fine," I tell her. "I'm not like you. You say you're who you want to be, but I don't know how to become who *I* want to be. I'm tired of being . . . " I trail off. I'm not even sure what I was about to say. Afraid, maybe? "Agapios said I'm like Reinhart, but I can't be like him."

Cass screws up her face as if she tasted vinegar. "Then don't."

She's not getting it. "Reinhart worked for Stripe," I say. "He stole the Greenhouse. He let Mom die."

"Don't say that!" Cass chews her lip. "That's not how it happened."

I bunch the pillow tighter. "How do you know?"

"You're not the only one who had their parent's coin in the Hotel."

Mom's coin. Of course. I'd completely forgotten. The Maid Commander took it after the Monastery, but Cass wore it in the Hotel for hours before that.

Cass picks at the divots in the foam of her chair's arms. "I felt her with me, when that Mr. Stripe showed up. I saw things too. Dad didn't push her . . . he was trying to stop her."

"Stop her from what?"

"She did it on purpose, Cam. Mom knew Dad had a contract with Stripe, and she did what she had to do to keep him from fulfilling it. And when she fell . . . all she kept thinking was that she wished she could've saved him, too."

I shake my head. "No. *He* signed the contract with Stripe. *He* made that choice, and she died because of it."

"He did it for a good reason."

"There's no excuse for what he did."

"Yeah, there is."

I scoff. "What could've possibly been that important?"

"It was me, all right!" she shouts. "He signed that contract because of me."

I scoot back, surprised by her outburst. "You don't know that. You were only there for what? A day? Day and a half? I was there over a week and didn't learn that much."

"Because you weren't listening!" Cass growls. "You never just listen. That's why Oma won't tell you what's going on with me. She knows that no matter how good a procedure might be for my health, you're going to pick apart all the reasons it's bad. It's like you believe you're the only one who knows the truth, and you won't even hear us when we tell you that I don't need your help all the time, or that you're wrong, or that things are better than you think. Dad's coin could've drawn a stinking map for you if you'd just stop worrying for a minute and let things be."

I start to argue, but is she right? Agapios had assumed that if the coin held the memory of what Dad did with the Greenhouse, I would have found it way sooner. Was I so busy worrying about what might happen that I missed the things that *were* happening around me?

She folds her hands, trying not to cry. "Look, Mom was the one who helped Dad break away from Stripe in the first place. He'd walked away from the Competition and joined the Hotel—like, was really *with* them. But when Mom told him I was going to be born with all this medical stuff, he freaked. She knew he'd go to Stripe, and she didn't get in his way. Stripe told Dad he'd heal me in exchange for the Greenhouse." She sniffles. "When things started happening, Mom realized they'd made a mistake. So she tried to stop him."

"Stripe *didn't* heal you, though," I say after a moment.

"Because Dad broke the contract. Mom knew he couldn't defy Stripe on his own. Mr. Stripe had messed with his head too much. The only way she could stop Dad from giving him the Greenhouse was to make sure her binding with Dad was stronger than his binding with Stripe."

I stare into the bed sheets. "So why did—"

Cass wipes her eyes and reaches for my hand. "Mom didn't die," she says. "I felt it on that elevator. Mom re-bound herself even more deeply to the Hotel. That way, with both her and the Hotel working together, Dad could resist Stripe long enough to hide the Greenhouse and get us to Oma. They did it together."

But in Reinhart's memories, Stripe was there too.

No. Not the real Stripe. More like . . . an impression. Like Stripe was *inside* Reinhart. That's why whenever Reinhart caught his reflection in the elevator doors it looked like Stripe, or Agapios. He was seeing deeper, into his bindings, as if his agreements with Agapios and Stripe were tug-of-warring inside him. Mom gave the Hotel side of him what he needed to win the tug, if only for a little while.

"That's why no one knew where the Greenhouse was," I say. "Mom was hiding it, through her binding with the Hotel."

Cass nods. "She made him promise, and that pact became a contract Dad couldn't break. They signed it by . . . " She doesn't finish, but she doesn't have to.

I look at my hands. The cut from my blood-bond with Nico is healing. It scares me to think what our contract might really mean.

"It worked, though," Cass says. "Dad never gave Stripe the Greenhouse."

"But I did. After Mom sacrificed herself to keep it out of his hands, I led him right to it. And you're not even healed."

"Forget about that," she says, her tone sharp again. "I'm me and you're you. What I am doesn't need fixing. We're just us. Mom understood that, even if Dad couldn't." She settles her gaze on me. "Even if you don't either."

Cass and I sit in silence for a long time, until eventually she rolls off to bed.

I don't want to sleep, though. Sleep is my enemy. It's coming to take away my memories. The adventures. My friends. But as the clock counts toward morning, I can't resist it anymore. I nod off, curled up in the knowledge of what Mom gave up, and what I did to ruin it all.

This time, there are no dreams.

27

A Knocked Door

A noise wakes me.

I look to the window, now glowing with the first rays of morning sunlight, and remember when Nico knocked at that pane and whisked me away. Despite everything, I kinda miss him. I don't know whether it's the blood-brother bond or something else, but part of me wishes he'd come back and say it was all a mistake.

At first I think it's my imagination when a familiar pin crackle comes from my door, but the knock makes it real. And a knocked door is always opened.

I hop out of bed, excitement tingling in my fingers, and throw it open.

It's not Nico, though. It's Rahki. And . . . Sev?

"We need to talk," Rahki says.

I shush her and motion them both into my room and off the snowy cobblestone street now bound to my bedroom door. I struggle to keep my voice down, but I'm so happy to see them, whispering is hard. "You're okay!"

"No thanks to you," Rahki grumbles, sitting down on my bed. Her uniform is messier than I've ever seen it, and her face is dirty.

"Do not be so harsh, Rahki." Sev claps a hand on my shoulder. "It is good to see you. I am very sorry for my part in Stripe's deception. *Delat iz muhi slona.* We have all made mistakes."

"Yeah, we have." I should be mad at him, but I can't. He tried to warn me, after all, when he came to my room that night. "It's good to see you, too. But what are you doing here?"

They catch me up on what's happened since I last saw them. Rahki keeps it short: Nico's sliver transported her to the Australian outback, where Sev was waiting for her.

"Waiting?"

"Nico slivered me first," Sev says. "He told me to wait, so I waited."

Rahki rolls her eyes. "Which, of course, you did. Without question."

"It is good I did. You would have been all alone out there. At least *I* knew where to go."

"Why would Nico sliver *you?*" I ask.

Sev explains that after he left my hotel room that night, he went back to tell Nico that Stripe wanted him to take Nico's family.

"Wait . . . so Nico knew what you were about to do?"

He nods. "Nico told me to do as Stripe asked. Which is good, I think now, because otherwise I would have lost myself."

"But did you . . . hurt them?"

He jerks back in disgust. "Of course not. The Jimenezes went willingly, because Nico sent me with a note for them, telling them to trust me."

"It looked like . . . " I stop. "Of course it did. . . . If Nico knew what was going to happen, he could've just made it *look* like a struggle."

"Exactly. When I came back to tell him it was done, he slivered me away to Australia with instructions to wait. A few maids appeared soon after, talking about Nico's betrayal in the Corridor, but I hid until they left. It was not until Rahki arrived that I knew my help had come." Sev laughs. "Though, I thought Rahki was going to bind me to the side of an angry bear when she saw me."

"I'm still confused, though," I say. "Nico lets you steal his family, then slivers you? Then he makes a mess and pretends he didn't know you'd taken them? Why?"

Sev shrugs. "Who knows why Nico does anything? I have never understood him. But when Rahki popped up in front of me and told me what happened, I knew it would not be long before the Hotel sent you away. Fortunately for us, Rahki had taken the pin I bound for you, which allowed us to come here."

Rahki interrupts him. "Point is, now we need your help. Nico or no Nico, we can't leave the Greenhouse in Stripe's hands. Or those kids."

Sev crosses his arms. "Agreed."

"So what do we do?" I ask.

Rahki holds her head high. "Objective number one: Get to Stripe's Museum."

I purse my lips. "You should be telling this stuff to the Maid Commander. Isn't that what the Maid Service is for?"

"Maid Service doesn't know where Stripe's Museum is," she replies. "The Corridor was the closest we'd ever come to finding it, and Nico's pin-snap closed that door. So even if we *did* know where it was, the maids couldn't get inside. The magic binding the great Houses is different from place to place."

Finally Sev pipes up. "What we need to know is, has your contract with Stripe been fulfilled? We cannot risk you going inside if he has control over you."

"Stripe never had me sign a contract," I tell him.

Rahki stiffens. "You mean you weren't under Stripe's influence when you stole the Greenhouse? You did all that stuff of your own free will, like a suit?"

I shrink back. "Influence? I mean . . . he lied to me. And I didn't steal the Greenhouse. Nico did."

"You let him in."

"Not on purpose!"

"Leave it alone, Rahki," Sev says. "We are all Stripe's victims here. Besides"—he turns to me—"that you did not sign a contract is good. If Stripe had bound you, it would have made you his docent, as he did me." He pauses. "However, since you did not sign a contract, we may have no way to get inside."

A dark thought hits me. "I *did* sign a contract. Just not with Stripe."

They shoot each other a worried look.

I show them my still-bandaged hand and explain the blood-brother contract with Nico. "It said everything that's his is bound to me. That's how Nico got into the Monastery—he was still bound to the Hotel because of our connection."

"Blood-brothers," Sev says, curling a lip. "That was reckless, Cameron."

"I thought I could trust him!" I sigh. "Thought I could trust you, too."

"Sev didn't have a choice," Rahki says. "His contract gave Stripe the power to manipulate him. Compelled him to do things he didn't want to." She gives Sev a sad look. "He couldn't help it."

"But Sev had enough control over himself to come to me. And to Nico," I say, trying to sort it all out.

"I did not, however, *break* my contract with Stripe," Sev says. "As long as I obeyed Stripe's instructions in the end, I could accomplish the task however I wanted."

Rahki continues to explain. "Stripe has direct control over his docents, but that control only goes so far. It's limited by how close you are to him, and whether he's talking to you directly. Beyond that, they make their own decisions. The contracts themselves, however, are *very* powerful. To break a contract that's magically bound can cause some really terrible things to happen. If Sev had broken his docent contract, even if Stripe wasn't around, Sev would've lost everything that makes him, him. He'd have become a mindless servant. And that's not the worst of it."

The slightest smile appears on Sev's lips. "Your bond with Nico is something else, though," he tells me. "What is bound to Nico is bound to you—and Stripe's Museum is bound to him. The Museum will trust you, just as the Hotel trusted Nico."

"But doesn't that mean Cam's bound to Stripe, too?" Rahki asks. "We can't risk a mistake like that."

Sev frowns. "I believe Nico's contract with Stripe is different, as well."

"Because Nico is Stripe's successor," I say. When I tell them everything Nico and Stripe said in Honduras, it all starts to click. "Stripe's been grooming Nico to take over the Museum ever since my dad failed him."

"So Nico's a true suit," Rahki says, quickly understanding where all Nico's cards are falling. "He's not a servant, like the docents. He's Stripe's partner."

"That makes sense," Sev says. "I missed it before, because I did not know how long Nico and Stripe had been together. I always wondered why he seemed so willing. Stripe needs Nico to make his own decisions. He would still have a contract, but that contract would allow more freedom than those of the docents. To Stripe, the ultimate possession is one that chooses to belong to you of its own free will. That is why Reinhart was able to break his deal with Stripe. He had a choice. As long as Reinhart did what he was contracted to do, Stripe could not control him outright."

"That's why Mom . . . ," I pause, not sure how to explain. "My mom knew that once Dad disobeyed, Stripe would gain control and he'd be forced to give up the Greenhouse. Either way, Stripe would win. But my mom made a new binding—no, she *became* a binding—between him and the Hotel. That bought him time to hide the Greenhouse, and bring Cass and me to Oma. He left their coins with us so he'd forget, and so he'd never be able to give Stripe what he wanted, no matter how much power Stripe had over him."

A dense quiet falls over the room.

"At least your dad did *something* right before Stripe took control," Rahki says.

I'm a little surprised Cass hasn't knocked on my door to see what's going on. We keep forgetting to whisper . . . and she's such a light sleeper.

Then it hits me. If Reinhart broke the contract with Stripe . . .

"Oh no!" I bolt for my door and throw it open, but it's still bound to the snowy street somewhere on the other side of the world. "Plug! Give me a plug!"

Sev digs the device out of his pocket and hands it to me.

I unbind the door and race for Cass's bedroom. But I'm too late. The room is empty.

"She's gone," I say, leaning against the wall and sliding to the floor as Sev and Rahki enter behind me. "He took her."

"Who did?" Rahki asks.

Sev grips my arm. "Reinhart. He must have escaped the Hotel and taken your sister back to the Museum."

"It's all my fault." I run my hands through my hair and squeeze a handful.

Rahki kneels next to me. "We'll find her, Cam."

I pull my knees to my chest, and something crinkles in my pajama pocket. An envelope . . .

And a coin. Nico's coin, right where it always is.

"That sneaky jerk." I hold the letter up so they can see my name in Nico's flowing cursive.

Rahki furrows her brow. "Where'd you get that?"

"Nico's trick coin." Now I get it. All this talk of contracts; I never fully understood what Nico and I did that night in Honduras. "When we signed the blood-brother contract, his coin got bound to me too. Everything he has, right? Whenever one of us pats our pocket, even accidentally, the coin returns to that person, along with whatever's with it."

She shoots me another disapproving look.

"I haven't *sent* him anything."

"Open the letter," Sev says.

I tear it open, but there's more than just a note inside. A silver key falls into my palm.

Hey blood-bro,

Sorry for how everything's turned out, but you know how it is. Gotta do what you gotta do. The exchange was the only way to get you your dad. I made a promise, and I kept it. Besides, I gotta make sure my family's taken care of too. Hope you understand.

The kids are in Stripe's Museum, and your dad just showed up with Cass. Stripe thinks he's won, which means he's as vulnerable as he's gonna get. I'll keep everyone safe as long as I can. If you're up for it, we can still have a little fun before my plan comes together. I don't really need the help, but if you wanna join forces and have an exciting ride, I'd be happy to have you along.

Whatever you decide, though. Don't want to make you work too hard, right?

Pretty much the greatest,
Nico

Rahki scoffs. "Does he really think you're going to buy all that?"

"Maybe." Something about the letter feels . . . I dunno . . . right. "What if he's telling the truth? I mean, he did tell Sev to wait for you. He set up the Jimenez house. And making the contract with me . . . helps us. That contract let him into the Monastery and the Hotel network, but now it'll let us into the Museum." I pause. "It's almost like he was planning this all along. Like it was all an act to deceive Stripe. Make him think he's winning."

"Nico *is* one to plot," Sev says.

"What if he's lying?" Rahki asks.

I examine Nico's silver key. "Isn't this why you came here? Nico just gave us a way in. He handed over the key to the Corridor, and he made *me* the key to the Museum. And anyway, Stripe's got Cass. I have to go."

This is where I usually start thinking through all the things that could go wrong, and all my fears culminate in one big, grand

No. Not this time. Sure, bad things might happen if we go, but something bad *will* happen if we don't.

"Sev, head back to the Hotel," I say. "Get help. Not the Maid Commander—Agapios will understand. Tell him we're going to find the kids and to be ready when we bring them home."

A smile spreads across Sev's lips. "I will."

"Rahki, you're with me. Let's find Nico and fix this thing."

28

Mapping the Maze

The door at the back of the hospital mocks me. It looks so big, and I feel so small. I never thought I could come to hate doors, but right now I could take every door in the world off its hinges and burn them on the hugest bonfire in history.

Nico's coin is missing from my jeans again. I call it to me with a pat, and my pocket inflates with another message.

Does this mean you're coming? We're gonna have so much fun.
Pretty much the greatest,
Nico

"What did he say?" Rahki asks.

"Nothing." I wad the note and toss it in a Dumpster. "Let's get this over with."

Nico's silver key unlocks the door to the Corridor in a shimmer of silvery foam, and I lead Rahki toward the end with the big, shiny M. The Corridor is as I remember it—peeling wallpaper, checkerboard tile—but my memories of it are fading, bound to the coin I no longer have.

I stop when we reach the M door. When I place my hand on the wood, I can feel my connection to Nico binding me to it, like ants crawling under my skin.

When I turn the knob, there's no flash or glitter. The door swings open on silent, oiled hinges.

Rahki pulls on her gloves. "Here we go."

We enter a large hallway. Thick carpet squishes like a sponge. Exhibits featuring centuries-old paintings line the walls, filling the air with the musty scent of things forgotten. Suits of armor. Weatherworn scrolls in display cases. Engraved silver nameplates on rounded cobblestones.

Rahki takes in the glistening fixtures. "Do you know your way?"

"No." I run my hand along a wall of hanging silver leaves set against a black background. It's interspersed with paintings of cities on fire, or crushed under tidal waves, or attacked by armies. "Stripe never brought me here."

Ahead, two kids pass in the adjoining hall dressed in spiffy suits. I pull Rahki into the shadows and wait for them to round the corner.

"Docents." She blows out a puff of air. "One step at a time."

We head toward them, staying on the balls of our feet. When we reach the corner, I spy a balustrade overlooking a foyer ahead. We must have entered on the second floor of the Museum. More turners, just like in the Hotel.

I motion for Rahki to stop. Below us, an enormous angel statue stands with arms outstretched over the foyer. Polished steel swords and spears and axes hang from the ceiling, reflecting the light off the silver electric candelabras. People—kids and adults, all dressed in the same suits—are everywhere. Some stand scattered around the foyer, staring into space with sad, vacant eyes. Others plod across the room carrying books and platters of food, dusting mantles, changing light bulbs.

Rahki tracks one of them with her finger. "See how they don't even look around? These docents are bound to this House, and not in a good way. I've heard rumors about the Competition's influence over others. They might as well be furniture."

One of the docents rounds the corner on the upper level and turns toward us. The boy walks past carrying a pail of cleaning supplies. He doesn't react to seeing two people who obviously don't belong here. In fact, he doesn't acknowledge us at all.

"Can he not see us?" I ask.

"He sees, but he's lost control over his mind. What's left of him only knows what he needs to know." She points to a hall leading off the foyer. Docents stand guard on either side of the entrance. "Looks like they're protecting something."

After a moment, I recognize one of the guards. "Is that . . . Orban?" The Hungarian with the fur-patched cheeks stands beside the door, hands clasped behind him, gazing into space.

Rahki clenches the rail. "I knew it didn't make sense for Orban to turn on us. He's under Stripe's control too."

"Back in Budapest he was trying to tell me to get away from Stripe. If only I'd listened."

Rahki considers this. "I'm going to figure out a way around them."

I stop her. "If this place follows the same rules as the Hotel, wherever those doors lead shouldn't have a back way in," I say. "They're probably like the sub-level to the Concierge Retreat. One way in, one way out."

"We need to get in there."

I lean against the door beside us and listen to the hum of its binding—that calming, unique sound of magic coursing through it.

"Do you still have that plug?" I ask.

"Mine and Sev's." She pulls the devices from her coat pocket.

I drag her into a nook and explain my idea.

"You want to unbind the Museum doors?" she says, obviously not convinced.

"I want to set a trap. Like the trap in Budapest. The Museum works against us because we don't know our way around, but it's one of the great Houses, right? A bunch of doors bound together over time. If we rearrange the pins . . . "

"We rearrange the House."

I smile, and it feels good for once. "We don't have to know where everything goes—just scramble the doors and the docents will be as lost as we are."

"Wouldn't that take a lot of time?"

"Nuh-uh." I point at the double doors leading from this wing to the foyer's upper level. "As long as we un-pin those doors, *and* the same ones on the lower level, this whole wing will be cut off from the rest. Like the wings the Hotel lost in the pin-failure."

"Unless other doors lead back here."

"We just need to buy some time. You said it yourself—these servants don't exactly think on their feet. We mix up the doors, and that'll give you the opportunity to find the Monastery kids and me to go after Cass and the Greenhouse."

I'm hoping Rahki doesn't realize the one big flaw in my plan. If we trap all the docents on this side of the Museum, they'll be stuck between us and the Corridor—our one reliable escape route. We'll have to find another way out. But as many doors as there are in this place, getting out shouldn't be a problem.

"Okay," she says. "Let's rearrange some pins."

I bend down to retie the laces on my Chucks.

Rahki has finished re-pinning the doors on this wing to make a loop that should keep the docents occupied for a while. Our trap is set.

"I'll draw their attention and lead them into the hall," I say, scanning the foyer below. "You hide up here, and plug the doors down there once they follow me inside."

She offers me a hand. "Good luck, Cam."

I shake it, and she takes her position at the top of the stairs. We're committed now.

I blow out the tension in my lungs and hurry down the steps, ready to start shouting.

But before I make it to the bottom, the guarded door opens with a clank, and a short, scrawny figure with gelled hair steps through.

"Hey guys!" Nico says, squeezing between Orban and the other guard with an awkward "excuse me." He looks so much like Stripe. Same satin pocket square in his striped vest, same squatty straw hat, even hobbling with a perfect replica of Stripe's rope cane. The sight makes my chest tighten. "Wasn't sure you'd make it."

"You told us to come," I say. No one else moves. The entire Museum holds its breath.

Nico waves to Rahki at the top of the stairs. "Hi Rahki! Why are you hiding up there? Afraid I'm going to get you back for hurting my ankle?"

I take a step toward him. "What are you doing?"

"Exactly what I said I'd do. Helping you take those kids off Stripe's hands." He pats Orban's shoulder. "But that's what makes this complicated. Gotta stick to the plan." He raises his voice. "Hey everybody! The future master of this House commands you to capture these two intruders and bring them to him!"

At once, the servants drop what they're doing and turn toward Rahki and me.

"Run!" Rahki yells.

I sprint for the hall, almost barreling straight into the hands of a docent built like a pro wrestler. He grabs my collar, and it rips when I duck under his arm. I stumble and turn, and what I see makes me freeze.

They're coming. All of them.

Rahki leaps over the balustrade, gloved fingers sparkling with binding dust, and slams her palm into one of the docents. He sticks to the floor like a mouse in a glue trap. "Go!"

And I do. A few more jukes and spins bring me to the double doors leading to the hall. The docents follow, just like we planned, but they're too spread out. Some must've chased after Rahki. That'll complicate matters.

What's Nico thinking? He *told* us to come. Maybe he *is* being controlled in a different way, and this is all Stripe, but how would I be able to tell?

At the end of the first floor hall, I slip into the door Rahki re-pinned to upstairs. Our little escape hatch. The docents are hot on my trail, though. Before I can throw the door closed, the boy behind me slides his foot in the gap. No. No. No! I try to pull it shut, but he keeps pressing. If I don't plug this door, our trap will fail. I slam the door again, and again, but he remains strong. A girl appears behind him, adding her weight to his.

I stomp on the boy's foot and he pulls back, leaving his polished slip-on dress shoe behind. This is why you wear sneakers. I pull his shoe out of the way and slam the door.

The door's binding buzzes through me as I press myself against the wood, panting. The docents pound against the other side. If I can just get the pin out of the hinge. . . .

I fumble for the plug, struggling to hold the door closed and dropping Nico's coin in the process. The kids are strong, but my

Chucks provide enough traction to brace against them. I try to pop the pin, but with the boy fighting against me the spring isn't strong enough. It needs some extra force. A hammer. Something.

My gaze falls to the boy's shoe.

I swipe the hard-soled oxford off the carpet. The door opens a bit when I bend over, but I'm able to shut it just as quickly. Back pressed against the door, I line up the spike and knock it upward with the shoe. The pin pops up an inch. Carefully—I don't want to snap it—I give the pin two more hits, and it flops to the floor.

The binding drains away with a shimmer.

Success. The mob should still be in the downstairs hall, separated from me by the door I just unbound. We're not done, though. This door's unpinned, but there are still the doors on the lower level. Rahki was supposed to plug those behind me, but who knows what happened after Nico sicced Stripe's attendants on her.

I sweep the coin off the carpet and hurry down the stairs to where the chase started.

Nico's gone; the lower doors are still bound. I don't see Rahki, but scattered everywhere are docents who met the business end of her duster. A girl's hair is bound in a knot around a bannister. Another's hands are glued over her eyes, causing her to stumble aimlessly around the room. One guy's butt is stuck in a potted tree—leaving him rolling on the floor doing his best upside-down turtle impression—and a group of four are so twisted up in one another, I can't tell where one ends and the others begin. The giant angel statue at the back of the room almost looks like it's laughing at the scene. I have to remember never to tick Rahki off again.

I rush for the hall doors to lock the gathered docents inside, but Orban steps in my path. With his hairy knuckles clenched, brow furrowed, hand bound to a bit of wall he's since ripped free, he swings his drywall-bound fist at me, and I barely miss being clocked.

Down the hall, the mob turns. No way can I unbind those doors while under attack from the lumbering Hungarian. It won't take those docents long to make it back to the foyer. If only I was stronger.

My attention flits to the angel statue, and the stone slit near the bottom of its robe. Sana said the coins bind us to the icons. The Hotel took my coin, but I still have Nico's. And thanks to the contract, it's bound to me by blood.

Time's running out.

I roll out of Orban's reach and bolt for the angel.

As I slide the coin into the slot, the stone monstrosity stirs. Marble robes shimmer and turn to white fabric. Pale gray sculpture transforms to soft brown flesh. The icon strikes an attack stance and starts to draw a curved, flaming-white blade from its scabbard, but I will it to stop. I don't want to hurt Orban or anyone else under Stripe's control. I only want to keep *them* from pounding *me*.

Orban snarls and charges.

The angel zooms between us, smacking Orban in the chest and knocking him into the hall with the rest of Stripe's servants. He rolls to a stop at the feet of the angry mob.

With one last thought, the angel slams the doors and braces against them with its enormous hands. The docents crash into the other side.

I give the icon a pat and a "Great job, buddy," as I yank Nico's coin from the slot. The magic dissipates, and the angel transforms back to solid marble. No matter how solid the statue is, though, in time that mob will still break through. I have to unbind the door. I just hope Rahki's not on the other side.

"Sorry, Rahki," I say, knocking out the first hinge-pin. "You're on your own."

I remove the final pin, and an eerie silence falls over the Museum.

"All right, time to find Cass. In a creepy museum. Alone."

29

Here's the Beef

As I head into the newly unguarded hall, the pins from the severed doors burn in my hand. Teal and white mosaics laid like wisps of wind draw me deeper into the Museum. Arched doors tower on either side, older even than those in Stripe's Corridor.

The missing kids are probably hidden behind one of these doors.

I grab the handle on the first one, and I'm surprised to find it unlocked. When your entire security force is mind-controlled, I guess you don't need to lock things.

The heavy wood glides open to reveal a dusty hill—an old, packed sand dune. I leave the door cracked open and climb to the top.

The peak overlooks an enormous hole in the barren landscape. It's a quarry, filled with kids trudging up and down ramps, lugging heavy tools, digging into the exposed rock. The shirts of those who actually have shirts are sweat-soaked and riddled with holes. The rest are bare-chested, bare-legged except for small bits of cloth wrapped around their midsections. They all glisten with sweat from the hot sun.

I want to look away, but I can't. Many of these kids could've sat beside me in school. They look dirty, and . . . sad. Stern-faced men watch over them, making sure they keep working.

Rahki said she was in a bad situation before the Maid Commander brought her in. How many stories like this are walking around The Hotel Between? How many people did Agapios's House help before I gave the Greenhouse to Stripe? I always thought dying by one of the thousand-plus ways on my WWTD list was the worst thing that could happen to a person, but I was wrong. This is worse than all those ways to die, because these kids don't have a life that's theirs to begin with.

"Looking for me, Mr. Cameron?"

I turn to see Nico leaning against the door leading back to the Museum, cane in hand. He straightens his vest, a snotty grin plastered across his face.

The eyes of the kids from the Monastery flood over me again, and all those scared faces solidify into one clear impulse.

I'm going to knock Nico's stinking lights out.

I guess he doesn't see it coming, or doesn't think I might actually do it, because my fist slams into his chest with a loud *pap!*

His cane clatters to the floor and he stumbles back into the hall. "Whoa, whoa, whoa! What's that for? We got no reason to fight."

"No reason?" I shouldn't be screaming, but I'm so mad I don't care.

"It's all turned out okay," he says.

"How is this okay? You lied to us. To me! You even sicced Stripe's henchmen on me."

Nico scoffs. "Hey, there were hench-ladies, too."

"And these doors . . . all those kids . . . " I chew my tongue just trying to stand still. "How could you be involved in something like this?"

He sweeps the cane off the floor. "Same as I picked out this tie," he says. "One of many options."

I want so much to hit him again—to make him stop smiling. "You're not even taking this seriously."

Nico's expression dims. "Yes I am. You don't even know how serious I'm taking it. You have to trust me."

"Trust you? *Trust* you?" My chest wants to explode. "You betrayed me. We were supposed to be blood-brothers."

"We *are* blood-brothers." He limps toward his hat. "I only kept things from you to protect you, kiddo."

"You didn't protect me! No one protects me. I'm always pro-tecting everyone else. And *stop* calling me *kiddo!*"

Nico sighs, and it sets my blood on fire. "You don't know Stripe. What it'll take to stop him."

"But *you* do?"

"I do." He brushes his hat off and slicks his hair back. Then he pulls his coin from his pocket and gives it a flip before starting down the hall, waving for me to follow.

"You think I'm going to go anywhere with you?"

"Yeah." His voice is serious. Quiet. "What other option do you have? You want to get Cass back, right?"

My face warms, but I hold my anger in. He's right.

He lowers his voice, rolling the coin over his knuckles as we walk. "Here's the beef. With Stripe, everything has to be bought. He has to think he's winning. As far as he's concerned, he owns everyone he's taken, just like he owns the docents you booted out of the Museum with that primo door trick. But that's where I come in. If we want to get all of you out of here with your backsides attached, someone's gotta pay. I mean, Rahki's great and all, but you can only get so far beating your enemies with a duster." He stops. "That's why I needed you."

"You're full of lies."

"Not a lie," he says. "When I made that contract with you, I told you I was looking for someone who could trust me, no matter what. That's still what I need."

I meet his gaze. "How can I ever trust you again?"

Nico's smile wavers. "You can't. But I hope you will. We've got one chance to get this right. If you don't believe me, then believe the contract between us. I promised to do everything in my power to find and protect your family. It's a pact I can't break." He points his cane to the door at the end of the hall. "Go on. Stripe's waiting."

30

Binding in the Greenhouse

The Greenhouse dome looks different from the first time I saw it behind the armoire. Dusky sunlight streams through the branches of the Vesima tree, warming the humid air. Leafy plants and flowers drip with condensation as though they're sweating.

But the plants are anything but green now. A dull, black residue drizzles off the leaves, snaking in murky streams down the hillside. Scattered flowers—so bright and colorful before—lie wilted in the dirt. Even the branches of the Vesima hang limp and withered, dripping with rotten fruit. Many of the lowest branches have been sawn off, left in scattered piles.

"What happened to it?" I say.

Nico shushes me and points to Mr. Stripe, who's rummaging through baskets overflowing with fruit at the foot of the tree. Roots carve through the earth around him like a giant octopus pulling apart a ship.

"Please excuse, sir," Nico says, marching up the dirt path. "Cameron Kuhn is here to see you."

Stripe throws up his hands in delight. "Dear Cameron, what a pleasure! And so soon."

I nod, trying not to step in the streams of black bleeding across the path. "Mr. Stripe."

"Oh dear," he says, "we both know that's not my name. Although I daresay it's one of the better ones I've been given."

Nico shifts next to me. It's hard to think this awful man raised him to be who he is.

"Our guest looks thirsty, Nico. It wouldn't do to make him uncomfortable." Stripe turns to me. "Would you like a soda? Tea? Or something more your style, like an icy, tangy Creamsicle?"

He's showing off, flaunting the fact that he knows everything about me. Who I am. Who I've always been. But I refuse to let him or anyone else define me. He doesn't know who I really am. Only I know that.

"I don't need anything, thanks."

Stripe's grin vanishes. "Oh, but you do. . . . That's the reason you're here, isn't it?" He nods to Nico. "Fetch the family."

Nico limps away through one of the doors.

Stripe's not even pretending to be the kind, caring person I met before I came to the Hotel. He watches me with the same smug face Nico gets when he knows he's made a good joke.

"Why'd you have Reinhart take her?" I ask. "Didn't you get what you wanted at the Monastery?"

Stripe laughs. "Reinhart? Calling your father by his first name, now that you've met the real deal? Did Daddy not turn out to be what you hoped?"

"What do you want, Stripe?"

"Oooh." He shivers dramatically. "So bold and brash. Sounds like my boy Nico's rubbing off on you."

He grabs one of the nasty, soft fruits from a basket and takes a bite. I gag as the rotten juice drips from his chin.

"The real question is what do *you* want?" Stripe says with his mouth full. "*I'm* only looking to make a deal. The way you care for your sister fascinates me. Mother Melissa, dead in a pit with her ideals. . . . Daddy Reinhart, running away as fast as he can. . . . Yet there you are, taking care of your sister like a good brother." He swallows. "It's no surprise the Hotel was interested in you, even though no one else appreciates you."

He's baiting me. Keeping me angry, just like Nico does by calling me "kiddo." But I can see through it now. He's trying to manipulate me, but I won't be yanked around anymore.

"See, your problem is that you're afraid to want anything, because you might not get it. Or it might not turn out to be what you wanted in the first place." He closes the distance between us, and the juice squirts when he takes another bite only inches from my face. "I think what you really want"—*squish, slurp*—"is to be free."

"I don't think I'd like your kind of freedom."

"You'd be surprised." Stripe tosses the half-eaten fruit into the wilted grass. "I can provide safety. Here, all the responsibility is mine. And I take care of my possessions."

"You use them." I reach for the coin at my neck, but of course it's not there. A pang of panic ripples through me, but I have to remember that I don't need Reinhart to be strong. He's not who I am. I'm just me. "Agapios says you want power."

"Oh, I do like you." Stripe laughs. "You like to keep things simple. Did Agapios tell you *why* I need power?"

"No."

He drags his finger along one of the sawn branches. "People always *want*, but never *have*. They want friends until they get them, then they decide they don't like their friends anymore. They want stuff, and then throw it away for more stuff. They get angry and sad and throw temper tantrums when they don't get their way." He rakes his fingers across the rough edge of the wood and jerks his hand back with a gasp of pain. "It gets under your skin after watching it as long as I have," he says, pulling something out of his finger and examining it. "People are like splinters. The world's infected with them."

"You want to get rid of people?"

Stripe sighs and flicks the splinter away. "I don't want to get *rid* of people. They're useful, if you can keep them under control. I just think it's time they were put to better use."

He eyes the Greenhouse door as it opens, and Nico rolls Cass through. Reinhart follows, head hung low.

Cass makes eye contact with me, but quickly looks away.

"Take your sister, for instance," Stripe says. "You've taken care of her thus far, but you can't take care of her forever. That's why you went searching for dear old dad. You're scared. But you've been so worried about losing her, you forgot to be happy about having her in the first place. I can free you from that worry."

"You're saying you can keep Cass alive?" I ask as Nico rolls her up the hill, Reinhart trailing behind.

"Better than alive! I can heal her. That's the promise I made to your father all those years ago. If he'd kept his contract, your sister would be happy and healthy, and all that responsibility you feel for her would be no more than a passing thought."

It almost sounds good. Almost. But I know there's a catch.

Stripe turns his attention to Cass as she and Nico reach the foot of the tree. "Cassia, you look so lovely this evening."

She doesn't. She's in her pajamas, and her hair is unbrushed. And she looks . . . sad.

"Are you okay?" I ask.

"No," she replies, but her tone says so much more, like, *You should never have left in the first place*, and, *This is your fault*.

I want to give her a silent, *I'm working on it*, but she won't look at me. I don't know how I'm going to make this up to her. But I have to try. I can't depend on Nico for help, either. He wanted me to follow his lead, but I can't let things just *happen* to me anymore. It has to be my choice. Not Nico's. Not Stripe's. Not Reinhart's or Cass's or Agapios's or the Hotel's.

This is *my* fault.

I turn to Stripe. "Let's make a deal."

Nico whips his head in my direction.

Cass sits up straight. "What?!"

But Stripe only grins. "A deal?"

"Yes." I swallow hard. "I want you to heal my sister, like you promised. And then I want you to release her, and end your contract with Nico."

What are you doing? Nico mouths.

I'm not sure, but I have to do something. I know I can't offer Stripe enough in exchange for all those children, but I can at least get Cass out of here. And if Nico's no longer bound to Stripe, maybe he can return to the Hotel, tell them everything he knows, and they can come back for me. It's a long shot, but if anyone's crafty enough to get it done, it's him. Rahki will have to get the Monastery kids out on her own, but she's more than capable.

Stripe laughs. "What price are you willing to pay for my protégé *and* the healing of your sister?"

For Cass? Anything.

"Me," I say instead. "I'll stay and work for you. I'll take Nico's place as your protégé. On my own. A willing possession—that's the best kind, right?"

"Cam, please," Cass cries.

"Oh!" Stripe claps. "Someone has done their homework! Has Nico been talking about my favorite things? No. Not Nico. I bet it was Sev."

"What does it matter, as long as you get what you want?"

"It doesn't!" Stripe exclaims. He walks over and throws an arm around Reinhart's shoulder. Reinhart doesn't move. He's like the docents, bound and thoughtless. "You know, I offered your father the very same deal all those years ago. I wanted this Greenhouse, sure, but I wanted him to give it to me of his own volition. There's something delicious about free will. The thrill of risk. I was so disappointed to have to take Reinhart's will away when he broke our agreement."

"So you'll do it?" I say. "Heal Cass and let me take Nico's place?"

"No!" Cass says.

"Don't argue," I tell her. "I know what I'm doing."

Nico holds Cass's chair still with one hand and adjusts his hat with the other. The look on his face tells me I've probably screwed up his entire plan, but it's my turn to take charge.

"You really are Reinhart's boy." Stripe's eyes narrow. "However, while I'd love the chance to see Agapios's face when he finds out I've turned his choice for a successor into my own"—he casts a side-eye at Nico—"I've grown terribly fond of Nico. Few have his talent for binding. And to heal your sister . . . well, things like that don't come cheap."

I shoot Cass a silent apology for drawing her into this, but she scowls at me. She's probably angry with me for making this about her.

"Here's a counter-proposal," Stripe says. "The only deal I could accept at your price would be for one or the other. In exchange for your unlimited, willing service, you can choose: Either Nico and dear Cassia go free, *or* I can honor Reinhart's agreement and heal your sister. Freedom or healing. Up to you."

I hesitate. I want Cass to be better, but I can't imagine making her stay with Stripe. "If I choose healing, would you bind Cass? I won't do anything where she's not safe."

"Wouldn't dream of it. She'll remain my guest, safe and cared for, as long as you and Nico serve me of your own accord. I'll build two Houses, now. Very exciting."

"What if I choose freedom?"

"Then Cassia and Nico may leave." He smiles. "You will be bound either way."

"And Reinhart?"

Stripe's eyes darken. "Your father hid the Greenhouse from me for twelve long years. His freedom will cost far more than you have to give."

Cass's glare burns through me. As much as I'm sure she'd love to walk and run and not worry about her complications, she'd hate me forever if I traded someone else's freedom and condemned her to living with Stripe for it. That's how this all started, with a deal to make her "well." To give her what I've always hoped she could have.

What *I've* wanted. Not what *she* wants. That's what she's always trying to tell me. She's happy being her. This is *her* life. She's the girl who wants to travel the world. The girl who's braver and stronger than I will ever be, and who values freedom above all else. And I love her. She is who she is. She doesn't need fixing.

"I choose freedom," I say. "Let them go."

Stripe smiles wide. "And you'll sign a binding contract?"

The sickness returns to my stomach. "I will."

"Wonderful. Nico, get some paper. I'm anxious to see what Cameron draws up."

31

Forever in Perpetuity

Stripe leans against the trunk of the Vesima tree as I burn out a contract in my scratchy handwriting. My fingers tingle as Nico's sliver sears the words onto the page, drawing the binding from me as I write.

"Let's see it," Stripe says as I finish.

I pulled a lot of the language from the blood-brother contract.

> I, Cameron Kuhn, freely give all rights to myself, and everything I have, to the Curator, Mr. Stripe, in exchange for the freedom of Cassia Kuhn and Nico Flores, and everything they have, forever in perpetuity.

I made certain to include the "forever in perpetuity" line to ensure he'll never bother Cass or Nico again. If I'm going to sell my soul, I'm going to do it right. I just hope this buys Rahki the time she needs to save the others.

Stripe scans the contract, then kicks his cane up and flicks a corner of its knotted head to produce his own sliver. "Very good," he says.

He holds the paper against his leg and signs on the line.

A crackle of energy pulses through me as the magic takes hold. It's different from my handshake binding with Nico, or the coins. I feel out of place, as if my brain stopped to reboot.

Images flood my head. Memories of an enormous tree—bigger even than the Vesima. An ancient city burning. Waves crashing through brick streets. A man with a quill, hunched in a dark cell.

"Cam?" Cass says. She's directly in front of me now, but I can't look at her. It's not just sadness I feel. It's shame. "Are you okay?"

No, I'm not.

More images flash. An army on a hill. A steel ship cutting across the ocean. And children . . . so many children.

The images are Stripe's. I'm seeing his mind, experiencing his memories, like I did with Reinhart. Only Stripe's mind is so much darker. I look at the man I've just bound myself to. I can't see what his goal is, or where he came from, but in this moment I know so much more about him. There's something ancient and terrible and greedy in Stripe's twinkling eyes. He's like the spirits Oma always warned me about, hungry to own all the things that don't belong to him. This is what she worked so hard to keep us safe from all those years.

"What a sad boy," he says, glimpsing my mind as well. I wonder what he sees there.

Cass wraps her fingers in mine. I'm glad she's here.

"What happens now?" I ask as Stripe's memories dim and the crackling in my blood fades.

"You say goodbye," he replies.

I look to Cass, still holding my hand. When I left for the Hotel, I knew I'd come back to her eventually. This is different. I might never see her again.

"Don't you dare tell me goodbye, you jerk," she says, eyes wet as I kneel in front of her.

"I'm sorry, Cass." And this time I know what I'm sorry about. I'm sorry I won't be there. I'm sorry I left.

I'm sorry I felt like I had to change everything.

"You can't do this," she says. "You're my brother. You can't belong to Stripe. You belong to me."

"No one makes me be who I don't want to be, right?" It takes all my strength to hold my fake smile. "Take care of Oma."

She shakes her head. "I hate you." But her look tells me she really doesn't. She just hates that I'm leaving.

I feel a hand on my shoulder. Nico's hand. "Thank you," he says. I can tell he means it.

When I look at Stripe, I feel a tug on my chest. A connection. But when I look at Nico, my connection to him pulls too. It's not the same, though. Stripe is my master, but Nico . . . he's my brother.

"Will you watch out for Cass?" I ask him. "Take care of her like she's your sister?"

He nods. "Everything we have?"

"Forever in perpetuity." No matter how many lies he's told me, he's bound by our contract to take care of her. I only hope that's enough.

"Always look for the opportunities." Nico winks and pats his leg. "It's the *key*."

That word jolts me back to my senses. Nico's not done. He's got another card up his sleeve.

Stripe gives a dismissive wave. "Take the girl and get out, Nico. Your service is concluded." He grips my shoulder. "Cameron and I have a lot of work to do."

After a glance back at Reinhart—who's still staring into space—Stripe guides me toward the doors on the opposite side of the Greenhouse. It's too late to argue. The deal is cut. All I can do is walk and wish. Wish I could leave with Cass and Nico. Wish I'd never joined the Hotel. Wish Reinhart had never left us twelve years ago.

"Hold on." Nico gives me that mischievous smile. "I haven't taken care of the business *I* came here for."

Stripe sneers. "You and I have no more business."

"Try again." Nico's smile widens. "And check your pocks."

Mr. Stripe releases my shoulder and pats the pockets of his pin-striped suit, slowly at first, then faster, until he's shoving hands in pockets he's already checked in a panic.

Nico reaches into his own pocket. "Looking for this?" He pulls out a key. But not just any key. Stripe's black iron key, the one he used to conjure the fragment tree in Honduras, and to destroy the doors.

Nico stole it. He deceived the deceiver.

Stripe's eyes burn with hatred. "Give it to me."

"This key's special, isn't it?" Nico traces the metal with his finger. "It's your key to unbinding the world."

"Give. It. Here."

"You signed it away," Nico says, his tone playful and light. "It's mine now."

At first I'm not sure what he's talking about, but then it hits me. The contract. The words I copied from my binding with Nico, almost word for word. I say them aloud from memory. "In exchange for the freedom of Cassia Kuhn and Nico Flores, *and everything they have*."

"Exactly." Nico shoots me a wink, and then focuses on Stripe. "You gave up the rights to everything I had on me when you signed Cameron's contract. That includes the topscrew I swiped from your pock earlier." He looks the key over. "It's a shame. . . . I'm sure you'll miss it. Your prized possession."

Stripe growls and steps toward him.

"Nuh-uh-uh," Nico says, wagging a finger. He waves his hands, and the key disappears. "Come any closer and I'll destroy it. Who knows what that would do?"

The look on Stripe's face tells me Nico won't be able to keep the key long. Knowing Nico, though, that's all part of the plan. He must have a way out.

Or . . . *I'm* his way out.

I check my jeans, and for once, Nico's coin isn't there. He called it back. If he managed to move the key to join with the coin . . .

Stripe marches forward and throws Nico to the ground.

I pat my leg and feel an added weight drop against it.

"Give it to me!" Stripe yanks Nico to his feet by his collar and searches through his suit.

I slide my hand into my pocket and feel the coin. And the key.

"I don't have it," Nico says as Stripe rifles through his clothes. "I magicked it away."

If Stripe figures out I've got the key, it's as good as his. My contract with him encourages me to give it to him even now. I feel the thoughts pulsing through my mind, my fingers, urging me to hand it over. This must be what Nico felt. What Reinhart felt. Their deals with Stripe were made by choice, of their own free will. Even though they weren't bound as docents and *forced* to follow him—like Orban was—the binding still influenced them, like it's influencing me now.

If I break my contract with Stripe, he'll gain control over me like he did Dad. I'll become just another docent. That's why Nico followed his orders—so Stripe wouldn't control him. Nico's only able to disobey now because I freed him.

I have to resist these urges long enough for him to see his plan through. And I can, because the blood-brother contract gives me what I need to do just that. Mom used her binding to give Dad the strength to resist Stripe long enough to save us and the Greenhouse. Now Nico's given me the strength to defy Stripe, too. Stripe may be my master, but my bond with Nico is greater. Because we're family.

Stripe drops him to the ground and bares his teeth. "What did you do with it?"

Nico dusts himself off. "I'll tell you *after* we make the deal."

"What deal?"

"The deal where you give me what you promised. My own House. The Museum."

It was all true. Nico said he wanted to be master of his own House, whether the Hotel or the Museum, and now I've given him the opportunity. And the look on Stripe's face says it just might work.

"Oh, and everything bound to the Museum, too," Nico clarifies. "The docents, the kids and their contracts. Cam, Cass, Reinhart, every person and room bound to this House. I want it all."

Stripe clenches his cane. "You greedy little—"

"Oh, you haven't seen me be greedy." Nico runs his finger along the brim of his hat. "You and I both know that key's worth far more than I'm asking. You're getting a steal."

I can't help but laugh at the joke, but Stripe's hateful glare shuts me up.

"Fine," he snarls. "I accept your terms."

"Good." Nico nods to me. "Cameron will draw up the contract."

Stripe's lip curls. We've won.

Another jolt zips through my body as Stripe signs the new contract and the weight of my connection to him lifts. I'm free.

"Now that's done," Nico says as Stripe hands back the contract, "Mr. Cam, if you'd please give Stripe his key."

"What?"

I grin and pull the key from my pocket.

Stripe bares his teeth at me. "*You* had it."

He marches toward me, cane raised, fire burning in his eyes.

I back away. There's murder in that face. This was a mistake.

He draws back, ready to strike. This is it. This is how I die, beaten to death by a man in a pinstriped suit.

But it never comes. Before his cane makes it halfway to my head, a blinding flash forces me to close my eyes.

When I open them again, a shimmering, golden mist encircles my body. Glowing particles float like dogwood spores in the air, spinning around me, shiny as coins.

The light fades, gradually, and I realize it's not just light—it's roots, too. The gnarled, sickly roots of the Vesima tree curled up from the ground and twisted in front of me to weave a solid shield to stop Stripe's cane.

The tree . . . it protected me. How? Why?

Mr. Stripe steps back and scans the branches overhead, teeth clenched. "So, you're not gone after all, are you, Melissa?"

"Melissa?" I spin around to take in the enormous tree as the roots slowly twist and dig back into the earth. "Mom?"

The tree towers above us, shading us from the harsh sun. I can almost see those weak branches reaching for me, dripping with whatever sickness Stripe's infected it with.

A strong, warm hand grips my shoulder. "She did this for us," Dad says, gazing up into the canopy. "All the things I couldn't do. Melissa bound herself to hide the Greenhouse, and ended up becoming a part of the tree itself. To watch over our family. To protect you."

I can feel her. In the tree. Inside me. It's an electric buzz with every beat of my heart that says, *I love you, Cameron. I've always loved you. And I will always be with you.*

I swallow the growing lump in my throat and turn back to Stripe. "I guess this is yours."

The man in the pinstriped suit glowers as he takes the iron key from me.

Nico holds his head high. "Now, Mr. Stripe, I think you know the way out of my new home."

32

Your Destination

Well, that turned out better than I thought." Nico gives me a hearty pat on the back. "You had me worried for a minute. I wasn't sure we could pull it off when you went rogue."

Dad squeezes my shoulder. "You okay, son?"

I bite my lip and look up at him. He's free of Stripe's control now, and he's . . . smiling. I want to say something to him, but what? I don't even know how to feel. Am I angry with him for stealing Cass, even though it wasn't his fault? Am I happy he's finally free?

After everything that's happened, can I . . . forgive him?

I glance over to see Cass staring at the tree roots, eyes glistening with tears.

I rush over to check on her. "What's wrong? Did Stripe hurt you?"

"No." She wipes her nose. "It's just . . . "

Nico places a hand on the arm of her chair. "Stripe never intended to heal you, Cass. Even if he had, it wouldn't have been the kind of healing you want."

"I know," she sniffs.

Dad squats down in front of Cass and speaks to her so softly I can't hear him over the rustle of the leaves in the wind. My whole body tingles with warmth as I watch them. When I look up at the Vesima tree waving in the breeze, I feel like my heart's going to explode.

It's then I realize there *is* no breeze in the Greenhouse. The tree is moving on its own, silently communicating through its shivering leaves. What happens to it now? Can it be cured of whatever's making it sick? Can Mom . . . come back to us?

Dad stands back up and looks at me with sad, wet eyes before placing his large hand on my head. "I am glad to see the man you're becoming," he says. "You and your sister will do well without me."

"Without you?" I ask. "Where are you going?"

"I broke my agreement with the Hotel," he says, looking up into the branches of the Vesima. *Mom's* branches. "I endangered everyone. Melissa gave up her life to protect you and this place from my mistakes. Your Oma's done a great job raising you both. You deserve better than me."

"So you're just leaving?" Cass says.

Dad shakes his head. "I need to go to a place where I can't mess things up. Look what I've done to our family so far."

I get it. He feels the way I felt. He's afraid, and thinks he has no choice but to go somewhere he doesn't need to be afraid.

But our destination doesn't choose us. It doesn't pick us up out of nowhere and lock us into a contract. It doesn't determine who we're going to be. We set our own destination.

"You belong with us." I can't believe I'm saying this, after everything. But even Cass showed Dad compassion at the Monastery. We're bound. It's why I always hoped he'd come back. That bit of magic holds our family together, no matter what. I've wished for so long that he was here to take care of us, but maybe that's not the way it works.

Maybe we're supposed to take care of each other.

"I want you to stay," I say. "We'll take care of you. Me, Cass, and Oma, one big family."

Cass nods in agreement. "Unless Oma kills us first for giving her a million heart attacks in the last week."

I smile. At last, our family is complete.

Nico stands next to me and bumps my shoulder. "You three should get going. Rahki found the kids, and she'll need help leading everyone back to the Hotel."

I give him a confused look. "How do you know?"

He taps his head. "This is my House now, and I know what happens in my House."

"You're staying?" Cass asks. "You won't come back to the Hotel with us?"

"I never really belonged there," Nico says. "I think that's why your mom led me to you."

I blink. "She . . . what?"

"At first I didn't understand. I knew Stripe wanted the Greenhouse, so it didn't make sense that the Hotel would send me—its enemy—to follow you." He shrugs. "Now I get it. It was *her*. She made the Hotel visible to you because she knew who you were. And the Hotel kept you because it knew who you could be."

"How do you know what the Hotel wants?"

Nico grins. "Maybe one of these days you'll find out." He stuffs his hands in his pockets. "My ambition's too big for that stuffy old joint, anyway. It's time to start building my empire."

Somehow, that doesn't sound crazy.

"You know, Cam," Nico says, his tone serious, "you're the reason I was finally able to turn against him."

"I am?"

He looks up at the branches still dripping with Stripe's sickness. "For a long time, Stripe was my only family. Getting to know the Jimenez family made me realize what it would be like to be free of him. But you . . . When you bound yourself to me, I started to feel what you feel. The love you have for Cass . . . Stripe doesn't get that. He never will. You showed me I couldn't wait until he handed me his empire anymore. Every minute matters."

"Tear it down," I say. "Don't leave a single person bound."

"I won't." Nico holds up a finger, as if realizing something, and runs to one of the doors. He comes back a few seconds later and holds out two pins—one old and rotten, one fresh and new.

He raises the rotten pin. "This'll take you back to the Hotel. Use it once you get outside the Museum—don't want the MC trying to take what's mine." He holds up the fresh pin. "And this one leads here, to the Greenhouse. Wait a few hours for me to clear out some of this wood, then give it to Agapios."

I glance back at the tree. With it, the Hotel will be able to grow its mission again, just like Mom wanted. Make new pins. Bind new doors. Change new hearts. "Thank you."

"She's your mom. Besides, the Greenhouse belongs to the Hotel. Always did. Let's just hope the groundskeepers can remove Stripe's corruption." He digs in his pocket and places his trick coin in my hand as well. "And you keep this."

"I-I can't. You'll forget."

"We're blood-brothers. Everything we have." He pats my shoulder. "Keep it safe."

I run my fingers over the smiley face carved into the etching. Nico might have lied to me, but deep down, he did all that to help us.

"The truth is told at the thresholds," Dad says.

Cass looks up. "Oma used to say that."

I nod. I never knew what it meant before, but I think I'm starting to. It means we learn who people really are when things change. The last two weeks have been all about change. I've changed, and a lot of it is thanks to Nico.

Cass and Dad say goodbye, and Dad rolls Cass down the path away from the Vesima tree.

"Will I see you again?" I ask.

"My home is your home," Nico says. "We may be on different paths, but I'll be here. You'll just have to find me."

I give him a hug. "I'll miss you."

He hugs me back. "You too, brother. Now go. Find your destination."

• • •

That evening, the Old Man summons me to the Concierge Retreat.

"Come," Agapios calls when I knock on the underwater door to his dusty-plains office. He's seated in one of two leather chairs next to the wood-burning stove. He motions for me to sit in the other.

The retreat is quiet except for the crackling fire. He's going to give me the beef now, I'm sure. No matter how things turned out, it was still my fault. It's time for me to leave the Hotel for good.

Instead, he says, "Thank you."

I fold my hands and watch the fire, not wanting to look at him.

"You did much good today," he says. "Helped many people."

"I only fixed what my dad and I screwed up in the first place. If we hadn't been so dumb—"

He holds up a hand to stop me. "The Hotel is full of those who've made mistakes." His voice is soft. Encouraging. "If it kept a record of wrongs, there would be no one left to walk its halls."

"What about Mom?" I ask. "Will she—I mean, will the tree be okay? Can it be healed? Can she . . . ?"

Agapios purses his lips. "Time will tell. Your mother bound herself completely to the Hotel. She is in its walls, rooting the doors together. She and the Vesima are one and the same. They cannot be separated. But yes, I believe we can remove Stripe's corruption."

I watch the flickering flames and breathe in a little smoke.

"I have a proposition for you," the Old Man says after a

moment. "My offer to train you as my successor was genuine. In your short time with us, I saw much of your mother in you."

"I'm not my mom." The past few days pretty much proved that.

"Of course not. But neither are you your father. My proposition is not for Melissa, or Reinhart. It is for you, and you alone. The Hotel called you, and so you came. You see the dangers of the world, and seek to protect others from them. And when crisis comes—which it always does—you set aside your fears to face it." He settles back in his chair. "I have spoken with your Oma, and she agrees. You have much to learn, but I believe in time you could flourish as Concierge of The Hotel Between."

"You want to bring me back? Even after what I did?"

"Especially after what you did." The firelight dances on his sharp cheekbones. "You feel the responsibility of the world on your shoulders already. Why not embrace it as a gift? Focus beyond yourself and your sister, and help this greater world that's so much in need?"

"I-I don't know what to say."

"The appropriate response is none at all. Consider it. The Hotel can sustain Cassia's health, to a point, and your Oma's skills as a teacher would greatly benefit our young staff. Your father will need time to heal, as well. Regardless, there will always be a place here for you and your family."

A place for Oma and Cass. People to take care of them, and magic to keep them with me. And Mom . . .

"Thank you, sir. I'll think about it."

Though I already know what my answer will be.

. . .

I work in a magic hotel with doors that lead all over the world. An hour ago, I bought pretzels and schnitzel in Frankfurt, Germany. Before that, I led a lovey-dovey rich couple to Buñol, Spain, for a festival where everyone throws tomatoes at one another. And this afternoon I'll have a family picnic with my sister and Dad and Oma, drinking orange juice in the shade of a giant tree.

But right now I have to deal with the disaster in room 2078.

"I just came back from dinner and there they were," a guest with pouty lips and eyes as big as saucers tells me. Her neck drips with pearls, earrings sparkling against her dark complexion. "Where could they have come from?"

She's talking about the cats. Lots and lots of cats. They're everywhere. On the king-size bed. Drinking from the sparkling fixtures in the bathroom sink. Climbing the complimentary bath-robes in the closet like pirates swinging from the rigging.

When I took this job months ago, no one said anything about animal control.

"I don't know ma'am," I say.

But that's not entirely true. One of the cats perches on the ornate windowsill, licking itself and stretching to bite the playing card stuck to the back of its collar. They've all got one. Those cards tell me exactly who sent these felines to terrorize the guests of The Hotel Between.

I haven't seen Nico since the Greenhouse. No one has. The only way I know he's okay is these pranks he keeps playing on the Hotel.

"We'll have your room cleaned up as soon as possible," I tell the guest in my best Concierge voice as some of the cats engage in a hissing match on her bed. I shut the door, but not before a screaming seven of clubs escapes down the hall. "Maybe you'd like to take advantage of our spa services in the meantime?"

I lick the tip of my pen to infuse it with my binding and scribble a note telling the spa staff to give the woman in room 2078 the royal treatment, before starting down the hall.

"Wait," she calls after me. "You're just leaving?"

"Apologies, ma'am, but I have five more guests experiencing the same issue."

"What about my room? Can't you just fix it? With your magic or whatever?"

She points to the coin hanging from my neck. Not Dad's coin. It's Nico's trick coin. I had Sev put a hole in it so I could keep it with me as a memento. After so many years with Dad's coin, it felt weird to have nothing there.

"Magic can't fix everything," I say. "Some things we just have to accept." I give her a bow. "Have a good evening."

As I head for the Elevator Bank, I can't help but chuckle. Pranks aside, at least I know Nico's still out there. He's bound to me, another member of my family. The Museum doors may be closed off and hidden away, but that doesn't matter. If Nico taught me nothing else, it's that there are magics in the world; you just have to know where to look.

And when I finally find *him*, I'm totally going to wring his neck.

ACKNOWLEDGMENTS (THE GUEST LIST)

It takes a full hotel's worth of people to bring a book like this to print, and the writing doesn't happen in the space between doors. It happens where the people are—in lobbies and hallways and guest rooms—and the people there deserve a hearty thanks. To friends like David and Jamie Ake, Jason Stevenson, Gerardo Delgadillo, Daryl Miller, Lindsay Cummings, Caleb and Josh Slinkard, Tyler Hiott, John Paine, Crystal Summers, and Josh Torres—thanks for not letting me be a hermit. To writing friends like Dani Baxter, Diana Beebe, Mervyn Dejecacion, Alexis Lantgen, Sarah Mensinga, Brad McLelland, Jared Pope, Kristin Reynolds, and Holly Rylander—thanks for your coaching and encouragement. To my Pitch Wars cheerleaders and the Electric Eighteens—thanks for being my tribe. And specifically to Julie Artz, Cindy Baldwin, Eric Bell, Heather Murphy Capps, Jenny and Alex Chou, Amanda Rawson Hill, Kat Hinkel, Michael Mammay, Leigh Mar, Anissa Maxwell, Heidi Stallman, Emily Ungar—you were in the delivery room when this baby was born, and told me it was a pretty baby. I needed to hear that.

Endless gratitude to my previous agent, Erin Young, for giving me the keys to this car, and to Jim McCarthy, for stepping in and taking the wheel.

Thanks to my editor, Krista Vitola, for choosing to take this journey with me. You're an amazing navigator. Catherine Laudone, for keeping us running. Chloë Foglia, for giving the Hotel such a beautiful sheen, and Katrina Groover, for checking the locks so diligently. Lisa Moraleda, Anna Jarzab, Sam Metzger, Deane Norton, Emily Hutton, Diego Rodriguez, Anthony Parisi, Anne Zafian, and anyone I missed on the publishing team—thanks for opening all the doors. And to my publisher, Justin Chanda, for welcoming me into this House.

To Petur Antonsson, whose incredible artistry created a window into this world of doors. Because of you, many more will choose to enter.

To Mary Virginia Meeks and her middle-school beta readers: Yasmine Aditya, Juliana Cimo, Reagan Craft, Zachary Dunker, Gunnar Gfeller, Maximus Liando, Ella McManus, Delaney Mann, Simran Mondol, Ashley Nickolyn, Joshua Rule, Kristine Soriano, Jacob Stein, Viha Vishwanathan, Addie Whightsil, Yeji Yang, and Shannon Zimerman. Readers like you give me hope.

Lastly and mostly, to my family. Mom and Dad, you showed me a bigger world. Brandi, you're the best sister ever (and you like books—big plus). Mama and Papa, you showed me who I want to become. Kendrick, you're everything I could ask for in a son. I'm proud of you. God, you know all I have to say. And to Shelly: you're the story of my life, the Best One, my favorite. Without you this wouldn't exist, and for that you deserve cookies.